The Cuban

CW Browning

CW Browning
Visit my website at www.cwbrowning.com

First Printing: 2023

ISBN-13: 9798373975438

The Cuban

"The boundaries which divide Life from Death are at best shadowy and vague. Who shall say where the one ends, and where the other begins?"

~ Edgar Allan Poe (The Premature Burial)

Prologue

The man fell, landing heavily on the stone floor with a grunt. He was unable to lift his arms to catch himself, but even if he could, he doubted that he had enough strength to do much more than try to cushion the fall. As the gray stones rushed up at him, he managed to lift his head to prevent his skull from cracking forcefully into the floor. That was the extent of what his battered body was capable of, however. He lay on his side, blood seeping out of his mouth, and willed the throbbing in his entire being to stop. One eye was swollen closed while the other only allowed the merest sliver of vision. Through it, he concentrated on the wall a few feet away. He found a particularly long gouge in the cement, made by a former occupant driven by desperation and aided by either chemical means or sheer insanity. Staring at it, he forced himself to breathe steadily, trying to help his heart rate settle back into a normal rhythm.

The door behind him creaked on its ancient metal hinges as one of the guards began to pull it closed. They were speaking, and the man listened intently. They rarely spoke, but when they did, he struggled to hear. Every little bit that he learned was something he could use.

The accent was one he was used to and had no trouble understanding. In the not too distant past, he had walked among the people in Chechnya, drinking and laughing with them. Their dialect was one that he had adopted himself on occasion, using it to blend into the population. He strained to listen to it now, his breathing slowing.

"He won't last long," a voice beyond the door was saying. The speaker coughed, then spit. "They never do."

"He's hung on longer than the last one," the guard replied.

"How long has he been here? A week?" The other man scoffed and the prisoner heard a match strike against the wall. "He's stronger than some, but no one holds out for long."

"What's the standing record?" The guard asked.

"Before talking? I'm not sure." The other man was quiet for a second. "Ten days? Perhaps two weeks."

"And to live?"

"Four weeks to the day." That answer was immediate. "People don't linger here. Dragos allows them no such luxury."

There was a grunt and the door paused as the guard peered in at him.

"I wonder if he will be the one to outlast the others."

The prisoner felt rather than saw another pair of eyes join the guard at the opening of the door.

"Not likely. They all break." He moved away from the door. "Some faster than others, but they all end up in the ground. Come. Let's eat. I'm starving."

The door closed and retreating footsteps echoed down the corridor until, at last, there was silence. The prisoner shifted on the cold stones, grimacing as pain racked his body. Four weeks was the longest anyone had survived this place, and he had already been here a week.

Returning his limited gaze to the scratches on the wall, the man's swollen lips tightened just slightly. His people would find him. He had no doubt about that. He just had to hang on until they did.

Chapter One

Philadelphia, Pennsylvania

Michael O'Reilly stepped through the door to his condo and tossed his keys onto a table just inside. A handful of mail joined them as he pushed the door closed with his foot. A feeling of relief went through him, and he felt the tension leave his shoulders as he entered his alarm code into the keypad on the wall.

The flight from Heathrow to Philadelphia had been long— longer than normal. At least that was how it seemed. When he'd finally landed and made it through customs, he was looking forward to getting home and crashing in his own bed for the first time in six weeks. It wasn't meant to be, however. Traffic turned a ten minute drive into a fifty-five minute nightmare, a situation caused by the fact that the Eagles were playing Dallas at the Linc that night. The streets were clogged with fans, and even his cab driver was getting frustrated. By the time he finally entered the elevator to ascend to his home in a high-rise overlooking the city, Michael was hungry, tired, and longing for a hot shower.

He turned away from the alarm pad and slid his carry-on from his shoulder, leaving it on the floor against the wall as he carried his duffel bag out of the foyer. He glanced around the living room before turning to stride down the hall to his bedroom. He would drop his bag, shower, put on comfortable clothes, and then order dinner. He glanced at his watch. He might even try to stay awake long enough to watch the game.

As he dropped his bag onto his bed and turned towards the master bathroom, Michael found himself smiling despite his exhaustion. If only Dave and Alina could see him now: the Giants fan living in South Philly, surrounded by Eagles fans. They would both laugh, and probably plant Eagles gear in his house just for fun.

The smile faded and he exhaled. It still felt like just yesterday when Alina had handed him a 1911 pistol and told him to make every shot count. That night four years ago had changed the course of his destiny, and Alina and Dave had both faded along with his old life.

He was just pulling his sweater over his head when his cell phone began ringing. Reaching into his pocket, he pulled it out, glancing at the screen as he did so. It was Blake Hanover, an old friend and fellow Marine. He hesitated, then sighed again, pressing the button to accept the call. The man must have radar. How the hell did he know he was back already?

"Hello?"

"Hey Mike! How goes it?" A cheerful voice asked.

"It goes." Michael walked out of the bathroom, heading for his dresser. "How're things with you?"

"Oh, you know, same old, same old. Are you home or out gallivanting the world?"

"Just got back." Michael opened a drawer and pulled out a clean pair of sweats. "My plane got in two hours ago."

"You're back in town?"

Blake sounded surprised and Michael paused, his brows drawing together in a frown.

"Why do you sound surprised?"

"Because the Wifey said she had a feeling you were back, and now here she's right." Blake sounded like he was stepping outside, and Michael heard the distinct sound of a sliding door through the phone. "How the hell did she know?"

"I have no idea, Blake. Why don't you ask her?"

"And tell her she was right? I'm not a fool. I won't hear the end of it." Blake cleared his throat. "We haven't seen you in months. Where've you been?"

"I've been traveling a lot." Michael pulled out a T-shirt to go with the sweats and closed the drawer. "It would be easier to ask where I haven't been."

"Okay. Where haven't you been?"

"Philly."

"I knew it couldn't be that easy. Fine. Don't tell me."

Michael felt a twinge of guilt and turned back to the bathroom. Blake had given up trying to find out what, exactly, Michael now did a long time ago. As far as he knew, he'd left the Secret Service three weeks after Alina died, joining a security firm. He traveled a lot, never talked about what he did or where he went, and as the years slid by, their friendship had grown more and more distant.

The Cuban

"There's nothing to tell. It was a long and uneventful trip. That's all there is to it."

Blake let out a sound suspiciously like a snort.

"Now why don't I believe that? But look, I didn't call to go over old, tired ground. I called to see what you have planned for Thanksgiving. Are you going up to your folks?"

"No. They're spending it in Florida."

"Florida? What's there?"

"My Aunt." Michael dropped his clean clothes on the vanity in the bathroom. "They wanted me to join them, but I didn't think I'd be back."

"Great! Then you can come here! Steph's getting pissy that we haven't seen you in a while. She says you're being a recluse and that you need to come and be social."

"Is that right?"

"That's right. She seems to think that you're dying inside. Are you, Mike? Are you dying inside?"

Michael felt a ripple of humor go through him.

"Not that I'm aware of. Has she been talking to Angela?"

"She went up to visit her last week," Blake admitted with a laugh. "She has a new boyfriend and Stephanie wanted to put him through his paces."

"Did he pass?"

"Barely. He's a lawyer."

"Sounds perfect for her."

"Maybe. So, can I tell Steph to break out the Jameson for Thursday?"

"I don't know."

"You don't know? What the hell else are you gonna do? I'm offering a 23-pound bird, stuffing, cranberry sauce, yams with marshmallows…we got all the good stuff. Hell, I'll even throw in pecan pie from Johnson's Farm."

Michael grinned. "Aw, you're too good to me."

"I know. So, will you come? Steph said that even Lina asked about you last week."

Michael stilled as an indescribable feeling rushed over him. After a moment's hesitation, he exhaled loudly.

"I'll see what I can do. No promises. It all depends on work," he capitulated.

"It always does." Blake sounded downright triumphant. "I'll go pick up the pie myself. See you on Thursday at fifteen hundred hours."

He hung up and Michael set the phone on the vanity counter.

13

He pulled off his sweater and stared at himself for a moment, noting the tired eyes and the grimness about his lips. His gaze dropped down to the newest scar running across the left side of his abdomen. He stared at it pensively for a long moment, then raised his eyes back to his face.

The past four years had changed him. He didn't know the old Mike that Blake remembered anymore. If Michael had one regret, it was that his close relationship with the man who had been like a brother over the years had changed. He'd lost so much, and it had all begun off the coast of Georgia four years before.

After that fateful night in the Atlantic Ocean, Michael had been determined to discover the identity of Alina's mysterious boss. He didn't even have a name to start with, much less any other way to track him down. Charlie. His lips twisted now as he finished undressing and stepped under the hot stream of water from the shower. At the time, he had thought he was being extremely clever to discover the identity of the head of the secret organization that trained and ran assassins. Now, he knew that Charlie had allowed himself to be found.

In fact, the man had been expecting him.

Just three weeks after the yacht carrying the country's most devastating traitor exploded, Michael resigned his position with the Secret Service and walked into a clandestine training facility. Six months later, he was in Europe, working for the Organization, and answering only to Charlie.

No one knew what he did. Blake, Stephanie, his parents: they all thought he worked for an international security firm. They believed that he had been so devastated by the events in the ocean that night that he's simply walked away from the Federal government, disillusioned and bitter. They were half right, Michael reflected now, reaching for his body wash. He *had* been bitter, but far from disillusioned. Instead, he was determined to ensure that such a thing never happened again. Proper intelligence could have avoided the whole nightmare, and Michael knew he was good at digging out what people didn't want known.

Charlie had obviously agreed, recruiting him into the Organization, but not in the same capacity that Alina and the SEAL had been. He went to work as a spy, gathering the very intelligence that the assets used in their operations. If he had ever given it any thought, he would have realized that any organization that had trained assassins must also have spies. Alina had said often enough that her job wasn't to gather the information, only to dispatch the bastards to their just rewards. Michael was one of the many spies that got that information

The Cuban

for them.

He stood under the water and let the heat soothe sore muscles while he stared at the tiles. So many different roads had led him here, and he couldn't imagine any other life now. Blake had married Stephanie three years ago. He'd been the best man at their wedding, but when the weekend was over, it was with relief that he went back to work. His lips twisted again as he remembered Alina's reluctance to make a home in New Jersey, and her discomfort when none of them would leave her alone. It was a struggle that he now fully understood. He loved Blake like a brother, and Stephanie had become like the sister he never had, but they were part of his old life. Each time he saw them, it was like he was stepping into another world and another time.

And he'd just agreed to go for Thanksgiving.

Shaking his head, Michael reached out to turn off the faucet. Thursday was going to be a long day.

Berlin, Germany

His breath came fast and hard as he ran around the corner, ducking past a couple walking hand in hand along the pavement. The woman gasped in surprise as he barreled past, but the man ignored her. They could think he was a thief or a criminal, running from the law. He didn't care. He had to get to the train station before the energizer bunny caught up to him.

The man should be dead. He'd shot him himself. Yet when he left the restaurant tonight, he'd been waiting for him in the shadows. Not only was he not dead, but he was clearly pissed off into the bargain.

He shot a look behind him. There was no sign of his pursuer, but that didn't mean he wasn't there. Turning his eyes back to the sidewalk, he continued on. The station was three blocks away and the train for Cologne left in twenty minutes. He would make it in plenty of time. The trick would be evading his pursuer long enough to get onto the train undetected.

Gasping for air, he ducked into the mouth of an alley and leaned against the building, heaving. His chest was tight and he was having trouble catching his breath. It was all those damned cigarettes. If he made it to Cologne, he'd quit. They were going to kill him, if Frankenstein didn't first.

He reached into his jacket pocket, his fingers closing around a slim object. He should swallow it, just in case. It was too dangerous to carry in his pocket now. They knew he had it. There was nowhere he could hide it where they wouldn't find it if he was caught.

Sucking in a deep breath, his throat closed up and he began coughing violently. He let go of the object, bending over as he hacked uncontrollably. He couldn't swallow anything until he stopped coughing, and then he would have to get moving again. He'd wait until he reached the station. Then he'd make sure that the package was protected until he could get it to his contact.

The coughing eased and the man straightened up, peering around the corner of the building. There was no sign of the assassin in the street. He looked the other way, scanning all the people and faces, noting the moving vehicles in the road, and the shop windows along the boulevard. After a long moment, he leaned back and exhaled. He'd lost him.

Turning, he made his way down the alley. It would be faster to take the alley to the next block and cut across to the station from there. Now that he'd lost his tail, he didn't have to stay where there were crowds to hide in.

He was just approaching the other end of the alley when a tall shadow moved out from behind a large, square trash receptacle. He had time to suck in his breath as a light overhead glinted along the barrel of a pistol.

Then everything went black.

Washington, DC

The silence in the spacious office was broken only by the occasional turn of a page in a file. The man bent over the folder on the desk, his gray eyes focused on the typed pages before him and his lips pressed together. The sun was sinking below the edges of the buildings, sending a pale dusky light through the floor to ceiling windows behind him, but he paid no attention to the waning light. His full attention was on the report before him.

Dade had really delivered this time. He'd spent longer in Paris than Charlie would have liked, but it had been worth the risk in the end. The mark hadn't suspected a thing, and Dade came away with the information, just as he always did.

The Cuban

The telephone on his desk rang and he raised his eyes to look at it, seeming surprised that it dared make noise. After a second, he reached for it.

"Yes?"

"I have C on the line, sir," his assistant told him. "He says that it's urgent."

"Thank you." Charlie closed the folder before him and sat back in his chair. "Jack? What are you still doing at the office?"

"The British Secret Service never sleeps. You know that. How are you, Charlie?"

"I'm doing very well, thank you, although I sincerely doubt that you called to inquire about my health."

"Sadly true." Jack cleared his throat. "I thought you should know that there's been another death."

Charlie frowned and stiffened. "What?"

"Elijah Payne, managing director for Infil, was found dead in his car an hour ago. The DS on site says it's an apparent suicide. Single gunshot to the right temple, gun in his lap. The car was parked along a remote stretch of the river, not far from his house."

"But?"

"As you know, Infil is a subsidiary of BP. This is the second executive of BP to be found dead in three months."

"The gun?"

"Oh, I've no doubt they'll find only Payne's fingerprints on the weapon, but here's the sticky part. Payne didn't own any firearms, let alone pistols, and as I'm sure you're aware, it's not as if he could simply go down to his local shop and purchase one. We're not Americans."

Charlie's lips curved faintly.

"I'd noticed," he murmured in amusement. "Well? This makes fourteen energy executives dead in eleven months. Do you still believe nothing is happening?"

"I never believed there wasn't something fishy going on, Charlie. After the third one, it was obvious that something was brewing. But my hands were tied. You know that."

"And now they aren't?"

"Let's just say that I have some very powerful people looking for answers, and that makes my involvement more relevant than it was before."

Charlie chuckled.

"They hit you at home," he said. "I understand."

"I seem to recall that you mentioned that you had an operation already in the works when you declined to join forces with me last month," Jack said after a moment. "Is that still in play?"

"Yes."

"And your man?"

"Are you sure that you want to know?"

"I rarely make phone calls in the wee hours of the morning simply on a whim."

Charlie raised his eyebrows and glanced at the clock.

"You're not in England?"

"Not presently, but I'll return shortly. I'd like to have something in place when I do. I know you didn't want to be involved before, but I'm rather hoping that these latest developments will sway you."

"I won't commit to being swayed, but I'm willing to discuss it with you, at any rate. When will you be back?"

"Tomorrow evening."

"I'll be on a flight in the morning."

There was a short silence on the line, then a very faint sigh.

"That bad?"

"There's been a development. If there's the possibility of you coming onboard, I have to read you in personally."

"The last time you said that we both lost good men before it was over."

"I'll repeat my question: are you sure you want to know?"

Jack let out a grunt.

"I'll see you tomorrow. Will you stay at your usual place?"

"Yes."

"I'll send a car for you around eight."

Chapter Two

Marlton, New Jersey

"It's about time you came to see us! God, you look like hell. Come inside before you scare the neighbors." Michael grinned as Blake wrung his hand and pulled him into the house.

"You look like you've gained some weight," he retorted. "Are you getting sloppy on me?"

Blake threw back his head and laughed.

"The cost of having someone to cook for me." He sobered and studied Michael in the hallway as he closed the front door. "You look tired. You okay?"

"Never better." Michael turned away as a woman emerged from the living room. "Hi, Steph. Happy Thanksgiving!"

"It's about time you came to see us!" She shot back before coming up to hug him. "God, I've missed you! How are you?"

"Busy, but alive." He held out a bottle of wine. "I brought red. I know you prefer it."

"See? I told you he'd remember," Stephanie said, taking the bottle of wine and glancing at Blake. "At least we'll have one decent bottle. I'll save it for after we eat."

"The guy at the store said white wine with turkey!" Blake protested. "So that's what I bought."

Stephanie looked at Michael and rolled her eyes.

"Hopeless," she muttered. "Come through to the kitchen, Mike. I have a beer waiting for you."

Michael shrugged out of his jacket and tossed it to Blake with a grin.

"Take care of that, will you? I've been summoned for some liquid refreshment."

"Ass." Blake caught his jacket with one hand. "Why did I invite you again?"

"Because you miss me," Michael said over his shoulder,

19

following Stephanie down the hallway.

He glanced at the framed photographs hanging along the wall. Wedding photos mixed with photographs of friends and family, and his eyes went straight to the same one that always grabbed his attention: three women standing on a boardwalk with their arms around each other, the wind blowing their hair as they laughed at the camera.

Stephanie glanced behind her as his stride checked and she caught him looking at the snapshot. She paused and smiled, turning back to join him.

"You love that picture," she said unnecessarily. "Every time you're here I catch you looking at it."

He smiled ruefully and shrugged.

"You're all so young. I guess it takes me by surprise every time I see it."

Stephanie looked at the photo and smiled wistfully.

"We *were* young," she agreed. "That was taken right before Alina joined the Navy. We were down the shore for the weekend. I'm pretty sure she got wasted that night and passed out on the beach."

Michael looked at the dark-haired woman on the end. Dave's sister had looked just like him, but her features were softer, and she was laughing in a way that Michael had never seen her laugh in the few, short months he'd known her.

"She looks just like Dave, there," he said, turning away. "It's still crazy to me how much alike they were."

"You should have seen them together." Stephanie continued into the kitchen. "They even laughed the same. Those were good times."

Michael looked around the spacious kitchen as the smells of turkey and stuffing assaulted his senses. Foil covered dishes sat on the island, waiting to be reheated just before they sat down, and three different pies graced the other end of the countertop. He raised his eyebrows, going over to investigate.

"Yes, we got the pecan pie from Johnson's Farm," Stephanie told him, opening the refrigerator and pulling out a bottle of Yuengling. "I made the pumpkin, and the apple came from the grocery store."

"Best pecan pie I've ever had," he said with a grin. "That pumpkin looks legit, too."

"Now you know why I'm getting fat," Blake said, coming into the kitchen.

"You're getting fat because you stopped running," Stephanie told him, popping off the cap to the beer and handing it to Michael. "I keep telling him that he can't eat like he does and expect to stay thin

The Cuban

"Did you just wake up from your nap?" he asked.

She nodded again, big brown eyes fixed on Michael.

"Do you remember Uncle Mike?"

The nod was slower this time and Michael laughed.

"That doesn't look convincing," he said. "It's okay, squirt. It's been a long time."

"Baba," the little girl said decisively, nodding her head. "Baba."

Michael raised his eyebrows and looked at Blake for help.

"Baba is the sheep blanket you gave her on her birthday," he said helpfully. "She calls it Baba, and sleeps with it every night."

"You do remember me!" Michael smiled at the toddler, feeling ridiculously happy that the two-year old knew who he was.

"Lina!" A voice bellowed across the backyard. "Blake, is she with you?"

"Did you run away from Mommy?" Blake demanded, heading for the door. "Did you escape?"

Lina giggled and squirmed in his arms.

"I've got her!" he called back to the house, stepping out of the garage.

"Alina Renée, you get back in here so I can dress you!" Stephanie yelled, standing on the deck with her hands on her hips. "You look like a homeless waif!"

Blake set the little girl down and she started running towards Stephanie. Halfway across the yard, she stopped and turned to look at Michael.

"You come!" she shouted, drawing a laugh from him.

"Yes, ma'am," he murmured, starting across the grass with Blake. As soon as she saw him following, she turned and started running again. "Bossy little thing, isn't she?"

"You have no idea. I give you one guess where she gets it from."

"Blake, get the turkey out to rest while I'm getting her dressed," Stephanie called. "Ryan and Nicole will be here any minute and I can't have her running around looking like this."

She grabbed Lina, swinging her onto her hip, and turned to disappear into the house, leaving the back door open for them.

"You're in for a hell of a life, Hanover," Michael said, unable to hold back his grin.

"Tell me about it." Blake sounded downright cheerful. "That's why I have the garage."

25

Sugar Land, Texas

Flashing red and blue lights lit up the night as emergency vehicles converged in front of the sprawling two-story house. Yellow police tape cordoned off the entire front yard and sidewalk and, as two officers emerged from the house, a coroner's van eased through the collection of vehicles in the street.

They stopped and watched as the van began to back slowly onto the front lawn, its lights adding to the chaotic display of color. The younger of the two police officers made a sudden noise, and his partner watched as he rushed over to a shrub beside the porch, bent over, and heaved up his dinner.

Behind them, a detective stepped out of the house, stripping off blood-streaked latex gloves. He watched as the young patrolman finished, finally straightening up, his face white and glistening.

"Is this your first multiple homicide?" he asked.

The man nodded, then took a deep breath. "Yes, sir."

The detective sighed.

"I wish I could say that it gets easier, but it doesn't, especially when children are involved." He tossed his gloves into a portable trash can that had been placed outside the door. "And on Thanksgiving, too!"

"Peters! What do you have?" a voice called across the lawn.

The three men turned to watch as the police chief made his way up the driveway. Detective Peters motioned the officers away and waited for his boss to join him on the porch.

"What brings you out on Thanksgiving, sir?" he asked as the older man stepped onto the porch.

"Some pretty important people want to know what happened. I guess your victim belonged to the right country club." The older man watched as a technician came out of the house carrying a box filled with evidence bags. "What do you have?"

Detective Peters shrugged.

"Looks like a murder suicide," he said grimly. "Husband, wife, and little girl. The husband shot his wife and kid, then hung himself in the garage."

The chief scowled. "The kid too?"

"Yeah."

"Hell of a way to celebrate the holiday," he muttered. "Any

signs of forced entry?"

"None. We're still processing everything, but it looks pretty straightforward." Detective Peters tilted his head. "Wife and daughter are in the living room, together on the couch. The husband left a note on the work bench near where he was hanging."

"That seems pretty straightforward," the chief agreed. "I'm sorry to call you out for this. How's Mary taking it?"

"She's not happy, but she understands. Her folks are there, and we'd finished eating, so it wasn't too bad." The detective looked at him. "And you?"

"Oh, Janet's used to it after all these years, but if you've got this in hand, I'll mosey on back for some pie."

"Go on home and relax, sir. There's no reason for you to be out on Thanksgiving just because some selfish bastard decided to off himself and his family." Detective Peters spit into the bushes. "Damned disrespectful is what it is."

"Well, wrap it up as soon as you can and get on home. Give Mary my regards."

Chapter Three

Arlington Cemetery, Washington, DC

Michael stared down at the white headstone that looked just like every other headstone in the sea of graves. While the rest of the country was recovering from Thanksgiving dinner and Black Friday sales, he was where he always was on this weekend. It had started years ago, when he moved to DC to take a position with the Secret Service. He would come to visit Dave, his best friend, who had died in Iraq years before, and reflect on the fact that he could no longer enjoy turkey and stuffing. And Dave had loved his turkey and stuffing, even when served on Styrofoam plates with plastic forks in the middle of the desert.

Now Michael came to pay his respects to Dave's sister as well.

He had no idea if she'd loved turkey and stuffing. Somehow, he didn't know much about her at all. The woman who had managed to have such a profound effect on his life had been an enigma right until the end. Michael stared at the name pensively.

Alina Renée Maschik.

Viper.

When he served with her brother, Dave had made him promise to look out for his sister if anything ever happened to him. Michael had been unable to honor that promise when Alina joined the Navy shortly after Dave's death, disappearing for ten years. When she found him five years ago, the little sister had turned into a government assassin, and she had absolutely no need of being looked after. On the contrary, she had ended up looking after all of them, protecting them and ensuring that they were safe right up until the very end.

Right up until that yacht blew apart in the water.

FREEDOM ABOVE ALL ELSE.

His eyes dropped to the single line under her name, rank, and dates of existence. His jaw tightened as he stared at it, his face hard. Freedom was what she'd always fought for, but it was never for her own. It was always for someone else's, and then she had lost hers in the end.

Michael pulled his hand out of his jacket pocket and opened

his fingers to look down at the dog tags that he always brought with him to the cemetery. She'd left them on Dave's grave for him to find after she was gone. He rubbed a thumb over the stamped metal and then shifted his eyes back to the headstone.

"You were a dramatic pain in my ass, you know that?" he asked out loud.

A stiff breeze rustled leaves across the grass and he sighed, shaking his head. She'd left the tags for him as a final goodbye. She knew she wouldn't be coming back, and she wanted to make sure that he knew that as well. It had taken months before he realized that it hadn't been a sign of her knowing that she was going to die.

It had been a warning not to come looking for her.

He'd told Blake that he'd moved on, and in a way he had. After her funeral, and after his training at the facility, Michael had begun searching for her. He hadn't told Blake, or Stephanie, or anyone, but he had quietly begun a hunt that he was still following to this day.

Alina wasn't dead. He could feel it in his very being, the same way he had known Dave was gone before he ever reached him in Iraq all those years ago. Somehow, she had made it off that yacht. He had no idea how, but he knew that she had.

After the yacht sank off the coast of Georgia, days had turned into a full week of searching by the Coast Guard. Alina had last been sighted by Stephanie and Blake on the deck of the yacht as it exploded. Neither her body, nor that of her ever-present SEAL, were ever recovered. Yet they had found pieces of everyone else that was on that boat. Hell, even Harry Shore's head had survived, fished out of the ocean on day three of the search. Yet there was no trace of Alina or Damon. They had vanished.

Stephanie and Angela, Alina's oldest friends, had been forced to accept that their best friend was truly dead when her agency approved the burial in Arlington. Blake had accepted that no one could survive an explosion at that close range, and had eventually convinced Stephanie that her remains weren't found because there were none. He argued that what wasn't incinerated in the blast would have burned in the fire on the water's surface. Eventually, everyone had accepted that as the truth.

Everyone except Michael. He knew there was another story.

When he completed his training for the Organization, Michael had been sent on his final test, and first mission, to Havana. While there, he overheard the hotel manager speaking to one of her associates. She had told the subordinate to cancel the reservation for Raven Woods. The guest had had to change her travel plans at the last minute and wouldn't be staying with them.

Raven Woods. The name had been the alias Alina used to purchase her property in New Jersey, and Michael had felt like a ton of icy water had been dumped over him when he'd heard it in Cuba. Upon his return to Washington, he'd gone to Charlie and demanded to know if Viper was still alive. Charlie had told him bluntly to stop chasing ghosts, and to leave the dead to rest.

"But you're not dead, are you?" Michael exhaled and crouched down before the headstone. "Charlie tipped you off, didn't he? And you haven't used the name Raven Woods since I demanded answers from him. I suppose I can understand it. He's protecting his assets."

A leaf blew onto the stone and Michael reached out to brush it off.

"I went to the apartment in Sorrento. You were long gone." He tucked the dog tags back into his pocket and stared at her name pensively. "I just missed you in Dubai. The building manager said the lease had been terminated the week before, but you didn't leave a trace behind. I switched direction after that. I decided to focus on Damon. I think I was close in Singapore, but then I lost his trail as well."

Michael lifted his gaze to the overcast sky. Anyone else would have given up after four years. He acknowledged that he was being bull-headed and stubborn. If Alina and Damon were still alive, and he absolutely believed that they were, they clearly didn't want to be found. He should do as Charlie had advised years ago and leave her to rest in peace. She'd earned that much. They all owed her more than they could ever repay. The least he could do was allow her to live out her retirement in privacy.

He shook his head and lowered his eyes to the headstone again.

"I'm sorry, Lina. I need to know what happened, and that you're safe now. I made a promise, and I have to keep it. If you're happy and the SEAL is taking care of you, I'll leave you alone. But I have to know for sure."

He got to his feet and turned to make his way out of the row of identical tombstones. One day he would find her, and then he would be able to move on.

The Cuban

London, England

Charlie moved unhurriedly through the crowded pub to the back corner where a booth was partially concealed by a huge potted tree. The corner was dark and, at first glance, it appeared the booth was empty. But he knew otherwise. Deep in the shadows waited one of the most dangerous people it had ever been his pleasure to know.

If he felt any qualms over meeting in public like this, they were set aside by virtue of the simple fact that it was necessary. He had already ensured that this meeting was secure, and he knew without a doubt that his companion had also made their own security sweep. This meeting place was as safe as any other, and the crowded pub offered them both a measure of comfort. They both felt most at home in the perfect anonymity of a crowd.

"Viper."

He set his pint down on the old, heavily scarred wood table and slid into the booth opposite the woman concealed by shadows.

"Charlie."

She sounded amused and Charlie allowed himself to crack a smile. Viper, or Alina Maschik as she was once called, studied him across the table with a faint smile.

"Do you ever wear any color other than gray?" she asked.

"I wore black to your funeral."

That surprised a laugh out of her and she visibly relaxed.

"I'm honored."

Charlie studied her across the table. Her hair was cut short, hanging just below her ears and giving her a decidedly European look. The color was dark, but the shadows made it impossible to tell if it was brown or black. His attention was drawn away from the hair, however, by the intricate tattoo that snaked down the side of her neck to disappear beneath the collar of her black jacket. It hadn't been there the last time they met.

"You look well."

"Thank you."

"Jack was asking after you. He wants to see you while you're here."

"I've already been. I surprised him at his club."

Charlie was betrayed into a laugh.

"Of course you did. How was he?"

"Very helpful and concerned, but you knew that as well." She tilted her head to the side and studied him. "Why are we working with MI6 again?"

31

"I prefer to think of it as them working with us," he murmured. "They've proven themselves useful before. I'm hoping that they will do so again."

Viper was silent, offering no comment, and he smiled faintly. "Ever the cynic."

"Wary. You know I don't like working with people."

"Some things never change." He pursed his lips and watched her for a moment. "How long has it been?"

The amusement was back in her eyes, and a faint smile crossed her lips.

"You know exactly how long it's been," she said softly.

"Over a year," he acknowledged. "I've missed your assistance running ops over the past few months. I had one in Marrakesh that would have benefited from your expertise."

"You agreed it was time for a break."

"So I did." He sipped his beer and looked at her thoughtfully. "And yet here we are."

"Yes."

"I reviewed your test scores this afternoon. They were outstanding, but I hardly expected anything else. I think Jack was surprised."

Her lips curved faintly.

"I think Jack had written me off as broken and washed up," she replied. "Was it your idea or his for me to take the MI6 qualifying evaluations as well as our own?"

Charlie chuckled.

"Both. I knew that you would pass without any problems, but I wanted him to be assured as well. I'm told that you're in excellent company within his agency. Only four other MI6 operatives have scored as highly. Congratulations."

"They're not warranted. Their exams were not as difficult as yours."

"I should hope not. I train my people to be the best in the world." He took a drink and set the glass down with a click, shooting her a sharp, searching look under his brows. "Now that you've officially been cleared for active duty, how do you feel about getting back into the game?"

"I'm looking forward to it."

Her voice was steady and unemotional, and he nodded in satisfaction. If he'd had any doubt about her getting back to work, her even tone dispelled it. She was nothing but focused and ready to move.

"Where are we with The Cuban?"

32

The Cuban

"I haven't learned anything new, but I don't have a good feeling. I want to move quickly, before he disappears forever."

Charlie nodded and reached into the inside pocket of his suit jacket, pulling out a thick envelope. He slid it across the table.

"Everything you need is inside," he said. "I want you to remain invisible. Move swiftly, but silently. Get in, find The Cuban, and get out again. We can't afford for anyone to realize what's happening, or connect it back to us."

"Of course."

"I'm aware that you know this, but it's worth repeating. If you're captured or uncovered, the US government has no knowledge of this operation."

The look he received across the table made him laugh.

"Very well. I won't mention it again." He watched as she drank her lager. "Is Jack aware of the situation?"

"Not entirely. He knows what he needs to know. Nothing more."

He was betrayed into another chuckle. "You haven't changed at all, have you?"

She looked faintly horrified.

"Good Lord, I should hope not!"

"It's good to have you back."

"I'm not back, Charlie. I'm taking care of The Cuban, then I'm going back to my quiet and anonymous existence."

He smiled faintly and finished his beer before standing. Buttoning his suit jacket, he looked down at her.

"Give 'em hell."

The look in her dark eyes was decidedly dangerous and she smiled coldly.

"Oh, I will."

Chapter Four

Michael tossed his keys on the table inside the door and went into the kitchen, wiping sweat off his forehead with the back of his hand. He'd been up at five, and in the gym located in his building by five-thirty. After half an hour of weight training, he'd run seven miles before wrapping up and coming back to his apartment to shower. Opening the refrigerator, he pulled out a bottle of water. The gym was the main reason he'd chosen this building when he was looking for a place in the city. If he had to live an anonymous life in a concrete jungle, giving up his garage workshop, then he was damn well getting a gym in exchange.

Twisting off the cap, Michael gulped down the water. He missed his wood-working, but it wasn't practical anymore. Not only did he not have the space, but he was never home to work on anything. One day, he promised himself, he'd get back to it.

If he lived that long.

The watch on his wrist vibrated and Michael glanced at the flashing alert with a frown. Charlie wanted to speak to him. With a sigh, he drank some more, then carried the bottle over to the counter. He pulled out his phone and swiped the screen. A moment later, he was being prompted for his security code. Once he'd logged in, he put the phone on speaker and set it down, turning to pull a bag of coffee out of the cabinet. There was no hold music, no automated please wait message, and nothing to indicate that his call was in the process of being routed through layers upon layers of security and patches until it would end up on Charlie's line. If a person had got this far on the phone number, there was no need for anything else. They already knew their call was being processed.

As he scooped coffee into the gold-tone filter in his coffee maker, Michael remembered the first time he'd unpacked the watch and phone provided by The Organization. A shock had gone through him at the watch. He'd seen the same one on Alina and Damon's wrists but had never realized that they were work issued. They looked just like any other high-end, smart watch. Now he knew just how different they were, and he smiled faintly as he turned to the sink to fill the carafe with water. Now he was part of their world, and they were not. Funny how things worked out.

"Are you secure?"

Charlie's voice interrupted the thought and Michael turned off the faucet. He reached out to type a code into his phone.

"I am now."

"How was Arlington?"

Michael frowned swiftly and carried the water over to fill the coffeemaker.

"Mind telling me how you know I was there?"

"I wouldn't be very good at my job if I didn't know you went every year the weekend after Thanksgiving," Charlie said, sounding amused. "When did you get back?"

"Last night."

"Well, I hope you got some rest because I'm afraid you're leaving again."

"When?"

"Tonight. You're booked on a British Airways flight out of Philadelphia."

Michael leaned against the counter, his brows coming together in surprise.

"Where am I going?"

"London. The reservation is on BA 0812 under Ronald Hastings, leaving at six-fifty."

"Passport?"

"In the usual place."

Michael shook his head. When he left unexpectedly at the last minute like this, Charlie deposited all the credentials he needed in a locker at Penn Street station. He'd given up trying to figure out how he did it, or who he sent. At one time he'd been so curious that he'd set up surveillance on the locker, but to no avail. It was almost as if the sealed envelopes with passports, ID cards, and currency just materialized.

"And when I get there?"

"You'll be picked up by a driver wearing a rainbow scarf. He'll take you where you need to go."

"Anything else I need to know?"

"You won't be coming right back, so tell Hanover that you'll be out of reach for a couple of weeks."

Michael sputtered, but Charlie had already disconnected. He put the phone down and turned to get a mug out of the cabinet. How the hell did the man know everything? Did he monitor his phone? His email? How the hell did he know that Blake still contacted him regularly? A frown settled on his face as he interrupted the brewing coffee to pour himself a cup.

And why wouldn't he be accessible for a couple of weeks?

Somewhere in Belgium

Alina Maschik-Miles watched the road, white-washed by her headlights, as she sped along the E40 on her way through Belgium. She would be in Berlin by breakfast, and then she would sleep for a few hours before getting to work. She reached for her bottle of water and took a sip, never taking her eyes from the road. It felt good to be moving again. She set the bottle back in the cup holder and smiled faintly. Who was she kidding? It felt good to be back at work again.

She'd been amused at the hoops both Charlie and Jack had made her jump through, with their qualifying physical tests and psych evaluations. They had both required them before they'd allow her back into the game. Her lips curved suddenly in a grin. As if they ever had any choice. They couldn't keep her out of it, even if she'd failed every damn test they threw at her. But of course, that had never been a possibility.

They wanted to make sure that she was still sharp, and still up to the physical and mental demands that she'd undoubtedly face. If either of them had any idea of the amount of training she did with Mossad agents on a bi-monthly basis, they wouldn't have doubted her ability after a four-year hiatus. The fact was, she had never *been* on hiatus. Not really. Her vacation, such as it was, had lasted exactly three months, at which time both she and Hawk were growing increasingly bored with the sedate and predictable life of a married couple. She had gone back to work running ops for Charlie on a contractual basis, and Hawk had made himself available to Western governments much in the same capacity as he had been for the Organization. Charlie had even used him on numerous occasions, all off the books. The sad fact was that people like them never retired. They could take breaks, and pretend to disappear, but they always ended up working again. It was in their blood. They didn't know any other life.

Even when they almost died under the waves of the Atlantic Ocean.

The Cuban

Alina still didn't remember much about the swim from the wreckage of the yacht to the underwater delivery vehicle waiting from the submarine. Her wounds, mostly incurred when the yacht exploded as she was jumping off the stern, had been extensive. She'd been told that when the charges decimated the yacht, she had been skewered with debris. A long piece of metal had penetrated her torso, puncturing her lung, while another chunk had embedded itself in her leg. Those were the worst injuries from the explosion, but they hadn't been the only ones she suffered that night. Harry Shore, her mentor and trainer, had sliced open her leg with a broken bottle, coming dangerously close to her femoral artery. In fact, the surgeon believed that the gash had facilitated a small piece of metal nicking the artery once she was in the water. A stab wound in her side, courtesy of a Mexican cartel lieutenant, had seemed like the worst of her problems when she went into the water. In the end, it turned out to be the least of them.

Hawk had been waiting in the SDV for her, but when he saw the blood trailing behind her, he got out and swam to meet her. If it hadn't been for him, Alina wasn't sure she would have made it. She was in and out of consciousness at that point, and it had only been sheer willpower and stubbornness that kept her swimming towards the flashing dot on her watch.

She exhaled and shook her head. She supposed, in retrospect, she couldn't fault Charlie and Jack for questioning her physical ability, though she'd have thought Charlie would have had more sense.

After healing enough to begin physical therapy, Alina had exceeded all the medical expectations of her team of doctors and therapists. She'd had the best that money could buy, Hawk had seen to that, and they were blunt with their patient. They had told her that the amount of muscle that had been damaged was extensive, and she would never have full movement of her leg again.

She was back to practicing yoga, unimpeded, within six months.

They had told her that her lung was irreparably damaged and that she would never have full capacity again. Long distance running was a thing of the past, and she should prepare herself for the possibility of severely restricted aerobic activity going forward.

She was back to running five miles every morning after eight months.

Everything that her doctors told her she couldn't do, she did. Hawk had watched it all with amusement, pointing out that instead of competing with him, she seemed to be taking on herself this time around. Alina didn't deny it. Her own limitations were driving her insane, and she had only one goal: to get as close to 100% as she could, as quickly as possible. And she'd pushed her body accordingly.

The mental healing had taken much longer. It was two years before she would even mention Harry's name, let alone discuss what happened aboard the yacht that night. Her fingers tightened on the steering wheel, and Alina frowned. Even now, anger still burned where it had been buried deep down inside her.

She'd thought that killing him would lay it all to rest: Dave, John, the attacks on everyone she held dear. They had all been avenged, and justice had been served. Years of intrigue and cover-ups had ended, and the man responsible for killing her brother was dead. She should have been able to move on without looking back.

But the bitterness wouldn't leave her. Stephanie and Angela, her two best friends from the time she was old enough to form friendships, believed that she was dead, killed in the same explosion that killed the man trying to kill them. She had planned it down to the last detail, right down to Stephanie witnessing the explosion so there would be no doubt that she was dead. She had done it so that they would be safe from any long-reaching plans that Harry had made. If Viper was dead, so was any interest or threat to those closest to her. Then, once the world believed the lie, Viper had done what Viper did best.

She disappeared.

Stephanie and Angela had grieved deeply. They had lost their childhood friend, and they'd lost her knowing that she had been saving both their lives. They'd attended her funeral, grieved with her parents, and slowly tried to put their lives back together after a horrific year consisting of one traumatic experience after another. Their devastation was something that would weigh on Alina until the day she really did die, the guilt warring with the knowledge that it had been the only way to ensure their continued safety.

And it was all thanks to a traitor who had destroyed her life without blinking an eye.

Alina knew that she would never be rid of the anger and bitterness, but she had learned how to live with it. Hawk had helped tremendously in that regard. He'd refused to allow her to fester, but had made sure that as soon as she could, she talked to him. It had taken two years, and he had been unbelievably patient, but in the end, he'd helped her process the feelings. He'd been a rock for her to lean on, and she was able to build a new life for herself.

And for him.

Her lips tightened and she rolled her shoulders, relieving some of the tension in her neck. Now that life they'd created was on hold, and she was back in the game. It was unplanned, and unexpected, but here she was nonetheless, with a job to do.

Viper was back.

Chapter Five

London, England

J ack sipped his drink and set the glass down, reaching for his utensils. He was seated across from Charlie at his favorite table in a restaurant well accustomed to seeing him dine with various dignitaries and anonymous men and women alike. They were almost concealed from the other diners in the large dining room by an ornately painted screen on one side, and the wall on the other. The screen helped to muffle the noise from the restaurant, and offered a sense of security and privacy, both things Jack held in very high regard.

"Has our intrepid friend got underway?" he asked, glancing up.

"A few hours ago."

Jack nodded and was quiet for a moment. When he looked up again, his eyes were grave.

"Is she up to the task?"

Charlie shot him an inscrutable look.

"You saw her scores."

"Yes, but we both know that exam scores don't tell the whole story, regardless of how freely we use them to gauge the efficiency of our operatives. You know her better than anyone. Is she truly ready?"

Charlie swallowed and laid down his utensils, reaching for his wine.

"If she isn't, there's very little we can do about it now. We both signed off on it, and she's halfway across Europe at this point." He sipped his wine, his eyes studying Jack over the rim of the glass. "If you truly had doubts, you would never have agreed. What's on your mind?"

Jack smiled and set down his knife and fork, pushing his plate away from him.

"When I met with her this morning, she reminded me very forcibly of the woman who pulled me out of a pit in the middle of a Taliban encampment," he said slowly. "She had the same intensity today that she had then. It occurs to me that that level of concentration and focus has to come from a place of emotional, shall we say,

40

The Cuban

instability?"

"You think she's emotional?"

"I merely acknowledge the possibility."

Charlie smiled faintly.

"The intensity, as you put it, is Viper. When she works, she shuts off everything else and focuses only on the job. She puts blinders on. It's what makes her so effective. Nothing can sway her from her course, and woe betide anyone who tries to get in her way. I've found, over the years, that it's best to leave her to it."

Jack stared at him for a long time, then nodded slowly.

"Fair enough."

"In any case, even if we hadn't signed off on her involvement, she would have gone anyway." Charlie picked up his utensils again to finish his dinner. "She wasn't about to sit this one out. We're lucky that we were able to corral her into an official operation."

Jack raised an eyebrow, amused.

"Official?" he queried. "I rather thought we were embarking on what you Americans like to call a black op."

Charlie was betrayed into one of his rare smiles.

"So we are. My mistake."

Jack shot him a keen look, then reached for his drink.

"I feel obliged to tell you that I'm bothered by the whole mission," he said. "I'm not happy with all the risks being taken by your people. I'd rather I had one of my own involved. I have three candidates that you can pick from, all exemplary men."

"I'm sure they are, but Viper prefers to work alone. She always has."

"That's not always possible, or advisable. I'd direct your attention back to her last official mission. The only reason she succeeded was because she had help."

"Help that she trusted, and he's the only one." Charlie's voice had a sharp edge to it and Jack exhaled. "He was always the only one she trusted."

"Very well. She does it alone. But should something happen and the need arises, I can have men in the air and enroute in a few hours."

"That is much appreciated."

Jack nodded and they were silent for a moment. He watched Charlie finish his dinner, then picked up the wine bottle to refill both their glasses.

"Tell me, Charlie, what changed your mind?"

"Regarding?"

41

"When I asked you last month to join me in a joint operation to leverage both of our considerable assets to locate and apprehend The Cuban, you told me in no uncertain terms that it wasn't a possibility." Jack set the bottle down and looked at Charlie steadily. "Yet here we are."

"Yes." Charlie wiped his mouth with his linen napkin and reached for the wine glass. "When we spoke last month, I had the situation well in hand. However, certain events have transpired that now make it absolutely crucial that I find The Cuban as quickly as possible."

"That's why you pulled in your big gun?" Jack asked with a quick grin. "I must admit I was surprised when her name was dropped. Are things truly that dire?"

"I would never have brought her back otherwise."

Jack nodded, sobering.

"What's the plan?" he asked.

Charlie raised his eyebrows in surprise.

"Are you asking me a direct question? I seem to recall you assuring me that you would never do that. Even the President of the United States prefers not to ask direct questions."

"Given what I know of your operatives and how their operations usually play out, I'd rather be prepared in the event that things go sideways," Jack said with a shrug. "And this is, after all, my playing green. You're the visiting team."

Charlie was surprised into a short laugh.

"I do like you, Jack," he told him, his eyes lit with amusement. "I dread the day you're no longer in charge of MI6."

Jack grimaced.

"God-willing, that day will not be forthcoming any time soon. It will come very quickly, however, if I'm faced with a mess the likes of which you had four years ago. So please, do me a favor and keep this operation clean? For my sake?"

Charlie was quiet for a moment, then he let out an imperceptible sigh.

"I can't promise you a clean operation, but I can assure you that no hint of it will come back on your agency," he said quietly. "I'll know more very soon, and when I do, I'll share what the plan is and how we're proceeding."

"Soon? When is soon, exactly?"

Charlie looked at his watch and smiled faintly.

"In about eight hours."

The Cuban

Michael strode through Heathrow, easily avoiding the CCTV cameras and using the crowds to his advantage. He'd been trained to be invisible, and he was very good at it, moving with instinct more than intent. He'd become very familiar with this airport over the past few years, eliminating the need to search out the hidden, and not so hidden, cameras. He knew where all the blind spots were, and those were the spaces he occupied.

As he moved through the crowds, Michael was very aware of his surroundings and the people who filled them. He knew with one glance which ones were innocent travelers, which ones were law enforcement, and which ones were ex-military. He could tell instantly if they were someone to remember, or if they could be dismissed as a non-threat. Moving past the baggage claim area, he reflected that his instincts had saved his mission more than once, and probably his life too.

A few moments later, he walked through the doors into the arrivals area. A line of drivers stood along one side, holding signs with names, and watching the sea of humanity as they poured out from the doors. Michael scanned them, his eyes lighting on one halfway along. The man was slim and about five foot ten, wearing a black leather jacket. Hanging around his neck was what had to be the brightest, rainbow striped scarf that Michael had ever seen. A royal blue beret sat atop his head, and Michael tamped down a laugh. Charlie hadn't been wrong. That was most definitely a rainbow scarf.

He walked towards the man, and bright blue eyes met his as he approached.

"Mr. Hastings?"

"That's me."

The man held out his hand, looking at the single duffel bag in Michael's hand.

"I'm Richards, your driver. Is that your only bag?"

"I travel light."

Richards nodded and lifted the cord that separated them so that Michael could duck under.

"Come along, then. The car is outside."

They walked out of the airport and a brisk wind smacked Michael in the face. Inhaling, he lifted his face to the fresh air as Richards led him along the pavement to a black sedan parked alongside the curb. Two motorcycles were parked behind it, and Michael glanced at them as they approached.

"Do you ride?" Richards asked, catching his look.

"When I get the chance," Michael said. "Unfortunately, that's not as often as I'd like."

Richards grinned and reached for his bag, opening the trunk of the sedan with the press of a button. He deposited Michael's bag in the trunk and pulled something out.

"It must be your lucky day, mate," he said, tossing him a helmet. "Your bag will be taken to your hotel."

Michael caught the helmet in surprise, glancing at the motorcycles.

"You're serious?"

Richards pulled out a second helmet, pulling it over his head, and that was all the answer Michael needed.

Berlin, Germany

Viper stepped out of the innocuous looking building that contained the morgue and pulled her sunglasses off her head, dropping them onto her nose. She turned to stride up the sidewalk, lost in thought. The body she'd gone to see had been killed with a single round through his forehead, a .22 caliber bullet that left a small entry wound and no exit point. It was a caliber she'd used quite a bit herself. It was small, devastatingly deadly, and the preferred choice of assassins around the world.

The body belonged to a man named Marcel, and he was an Interpol agent. He had turned into a reliable source of information for her over the past year. Marcel had eyes and ears all over Eastern Europe, a fact that had rendered him virtually invaluable over the past two weeks. She'd last heard from him two days ago when he called to tell her that he'd found something. His tone had been uncharacteristically urgent when they spoke, but when she told him to send her the information, he refused. He said it was too dangerous. He'd bring it to her personally. They were supposed to meet in Paris, but he'd been killed before he could leave Berlin.

Viper stopped at an intersection and glanced behind her before crossing the street. Officially, Marcel had returned from a trip to

The Cuban

Poland the day he contacted her, but she knew that wasn't his only stop. He'd told her that much over the phone. The information he was bringing her had been found in Minsk. Marcel had crossed the border into Belarus during his stay in Poland, something that was significant in itself. Belarus had suspended its participation in the EU over the summer while it supported Russia's offensive in Ukraine. The country had been placed under severe travel restrictions, and that included most Interpol agents as well. Yet Marcel had followed a lead into Minsk, and come away again with something that he was convinced was too dangerous to transmit even through encrypted means.

Surprisingly, she'd learned of his death from his handler in Interpol. The man had gone through Marcel's laptop, pulling case files and information before wiping the hard drive, and had come across her number in relation to one of Marcel's cases. Performing his due diligence, he'd called her to find out who she was and what her connection to Marcel had been. He'd hung up again convinced that she was simply a nobody, a random witness that Marcel had spoken to six months before. He'd got no information from her, but she had learned all that she needed to know from him. Marcel was killed in an alley the same day he contacted her. His handler seemed to have no idea what he was working on when he was killed, but Alina did.

And so did the person who killed him.

She was two days behind the assassin, and Viper knew that that was two days too many. Every minute counted now if she was going to discover what it was that Marcel was trying to get to her when he died.

Alina went into a coffee shop and ordered a large black coffee. She needed to know what happened in that alley, and that meant knowing everything that Interpol knew. She couldn't call in a favor. There wasn't time. It would have to be done the old-fashioned way.

A few minutes later, she was seated at a table in the corner with her laptop open before her and her coffee next to it. It was time to get to work.

Chapter Six

T he pain didn't seem as bad as it had been.
That was the man's first thought as he slowly came awake, the comforting darkness of sleep evaporating despite his efforts to cling to it. He didn't know how long he'd been allowed to sleep, but he was awake now. His body was getting used to the irregular wake-up calls and was adjusting to sleeping in very short bursts to compensate. He wondered why they hadn't been in yet to drag him off for another pain-filled torture session. He supposed he shouldn't complain. Every minute they left him alone was another minute his body could use to try to regain what little strength he had left.

He lay on the floor against the wall, wrapped in a blanket, staring across the eight-by-eight cell. The thin wool did very little to keep the damp chill from the stone floor at bay, but the man was grateful for the soft barrier between himself and the stones nonetheless. It was the only concession his captors had made to his comfort, and he suspected that it was more due to the fact that they didn't want him dying from exposure before they got what information they needed and could properly kill him.

He shifted and sucked in his breath as pain seared through his side. So much for it not being as bad as he was used to. He frowned and moved his hand to the burning sensation, running his fingers over a raised welt about the size of a large sponge. Grimacing, he removed his hand and closed his eyes again, trying to remember the last session. What had they done to him?

They had asked about Igor. The thought popped into his mind and he opened his eyes, filing that memory away with a frown. If he ever managed to get out of this hell hole, that interesting little tidbit could be very useful. In fact, their entire line of questioning was interesting, and not what he would have expected. Of all the things that they could dig out of him while they had him, they wanted to know about a dead accountant from Belarus. Someone that he hadn't thought held any significance at all.

The Cuban

He stared across the cell. How had he even got here? He had
no idea. The last thing he remembered before waking up in this cell was
the hotel in Minsk. Where *here* was, exactly, was another question. His
interrogator spoke Russian with a southern dialect, but one of the
guards didn't have the same accent as the others. He sounded like he
was from Ukraine, but that seemed unlikely. Or was it?

Setting the question aside, the man shifted again, grimacing at
the dull ache that went through his body. He had no idea where he was,
or how he'd got here, but he knew that his time was very limited. He'd
heard the guards talking again when they threw him back in here. They
were impressed that he'd lasted this long, and they were even more
shocked that he hadn't talked yet. He was the subject of a wager,
apparently, and one of the guards was betting heavily that he would
outlast the longest record for survival. He'd already beaten the standing
record for keeping his information to himself.

The man felt his cracked and swollen lips curve into a distorted
smile. That was something at least. While his memories of the
interrogations were sporadic and interrupted with blank spots caused
by the pain or unconsciousness, at least there was no doubt that he
hadn't cracked yet.

And that made all the difference.

He forced himself to straighten his legs and flex his muscles,
grimacing as pain raked through him. He had to keep the muscles
moving as much as possible. He couldn't let them grow weak. Shifting
again, he struggled to sit up and lean against the wall. They had pumped
him full of some kind of drug this last time. He recognized the effects
as ones that he'd been subjected to before. In training, perhaps? Or in
the field? This wasn't the first time he'd been drugged. Obviously, the
chemical hadn't worked as intended, or there would be no wager
among the guards, and no need for the matching electrical burns on
either side of his rib cage.

Leaning his head back against the wall, he peered around his
cell tiredly. He would be very glad to see the last of this place…if he
could just stay alive long enough to get the hell out of here.

Michael stepped into the hotel suite and looked across the
room at the man standing in front of the window. He waited for
Richards to close the door softly behind him before speaking.

"The bike was a nice surprise."

"I thought you'd appreciate it." Charlie turned from the window and motioned him to one of the armchairs. "It was a precaution. I wanted to be sure that you weren't followed."

Michael raised an eyebrow and went over to seat himself. "Is that a concern?"

"It's always a concern, but let's just say that I'm not willing to take any risks at the moment." He sat down and crossed his legs comfortably. "Having our allies involved does pose the problem of greater visibility than I would like. I'd rather you remained invisible as much as possible."

"We're really working with MI6?" Michael asked, surprised. "I thought you never worked with other agencies."

"Work is a misleading term. I prefer to consider it a sharing of resources."

Michael grinned. "All right. What resources are we sharing, exactly?"

"Right now, only information. But we may have need of personnel before this is over."

Michael studied Charlie for a moment, then sighed.

"What's going on? Why am I here?"

"There's been another incident. Another executive was found dead, but this time it was on our turf."

Michael raised an eyebrow. "American?"

"Yes. He was found in his home in Texas. His wife and toddler were killed as well. It was staged to look like a murder-suicide. The local police believe he killed his family before hanging himself in the garage. He even left a note."

"But you don't think that's what happened?"

"Given the similar circumstances of several of the others, no."

Michael made a face and nodded.

"There were four others with the same MO," he agreed. "Seems to be a rash of murder-suicides sweeping across the world all of a sudden."

"This death brings the total to fifteen dead in eleven months. The international community continues to look the other way, but we no longer have that luxury. We have to find the person behind all of this. Fifteen executives in the largest energy corporations across the world don't suddenly become suicidal."

"Oh, but some were of natural causes," Michael pointed out, a tremor in his voice. "Don't forget the Chinese man who died of a sudden heart attack. Of course, it was most likely spurred on by the

The Cuban

fifty-foot drop from the crane."

"My mistake," Charlie murmured. "Of course."

"My personal favorite was the one from Moscow who committed suicide by shooting himself twice in the head."

Charlie grunted.

"The Russians certainly don't lack imagination. They've thrown them out of hospital windows, down stairs, shot them, poisoned them, and caused fatal car accidents, all of which were covered up by their state news outlets. If it wasn't so serious, and hadn't spread into the global energy sector, I would find it amusing."

"But it has, and now apparently even as far as Texas. Who was it?"

"William Mosley, a Vice President and senior consultant for the Federal Energy Regulatory Commission."

"And his replacement?"

"Is yet to be announced."

Michael exhaled and rubbed a hand over his face.

"No doubt they'll follow the same trend as all the others. Not that we know what they have in common yet, but it must be something. The only reason to purge so many high-ranking executives is to replace them with people who'll do what you want." He dropped his hand and looked at Charlie squarely. "Everything that I'm coming across is leading back to The Cuban. I really believe he's the one behind it all."

"To what purpose? Why would an international arms dealer be interested in energy?"

"I don't know, but all roads lead to him."

Charlie was quiet for a long moment, then he nodded slowly.

"I know they do. Have you uncovered any indication as to his identity yet?"

"Nothing substantial. I know he's a male, and I think he's either Russian or Eastern European by birth, but I believe he was educated in the States. Really, the man's a ghost. There are plenty of people who claim to have been in meetings with him, but all of their descriptions vary drastically. Most of his meetings are conducted by trusted associates, but there's no doubt that he runs his business with an iron fist. No one speaks without him first telling them what to say, and everyone is afraid of him. Hell, no one even knows his real name. The Cuban. That's all we have, and we only have that because he likes to gift a box of Cohiba Robusto cigars with large purchases."

"He's the master of the most extensive arms network in the world, and yet the man is an enigma."

"Yes. A dangerous one." Michael hesitated, then cleared his

throat. "But I think I might have a lead. I received a message while I was on the plane, from a contact in Paris. While I was there, I found what I thought might be another piece of the puzzle. I had someone look into it after I left."

"And?" Charlie prompted when he hesitated again.

"I think some answers may be in Minsk."

"Minsk?" Charlie repeated, surprised. "What do you think you'll find in Belarus?"

"I've been building a list of The Cuban's known associates, the ones he does business with regularly. It's not a long list. The Cuban is notoriously suspicious and picks his friends carefully. One of them, Pedro Merino, was in Zurich last week overseeing the sale of a shipment of guns. He cut the meeting short to board a flight for Moscow, where he caught a connecting flight into Minsk. Now, Pedro is a man of very strict habits. He wouldn't have cut the meeting short and departed at a moment's notice unless he was being summoned to another, more pressing meeting."

"And you think it was with The Cuban?"

"He was facilitating the sale on his behalf. It only makes sense that that would be who called him away."

"What's in Minsk?"

"A compound outside the city, in Dachnyi 6. Several other associates of The Cuban have traveled there over the past few months, and I think that's where Pedro was heading. If it is, it's looking more and more like that's where The Cuban meets with his executives and associates."

"It would be ideal. With travel so restricted in that area, there is little likelihood of any of them being followed into the country, much less apprehended."

"Exactly."

Charlie was quiet for a long time, then he exhaled.

"I'll make the arrangements for the papers and identifications," he finally said. "How's your Russian these days?"

"More than adequate."

"Good. Go and see what you can discover at this compound. I'll have one of the assets on standby in case The Cuban is there. If he is, don't be a hero. Let me know and I'll send help."

Michael made a face. "I thought we wanted him alive."

For the first time since he entered the room, Charlie smiled faintly in amusement.

"They're more than capable of extracting a target without killing them, Michael."

The Cuban

Michael grunted.

"Unfortunately, they tend to leave a mess behind."

"I can't say that that weighs very heavily on my mind." Charlie stood up and buttoned his suit jacket, the interview over. "I'll have your papers by this evening. Go and get some rest. You leave tonight."

Chapter Seven

Alina sipped her bottle of water, her eyes on the screen, while she sped through the black and white footage from the CCTV camera. It had been more difficult to get the footage than she'd anticipated, thanks to Interpol. Difficult, but not impossible. After some false starts, she'd finally located what she was looking for.

She capped her water and reached out to slow down the recording as the timestamp in the corner rolled over to the day Marcel had been shot. She jumped ahead to the evening, then sat back in her chair, propping her feet on the desk and crossing her arms over her chest. Settled in and resigned to watching at least an hour of the most boring television imaginable, Alina reflected that she missed her equipment. If she were home, she would have computers doing this for her, and it would be much faster. The time she was going to lose was time that she didn't have to lose, but there was no other choice. She had to know what happened in that alley.

It was over an hour later when Alina straightened up suddenly, dropping her feet to the floor. There, coming around the corner, was Marcel. The image was grainy, but there was no mistaking him. He was running, and he barreled past a couple on the sidewalk, looking over his shoulder as he ducked into the alley. He leaned against the building, undoubtedly catching his breath for a few moments before he looked around the corner. After looking up and down the street, he turned and walked further into the alley, disappearing from the limited range of the camera across the street.

Frowning, Alina went to another tab and searched for a camera angle from the other end of the alley. After a few minutes, she landed on another camera and pulled up the footage, speeding through to the time stamp from the first camera. Slowing the playback down, she searched the dark alley for any sign of Marcel. The picture clarity of the new camera was even worse than the other, and she pressed her lips together impatiently as she tried to discern any movement past the fuzzy images.

The Cuban

Before she saw Marcel, she saw the man standing behind the large trash receptacle. He drew her attention when he moved, breaking the almost total invisibility that he'd gained in the shadows. When he moved, Marcel entered the frame.

Alina watched the two grainy figures on the screen, her lips pressed together. The shadow behind the trash container stepped in front of Marcel, raising a gun and firing immediately. There was no time for conversation, and certainly no warning for poor Marcel. He was shot point blank in the forehead. As he fell, the other figure bent over him, catching and easing him to the ground. Alina watched as he went through the dead man's pockets quickly, extracting something small from one of Marcel's jacket pockets. Freezing the image, she zoomed in and went about trying to clean up the image enough to make out what the assassin had found. After a few moments, she tilted her head and stared at the enlarged gloved hand. The object was small, about the size of a flash drive, and Alina sat back thoughtfully. Whatever it was that Marcel had been trying to get to her was now in the hands of the people who'd killed him.

Lost in thought, she stared at the blown up, grainy image. Interpol would have seen this same footage, and they would know that they were looking for an assassin who had taken information off one of their agents. But there was no way they could possibly know what that information was, or who it was going to. As far as they would be concerned, Marcel was killed for one of the cases he was working on, and they would be poring through all his active files, looking for what it was that had got him killed. Their one connection to her had already been explored, and disregarded as incidental and unimportant. As long as it remained that way, they wouldn't be a problem. If that changed, well, then she had an issue.

Exhaling, Alina leaned forward and pressed some buttons on the keyboard, rotating the image on the screen. No matter how she rotated it, however, she couldn't get any kind of shot of the assailant's face. All she knew was that the figure was tall and slender. Thanks to the gloves on his hands, she didn't even know what ethnicity he was. She had nothing.

Except the knowledge that whatever Marcel had discovered in Belarus had cost him his life, and Viper had worked with less.

She closed out the tabs on her laptop and began to shut it down. The answer was in Belarus, and she knew just where to look.

Michael studied the stubble on his jaw thoughtfully in the brightly lit mirror. His overnight flight across the ocean, followed immediately by a meeting with Charlie, and then lunch in a pub near his hotel had left him little time for personal grooming. After his shower, he'd pulled out his razor to take care of the burgeoning beard, but now he hesitated, staring at his reflection. Perhaps he should leave it. He was heading into enemy territory, and the more ways that he could conceal his real face, the better off he'd be. After about four days, he'd look like a scruffy dock worker, but that could only be to his advantage.

The television in the hotel room droned in the background as Michael considered his options. He could not touch it and grow a full beard and mustache. Or he could trim it into a goatee. The full beard would offer more protection, but how many Russians were sporting full facial hair these days? With the war in Ukraine, all men of a certain age had been forced into military service, and with that service came clean-shaven jawlines. Perhaps facial hair would actually draw more attention to him.

He was still pondering the merits of increased identity protection versus anonymity when the reporter on the television caught his attention. Turning, he went into the other room, his eyes going to the screen as the scene switched from stock news footage in London to Washington, DC. The ticker at the bottom stated that it was live footage, and Michael stared at throngs of protesters clogging the streets around the White House.

After living in the Capitol for four years, Michael was no stranger to the large protests and marches that occurred almost regularly. They were hardly ever newsworthy, and most American media outlets didn't even mention them. This one, however, had gained the attention of the British media, and Michael picked up the remote to turn the volume up.

"'Over three hundred thousand protesters have converged on Washington, DC, today to protest the administration's attempts to close multiple coal mines across the United States. The President announced last week that the mines would be closed by the end of the new year, paving the way for more sustainable energy. However, the announcement comes at a time when the United States is struggling with skyrocketing costs of energy and fuel, in addition to inflation that is the highest the country has seen since the 1970s. The President's statement appears to have been made without the consultation of any of the energy companies in the country, or the approval of the Congress, leading to a bitter fight between the parties. This morning, hundreds of thousands showed up in the Capitol to voice their disapproval. Not only protesting the legislation against the use of coal, the march is also protesting the continued closure of the pipelines into America's oil supply. As the nation heads into a winter that is forecasted to be more severe than in recent years, Americans are worried about their ability to heat their homes. Food shortages are also becoming a concern as the truckers that transport goods across the nation are unable to afford the rising fuel costs.'"

Michael watched the crowds in the streets with a frown. He'd known it would have to come to a head sooner or later. The current administration couldn't continue to strangle the American people and force them into desperate situations without some form of backlash. The Americans weren't like the Europeans. They were used to their freedoms, such as they were, and they would only allow the government to push them so far. Faced with the prospect of having to choose between paying for heat or paying for food, the people were at their breaking point.

Shaking his head, Michael turned the volume down again and went back into the bathroom. Fifteen energy executives killed across the world, and now mass protests in Washington over the government's attempts to regulate energy and fuel consumption. There was no way anyone would ever convince him that the two weren't connected; they had to be. But how?

Who stood to gain from manipulating the global energy crisis caused by a pandemic that had brought all of humanity to a screeching halt two years ago? Who was behind this onslaught of deaths, and why? And how did The Cuban tie into it all?

Berlin, Germany

Alina moved along the sidewalk, her hands buried in her jacket pockets. The late afternoon sky was overcast and the shadows were already lengthening in the city streets. She walked with her head up and her shoulders straight, her eyes constantly moving over the faces around her. This constant need to memorize every face that passed her in the crowds was a habit born from years of living in the dangerous world of assassins and criminals. It had served her well on more than one occasion, enabling her to recognize a threat before it was too late, and in the four years she'd been officially dead, it had continued. Now, more than ever, Viper was on her guard.

As she strode past stores and restaurants, Alina remembered another day, in another time, when she and Damon had strolled down this very street, hand in hand. They had marveled at how different the city felt when they were there for pleasure and not work. A smile played with her lips as she remembered how they went to all the tourist traps, amusing themselves as they joined the rank and file of first-time visitors to the capital city.

The smile disappeared before it really got started. Now she was here alone, and Damon was—well, she couldn't think about that just now. She had to find out what was on that flash drive that had been taken from Marcel, and that meant finding the tall, faceless assassin that had killed him. As far as she could see, she only had one course of action: she had to draw the assassin out. Using herself as bait was the most logical way to do that, which was why she'd just spent an hour in an internet cafe, leaving breadcrumbs for him to follow. Now she just had to hope that he was cautious enough to monitor anything connected to Marcel. As long as he was keeping an eye on the ongoing investigation into Marcel's death, he'd run across her and her breadcrumbs. If he was half as good as she suspected he was, or his employers were, she wouldn't have long to wait.

She reached the corner of a busy intersection and stopped, standing with a handful of other pedestrians waiting for the light to change. Who the assassin was was immaterial. Viper was more interested in the people who hired him to kill Marcel and retrieve whatever it was that he'd found in Minsk. Had they followed him from Belarus? Had he given himself away? Or had they been waiting for him here in Berlin? She supposed she'd never know and, she thought dispassionately, it didn't really matter. All that mattered was that she know what Marcel had known.

A yellow and black, double-decker bus rolled up to the intersection, turning ponderously around the corner. As she watched, a reflection in the gleaming tinted windows caught her attention and Viper stiffened. Her heart thumped once against her chest before settling into a steady tattoo that she remembered from years past. There, about two hundred yards behind her, was a tall man wearing a dark jacket. In the last remaining inches as the bus finished making its turn, Viper estimated the height and build to be the same as the assassin from the camera in the alley.

The light changed and she crossed the road with the rest of the people around her. It could be anyone, but every hair on the back of her neck was tingling and Viper had learned not to discount this particular feeling. She was certain that the man hadn't been there before the internet cafe. Had she really been flagged that quickly? While she hadn't thought that it would take long, she also hadn't expected that the response would be instant.

Frowning, Alina strode along the sidewalk, her eyes moving around the street, looking for an exit. It seemed impossible. She'd been expecting to wait at least a few hours, but it hadn't even been an hour. There was no possible way that someone had flagged the cafe and then got there in minutes. Even Interpol didn't move that quickly, she reflected, her lips curving in faint amusement despite herself. No. She'd been seen before the cafe.

The morgue!

The thought came to her in an instant. They'd been watching the morgue! Something akin to laughter made her shoulders tremble. The internet cafe had been a complete waste of time, then. They were already coming to her. Any dismay she would have normally felt for not being more discreet in her first foray into enemy territory in four years was swept aside. It had been a mistake, obviously, and one that she would not make again. But it was over, and on a positive note, it had had the unforeseen effect of bringing her quarry to her faster than she'd originally planned. A happy mistake, to be sure.

Viper slowed to a stop outside a shop window and looked at the display, casting a swift glance behind her from under her lashes. The man was still there and had closed the distance to about a hundred yards. When she stopped, he slowed noticeably, and that was all the confirmation she needed. If it wasn't the assassin from the alley, it was *someone*.

Turning, she continued along the sidewalk. About fifty yards ahead was the opening to a very narrow alley. She would go in there and wait. He wouldn't be able to resist such a perfectly secluded space. He would follow.

Pulling her hands from her pockets, Viper let out an imperceptible sigh. She supposed the car parked in the parking garage a few blocks away was also blown. If they'd been following her since yesterday, they most certainly knew what she was driving. She couldn't return to it, which was a shame because she'd left her favorite sunglasses in the cupholder. It was hard to find a good, comfortable pair of shades, after all.

Reaching the alley, she ducked into it, sliding her hand under her jacket to pull her combat knife from the sheath at her waist. Her

into his chest, near his dislocated shoulder. He let out a low moan of pain.

"The next time, I press your shoulder," she promised.

"Where?!"

"Near Dachnyi 6!"

"And what do they call this person near Dachnyi 6?"

The man sucked in a breath and his lips parted, but the words never made it out. Alina felt rather than heard the shot that propelled a bullet into his forehead. His head snapped back against the building and she released him swiftly, spinning to look behind her. The alley was empty, but the shot hadn't come from the opening. The angle was downward. Her eyes went straight to the buildings across the street and she dove to her right just as another bullet tore into the building, where her head had been milliseconds before.

Gasping, Viper sprang towards the metal staircase, diving behind it for cover as another bullet dinged against the steel frame of the stairs. Her heart pounded against her ribs and she sucked in air, forcing herself to breathe. She slid her knife into the sheath at her waist and waited for another shot. Silence fell over the alley and she listened to the sound of her own breathing before realizing that the shooter had no shot. The staircase concealed her completely. Taking another deep, calming breath, she began running along the side of the building, staying in the shadows as she went down the alley towards the opening at the other end. She didn't look back, but moved swiftly in the murky semi-darkness until she reached the end.

Going around the corner, Alina swallowed and looked around. She was on another busy street and she moved into the crowds of pedestrians quickly, blending in with the people effortlessly. Glancing behind her, she pulled the hood of her jacket up over her head and exhaled. They would come after her. They knew she had to exit the other end of the alley, and they would have people waiting. She had to disappear.

Looking around, Viper caught sight of a cab and moved swiftly to the curb, raising her hand to flag it down. It pulled over and she got in, letting out a silent sigh of relief as she pulled the door closed behind her.

"Alexanderplatz," she told the driver in German. "Quickly!"

He nodded and pulled away from the curb as she leaned back on the seat. Turning her gaze out the window, Viper pressed her lips together thoughtfully. This was the second time Minsk had cropped up.

She was going to Belarus.

Chapter Eight

Dachnyi 6, Belarus

Michael zipped up his jacket and turned to make his way into the trees. His car was concealed from the road behind an old, abandoned building and he glanced over his shoulder to send one last searching look across the countryside. The road was empty, and the only other vehicle he'd seen on his way here was a beat-up, old truck lumbering in the opposite direction. Despite being only twenty minutes from the nation's capital, the area was almost desolate. Heavily wooded, it didn't lend itself to farming, and Michael felt as if he was in a forgotten pocket of land, trapped in the past.

It was the perfect place for The Cuban to call a safe hideaway. Aside from the small town that comprised a handful of houses and stores, there was nothing for what seemed like miles. It was close enough to Minsk to be easily reached, yet buried in woods that were unlikely to be explored by hordes of tourists.

Michael made a face as he moved through the trees. Not that many tourists were coming to Belarus these days. Travel restrictions imposed by the EU had taken care of people coming in. The Belarus government's support of Russia's war with Ukraine had cost them dearly, but he could hardly say he was surprised that they sided with the giant to the east. Minsk had been in Putin's pocket for as long as he could remember.

Who was The Cuban, really?

The question popped into his head as he moved silently through underbrush towards where he knew the compound was situated. Michael believed he was Russian, but admitted that his only reason for thinking so was because of how many connections the arms dealer appeared to have in that country. He could just as easily be European, although Michael would be surprised if that were the case. Even though he'd never even so much as seen the back of the man's head in a photograph, everything about him screamed Eastern European or Russian. The way he did business, the way he thought, the way he disciplined those who went against him: all of it smacked of the turbulent and violent history of that part of the world.

Charlie wasn't so convinced. Michael smiled faintly. He had the distinct impression that his boss was humoring him with this field trip, much the same way that he'd humored him with a trip four years ago to Sorrento, Italy. The smile disappeared. He'd come up empty-handed that time. He sincerely hoped he wouldn't come up empty this time as well. If he did, then he was out of tricks. If The Cuban wasn't here, he had no other leads.

And Charlie had made it clear that they had to find him.

A few minutes later, Michael caught sight of an iron fence through the trees and slowed. There it was. He'd pulled satellite footage of the area before he left Minsk and knew that the compound extended over two acres, surrounded by a security fence. The main building was fairly close to the front, with several smaller structures in the back. The rest of the land was woods. Although the compound was comprised of over two acres, he didn't have to traverse two acres to get to The Cuban. He only had to get to the main building.

He moved through the trees until he was just outside the fence and had a clear view of the road that went through the gate. A guard hut stood just inside, and as he watched, two large dogs ambled past the hut. Michael frowned. He'd known about the armed guards. He hadn't known about the dogs.

Pursing his lips, Michael hesitated a moment, then moved to his left. He'd make a complete sweep of the perimeter and see if he could get an idea of just how many dogs and guards he would have to contend with. Once he knew just what he was looking at with security, he could come up with a game plan.

Tonight, he'd return and get inside. If he got confirmation that The Cuban was there, he'd withdraw and contact Charlie. He wasn't trying to be a hero. He'd had his fill of that in the Marines. No. He'd wait for the asset to arrive, just as Charlie asked. They would extract the bad guy, and it would be another operation in the books. If The Cuban wasn't in residence, then he was back to square one, and he would withdraw back to London.

Either way, he didn't foresee any complications. It was just another day at the office.

The Cuban

Minsk, Belarus

Alina stretched and leaned back against the headboard, staring at the screen on her laptop thoughtfully. Spread around her on the coverlet were maps, satellite images, and forecasted weather patterns for the next twenty-four hours. She'd arrived in the city and checked into the hotel just after dawn, falling into a short, deep sleep as soon as she'd ensured the room was secure. By ten, she'd finished breakfast and was hard at work, locating the most probable site in Dachnyi 6 for someone to receive secrets from an assassin.

It was a compound about twenty minutes from the city center. Satellite images showed that it was the only structure of any note for some distance, and what made it so noteworthy was the eight-foot iron fence around the property. The armed guards were also a good indication that whoever was in that particular house did not want to be disturbed.

Alina stared at the image of the sprawling, two-story house. It was perfect, really. It was close enough to the city to be convenient for visitors coming and going, yet secluded, surrounded by woods to ensure complete privacy. The house was guarded, but there didn't appear to be any military vehicles coming and going, so that eliminated the need to take enemy forces into account. She chewed on her bottom lip for a moment, her mind going back to a similar compound buried in the mountains of Syria. The terrorist mastermind there had had a virtual army protecting him, but Viper had made it through to him just the same. It was what she was trained to do, and she was very good at it. But it didn't mean that she didn't appreciate easier operations without heavily armed, enemy soldiers; operations like this one appeared to be.

After studying the image for a long minute, she exhaled and swung her legs off the bed. It was almost too easy. While there were certainly armed guards patrolling the compound, it was hardly an imposing force. Was the person who ordered Marcel killed really that confident that he would never be found?

Alina reached into the mini fridge and pulled out a bottle of water, twisting the cap off. Or were they not there at all? Her eyes went back to the bed thoughtfully. Was that the skeleton crew? The ones who stayed behind when the boss traveled? Or was the boss never there at all?

She went over to the window and looked down into the busy city street below. The late afternoon sun was sinking over the tops of the buildings and she glanced at her watch. It would be dark soon, and then she would move, using the cover of night to her advantage. It made no difference to her if the boss was there or not. She was going for the intel that Marcel had died trying to get to her. If she lucked out and came across the boss, she'd consider it a bonus, but the priority was the intelligence.

Sipping the water, Alina watched as traffic streamed past the hotel on the busy thoroughfare. The intelligence was her link to The Cuban.

This morning, she'd broken a long-held habit of always ordering room service when she'd gone down to the restaurant for breakfast. She generally kept the number of people who actually saw her to a minimum, but this time it had been necessary. She needed answers that she would only get by interacting with the hotel employees. Luckily, she'd had success with her first attempt. She'd shown a photo to one of the waitstaff, asking if the young man had seen the man in the hotel in the past few weeks. If she hadn't been watching him so closely, she would have missed the flash of surprise in his eyes. He hadn't been expecting a photograph, which wasn't surprising. As far as she knew, she had the only photo in existence of The Cuban. Also not surprising was the young man's denial of ever having seen the man in the photograph. What *was* surprising was that a mere waiter in the hotel restaurant had not only recognized him, but knew to keep his mouth shut. And that told her that he was no mere waiter.

Her stomach rumbled and Alina turned away from the window. She would eat before she left the hotel, but this time she would order room service. If, by some miracle, she actually found The Cuban in that compound, there would be no time to eat later.

There would be no time for anything but fighting.

The sleek sedan moved through the streets, heading out of the city and into the rolling countryside. A lone occupant sat in the back, his head bent as he studied something on a tablet, a faint frown on his face. He was separated from the driver by a soundproof window that most times was open, but today he wanted his privacy. Things weren't going well, and he needed quiet to think.

Somehow everything had gone wrong three weeks ago. He had no idea where the system had broken down, but broken down it most definitely had. Not only had an Interpol agent been asking questions about something that he'd been assured was not on Interpol's radar, but then a disturbing report came out of Zurich regarding an assassin whom he had been assured was dead. While on the surface the two didn't appear to be related, it turned out that they were. How an Interpol agent had uncovered the link between a dead assassin and a network of prison camps across Russia and Ukraine was a mystery that he had to solve before the Heads found out. An involuntary shiver went through him. If they discovered that their invisible containment system was no longer invisible, there would be consequences. He didn't want to be caught up in those consequences.

His cell phone vibrated in his coat pocket a split second before the audible ring made itself heard. With a sigh, he reached into his coat.

"Hello?"

"I'm sorry to bother you, sir, but something's been brought to my attention that I thought you should know about."

"Well?" the man asked impatiently when the caller didn't continue right away.

"It's from one of our men in Hotel Europe."

"In Minsk?"

"That's right. Someone is there asking questions." The caller hesitated, then cleared his throat. "About The Cuban."

The man stilled and raised his eyes from his tablet, shifting them to the countryside speeding by outside the window.

"Tell me."

"It's a woman. She showed him a photograph."

"A photograph?" The man scowled. "There are no photographs of The Cuban."

"That's what I said, but the kid swears it was him."

The man was silent for a long moment, then he exhaled silently.

"Who is this woman?"

"She's registered under the name Elena Ivanov. That's all I know so far."

The man let out a curse.

"Of course she is. There must be thousands of women with that name." He drummed his fingers on the arm of the door for a moment. "See what you can find out about Ms. Ivanov, but I'm not holding much hope. I have little doubt that it's an alias, but see what you can uncover."

"And the woman herself?"

"Put someone on her. Make it clear that they are only to watch, not engage. Let's find out who she is before we do anything more. Keep her under surveillance and keep me updated."

"Yes, sir."

"And Josef?"

"Yes?"

"Pull the kid from Hotel Europe and place him somewhere else. If she suspects anything, she'll go to him first. Let's not risk him giving anything away."

"Yes, sir."

The man hung up and stared out the window, his mind spinning. There were no photos of The Cuban. He was sure of it. Yet a strange woman not only appeared to have one, but she had shown up at the hotel where The Cuban was known to stay frequently.

He lowered his eyes to the tablet again, his lips pressed together in a thin line. This mess was growing, and until he found the cracks, he had no way of containing it.

And that didn't bode well for his continued good health.

Chapter Nine

Viper watched as two new guards relieved the ones inside the gate, then turned her attention back to the main house in the compound. Shutters covered the windows, preventing any glimpse inside, but the telltale glint of light along the edges showed which rooms were lit and which were not. On the ground floor, most rooms had light, but the second floor was mainly dark.

She lifted a hand to switch her night vision goggles to thermal scanners, scanning over the lower level slowly. The heat signatures were concentrated in the rear, left quadrant, leaving the rest of the lower level clear. Clicking the goggles again, she went back to night vision and scanned the area around the house. Two armed guards were stationed at the gate while two more patrolled through the property. She'd seen two dogs when she did her first pass and, even with the addition of the canines to the four guards, she was surprised at how light the security really was. Granted, there were several people inside, and they were undoubtedly armed, but still. She would have expected more than this. This was almost a joke. They had to be the base security left behind when the boss wasn't in the compound, and if they were, then The Cuban wasn't there. Her eyes narrowed thoughtfully and she pressed her lips together briefly. It made no difference to her. Whatever the situation inside, they were about to be breached.

Viper shifted her gaze over to the far side of the property thoughtfully. The heavily wooded area was the most accessible entry point. She would be unlikely to run into the guards before she could reach the house, which would leave only the dogs to get in her way. Her lips curved faintly. She wasn't worried about them. They wouldn't give her any trouble.

Something moved and caught her attention on the property line and she frowned, turning her gaze to the left. A shadow was moving just outside the fence and, as she watched, it moved up the iron barrier and over the top, dropping down inside the fence. There it crouched in the shadows, obviously listening for signs that it had been spotted.

"Now who the hell are you?" she muttered, clicking to zoom in on the figure.

She sucked in her breath as she focused on the face of Michael O'Reilly.

"Oh, you've *got* to be kidding me!"

If there was a touch of her old Jersey accent lacing her tone, Viper ignored it as she watched Michael straighten up and move along the perimeter, keeping to the shadows. The last time she saw that face was over six months ago. He'd been crossing the street in Prague, having just left the exclusive apartment building where she and Damon kept one of many safe houses. She'd been half amused and half annoyed at the time. It had been the tenth safe house that he'd hunted down in his relentless search for her. While he'd never found them, they'd been forced to replace each residence that he discovered. The Marine simply refused to give up, even after all this time.

Damon had wanted to put a stop to it three years ago when he'd come close in Dubai. He didn't care that he was one of Charlie's spooks now, he was sticking his nose where it didn't belong. She'd convinced him to let it go, but when Michael had almost caught up to them in Singapore, she'd had to admit that he was becoming a nuisance. Once again, Hawk wanted to take matters into his own hands, and once again, Viper had talked him out of it. If they did anything to stop Michael, any doubt that he might have that she'd survived would be gone. She'd argued that, so far, he didn't know for sure. It was best to leave him chasing a ghost. Unfortunately, it made their continued existence more complicated, and Michael had become something of a thorn in their side; a reminder that perhaps they hadn't left their life behind as cleanly as they'd thought.

Viper's lips tightened and she shook her head. Right this second, he was more than an irritation. He was a damned liability. Not only was he suicidal for breaching the compound alone and without any backup that she could see, but he was putting her own operation at risk.

"You're a fool, O'Reilly," she muttered, turning her attention back to the main house. "What the hell are you thinking?"

After studying the house for another minute, she exhaled and swung down silently from the high tree branch that had afforded such an excellent view. A few minutes later, she dropped noiselessly onto the ground and began running through trees. Somewhere in that house was either the information stolen from Marcel, or another link to get her to it. That was why *she* was here. Michael's presence, however, was a

The Cuban

mystery. She suspected his mission was tied up with The Cuban, but she had no real basis for thinking that. Hawk had heard rumors that one of Charlie's spooks was inordinately interested in the man, and now here was Michael, preparing to break into a location that was reputed to be one of The Cuban's preferred residences. It had to be the reason Michael was here. She couldn't think of anything else that would bring him to Belarus. Viper had seen absolutely no indication that the arms dealer was in the compound, or that he'd ever been here, but that was hardly surprising. The only way to know for sure was to get inside.

And she was going to have to do it before Michael did.

Michael dropped to the ground and stayed in place for a long moment, listening intently to the night around him. Getting over the fence had been the easy part. Now he had to get into the house without being seen.

He'd already hacked into the external security cameras, sending the live stream directly to his cell. He took it out and pulled up the camera footage, noting the locations of the two roaming guards. Sliding it into his jacket sleeve, he straightened up and began moving along the perimeter, staying deep in the shadows.

He'd hoped to avoid going into the house at all, but that hope was dashed when he realized that the security cameras inside must be on a closed-circuit feed. The shutters on the windows made surveillance visually impossible, so now here he was, moving through the darkness and questioning his sanity. If The Cuban was inside, he would have to get in, get out, and then get back in again without anyone knowing that he'd been there before. It was easy to be invisible once. It was damned near impossible to be invisible twice. If he had to return with one of Charlie's assassins, they would have already lost any element of surprise.

That was all assuming that The Cuban was inside. Everything he'd seen from the security made it doubtful, but he had to be sure.

As he made his way towards the house, Michael shook his head. A part of him had thought that the security would be heavier once the sun went down, but everything was just the same as it had been earlier in the day. If The Cuban was inside, he was clearly not concerned with intruders. Knowing how cautious the man was, Michael thought that highly unlikely. He didn't think the man was inside, but even if he wasn't, he might be able to find some intelligence to make his trip worthwhile.

With that cheering thought, he glanced down at his phone again, checking the positions of the guards. The path to the right was clear all the way to the house. Tucking the phone away again, Michael moved to his right silently.

All he had to do was get inside. The rest would follow. It always did.

Washington, DC

Charlie stood at the floor-to-ceiling window and stared down into the busy street below. The streetlights cast an unnecessary glow over the red and white colored lights from the traffic clogging the capital. His office was silent, but he could almost hear the sounds of the city: honking cars, yelling cab drivers, sirens, and the almost constant thump and bass of two-door imports into whose trunks the owners had installed what had to be stadium-grade sound systems. It was the noise of the city at night, and it was something he'd learned to tune out as he navigated the silent and dangerous shadows where he lived and worked. This was his city, and he was used to it.

But it was changing. Two days before, hundreds of protesters had been arrested during the march on the Capitol. The majority of those arrested had done nothing beyond show up with cardboard signs and try to make their voices heard, but that had been their mistake. This administration had no interest in allowing opposition to make their voices heard. While they couldn't stop over 350,000 people from pouring into the city to join the organized protest, they could, and did, arrest as many as they could. Unfortunately, those people were still being held. Gone were the days when protesters got rowdy, were held overnight, and then released with a warning. Now they were held indefinitely under the shadow of domestic terrorism. The entire system was a mess, and there was nothing he could do to prevent the inevitable conflict that was bound to arise because of it. The American people would only be held down for so long.

Yes, his city was changing. The shadows were darker, the enemies more numerous, and the ability to tell friend from foe was becoming more and more a game of chance rather than design. He was keeping more and more secrets to himself, and trusting fewer and fewer

The Cuban

allies. It was just the way of it right now.

Charlie tightened his lips and turned away from the window. How long it could continue was anyone's guess, but it wasn't his job to worry about the domestic war being waged outside this office. He couldn't do anything to help the innocent citizens trying to fight back against their government, but he could do everything in his power to protect them from external threats while they did it.

His eyes fell on the sealed manilla envelope on his desk. If he could discover what it was that Hawk had been on to, it would go far to securing what might be one of the largest threats the world had faced since the Cold War. He went over to sit at his desk, leaning back in his chair and staring at the envelope pensively.

Hawk.

He'd lost contact with Damon Miles two weeks ago. Three days later, Viper had shown up in Washington demanding answers— answers that he didn't have to give. Hawk had simply disappeared.

It had seemed impossible. The amount of security measures all his assets abided by virtually ensured that this would never happen, especially after he'd lost almost half of his assets to Harry Shore four years ago. Hawk, in particular, had been religious in following the protocols to protect himself and the Organization over the past few years. He'd almost lost everything to blown identities once, and he wasn't about to risk it again. Yet two weeks ago, he'd disappeared. His watch, cell phone, and even the biometric tracker placed in his thigh, had all gone dark. Just like that, he was gone.

His last officially known location was Berlin. The tracker had pinged in Minsk three days later, but there was nothing after that. The day after meeting with Charlie, Viper had landed in Berlin, looking for some trace that might lead them to him. Charlie had had every confidence that she would pick up a trail, but after two days of searching, she had nothing.

And the reality that Damon Miles was really missing set in.

Viper appeared to be taking it in stride, but Charlie knew that couldn't be the case. Not for the first time, he lamented the loss of Harry's psychological insight. His current in-house psychologist was no match for Viper, but it hadn't seemed to matter until now. She ran ops for him on a contractual basis, but had retired from the life of one of his top assassins. There hadn't been a need to constantly monitor her mental health and well-being. When Hawk disappeared, all that changed, but it was too late. He couldn't get any kind of read on her real thoughts on the situation, and his psychologist hadn't fared much better. For all he knew, he'd unleashed a demon on Europe when he allowed her back into the field.

His lips curved faintly. Perhaps that wasn't a bad thing. If it was possible for anyone to find out what had happened to Hawk, Viper was the one to do it.

Letting out a sigh, Charlie sat forward and reached for the envelope, breaking the seal. He pulled out a stack of glossy surveillance photos taken from a mix of satellite images and CCTV feeds, spreading them out across his desk. They had been taken in a variety of locations across Russia, the Baltic States, and Eastern Europe. Amassed over the past ten months, they were his only lead to what Hawk had discovered. Any other intelligence he'd gathered had been hidden, or destroyed, when he disappeared. These photos were all that remained, and they were all of the same face.

The Cuban. He was the key to everything.

Chapter Ten

Viper stood still and silent in the darkness, listening to the sound of heavy footsteps walking down the hall outside the door. The guard was moving towards the closet where she was concealed and she lowered her eyes to the beam of light along the bottom of the door. As he approached, the walkie-talkie clipped to his waistband crackled, and a voice spoke through it, sounding inordinately loud in the silence.

"Ivan, where the hell are you?" it demanded. "The stew is getting cold."

"Just finishing the ground floor sweep." The guard paused outside the door and Viper stared at the shadow in the beam of light under the door, her breathing even and silent. "Perhaps the taste will improve as it cools."

"It's terrible stew," the walkie-talkie agreed cheerfully, "but cold it will be even worse."

"I'm coming. God, you're worse than my grandmother."

The shadow under the door moved as the guard continued down the hall, and Viper listened as the footsteps went around the corner. After a moment, she cracked open the door. They had spoken in Russian, but that was hardly surprising. The majority of the people of Belarus spoke Russian. What was interesting was that they spoke with an accent that she couldn't put her finger on. It wasn't Belarusian, and it wasn't from Moscow. In fact, she wasn't sure that she'd ever heard that particular accent before, and that was saying something. After all, Hawk had taken great pleasure in taking her on a tour through the old Soviet block and Russia. While her area of expertise was the Middle East, his was Russia, and he'd enjoyed teaching her the different dialects and accents that he'd picked up. If he'd been here, he would know exactly where the guards came from, and that would be something that she could use.

But he wasn't here, and she was on her own.

Seeing the hallway empty, she slipped out of the closet and closed the door silently before crossing the hallway to the stairs. She went up them quickly, pausing at the top to look at her phone in her hand. She'd patched into the internal security cameras in the basement when she came in, redirecting the feed to her cell phone. The hallway was clear and she turned right, tucking the phone back into her pocket.

The security cameras showed what was happening in every corridor and every room in the house, except the one at the end of this hallway. That was the only room that wasn't connected to the cameras. Someone didn't want anyone to see what happened in that room, and that made it her first stop.

Viper moved down the hallway quickly, her heartbeat steady and her senses tuned for any sound out of the ordinary. There were a total of six guards in the house, and the four outside made a grand total of ten, all armed. While it was hardly heavy security, it seemed a bit excessive for what appeared to be an empty building. There was no sign of The Cuban, a boss, or anyone else besides the guards on the camera footage. Even if The Cuban *had* been here, he certainly wasn't now.

Where the hell was he?

Viper shook her head and reached for the door handle. That wasn't her problem right now. He wasn't here, but she hadn't really been expecting that he would be. It was the information she wanted, and that might be behind this door.

She stepped into the room, closing the door silently behind her as her eyes went quickly around the area. She was standing in a sort of office. A large, heavy wooden desk commanded attention at one end of the room, positioned in front of French doors that she assumed led onto one of the several balconies gracing the back of the house. A fireplace dominated one wall, and two leather armchairs were in front of the empty hearth, a round mahogany table between them. On the opposite end of the room from the desk was what looked like a small home gym, with a treadmill, stationary bike, and weight stand all positioned around a huge TV mounted on the wall.

In direct contrast with the rest of the rooms in the house, this room appeared to have been occupied recently. The faint smell of cigar still hung in the air, and her lips tightened imperceptibly as she crossed the room to the desk. There was no film of dust on the gleaming wood, and a quick glance at the table between the armchairs confirmed that it was also clean. An empty rocks glass sat on the table, but it was dry. Any liquid that may have been left had long since dried up and evaporated. The room had been occupied recently, but not too recently.

Rounding the side of the desk, Viper felt a surge of satisfaction at the sight of a computer sitting on the floor. Dropping into the chair, she bent down to press the power button, waiting while the computer booted. Her eyes went around the room again and she pursed her lips. It was more than an office. It was a retreat; somewhere that he could come and not be disturbed. Even the security had no eyes here. She considered the armchairs thoughtfully, her eyes going to the hearth. Despite the cold temperatures gripping the region, the fireplace was void of kindling or wood.

The monitor lit up, drawing her attention away from the hearth, and Viper reached into her inner jacket pocket to pull out a slim box with USB cable. Plugging it into the computer, she reached for the mouse. This was the only room in the house where Marcel's flash drive could have possibly ended up, and if it had, the contents would have been transferred at this computer.

A moment later, the entire hard drive was being copied onto her external drive.

Michael raised his eyes to the wooden beams above his head, listening as what sounded like two sets of footsteps crossed overhead. He could hear the muffled mumble of voices through the floor as the two men walked down the short corridor to the kitchen. That should be the last of them. The rest of the guards were already in the kitchen, gathered around a large table with food, cards, and beer.

He turned his attention back to the tablet in his hands as he finished transferring the closed-circuit feed to his device. Once he was locked into the security feed, he reached up and pulled the cable from the router, severing any link that would show that he'd hacked into their system.

As he wound up the cable and stuffed it into his pocket, Michael remembered how horrified he'd been the first time he'd heard that Viper had hacked into the FBI. He'd been offended by the illegal means both she and the SEAL used to gain access to systems and information. He grinned ruefully. Oh, how times had changed. Although, to be fair, he generally only hacked into enemy servers. He had yet to hack into the FBI, but he knew that if the need arose, he wouldn't hesitate. The Organization had dispelled any lingering ideas of ethics and legality from his mind. He used whatever means were necessary to get the information that Charlie needed. Period.

He frowned as he turned his attention to the tablet, watching the men in the kitchen for a moment before examining all the rooms on the ground floor. He didn't know why Viper had been on his mind

Chapter Eleven

Michael sipped his coffee, his eyes on the screen of his laptop. Dawn was just lighting the sky outside his hotel window, and he stifled a yawn. After sleeping for a few hours, he'd been up before the sun, plugging in the external drive that he'd used to copy the hard drive at the house the night before. He had no idea if there was anything on it that would help him find The Cuban, but the high level of encryption that he was facing was encouraging. Military-grade encryption wasn't needed if there was nothing to hide.

His eyes strayed to the window and he reached for his coffee again. When he'd got to the office last night, the French door to the balcony had been ajar. He'd skirted the room, careful to not be seen from outside the doors, and had arrived at the balcony just in time to see a figure disappear into the night, heading towards the trees along the perimeter.

Michael frowned now and sat back, shifting his gaze out the window to the gray light of dawn. It hadn't been one of The Cuban's men, that much was obvious. Who was it? And did they now have the very information he was trying to get to? What had they been doing there?

Another player was a complication, but not necessarily something to concern him. It didn't matter to him if someone else was looking for The Cuban as well. All that mattered was that he find the man first. What *was* concerning, however, was the level of professionalism that the intruder had displayed. There had been no trace of him in that office. Even the computer didn't appear to be touched, though he knew that had to be wrong. The computer was the only item in the office worth looking at. There was no safe, no books, nothing of any value other than the computer. Whoever he'd just missed, they had to have been there for that. Anyone who could cover their tracks that effectively was someone worth knowing about, and he knew absolutely nothing about them.

He turned his gaze back to the laptop as one of the decryption programs he was running stopped. Leaning forward, he set his mug down and clicked open the drive he'd just gained access to. He blinked at the sheer number of files and folders that streamed across his screen. It would take weeks to go through everything thoroughly, and he didn't have weeks. He didn't even have days. He was behind The Cuban, and he had no idea how far behind. The house seemed to have been empty for some time, but the smell of old cigar smoke had still lingered in the office. Perhaps a week? Two?

Michael shook his head and began sorting through the mass of files. Certainly no more than two weeks. Any more and he would have heard something somewhere. He had too many ears and eyes watching for the arms dealer to be in the dark for very long.

He would sort the files by date of the last accessed and start there. If nothing else, it would give him a good idea where to look. A moment later, he was clicking open a file cryptically titled, 'Cellars.'

Michael frowned as he stared at a list. He wasn't sure what he'd been expecting, but this certainly wasn't it. It had to be some sort of code, but he was damned if he could make head or tail out of it. The list was divided into two columns with a line of numbers in one and corresponding names in the other. It wasn't an itemized list of names. All the numbers repeated in a seemingly random order. The names were also strange. They were first names only, and some of them had strange symbols next to them. This was the last file accessed? There were fifteen numbers repeated and at least fifty names, but none of the names were repeated, only the numbers.

Sitting back, Michael crossed his arms over his chest and stared at the screen thoughtfully. Why use a code when the entire system was heavily encrypted? And what did it mean? Did the person who'd got there before him know the key? Were they looking for this as well?

And what the hell was it?

The man lifted his eyes from his laptop keyboard when his cell phone vibrated inside his jacket pocket. With a sigh, he extracted it, not taking his eyes from the screen in front of him.

"Yes?"

"You wanted to be kept informed of the movements of the woman asking after The Cuban."

"Proceed."

"She left the hotel last night and, well, we lost her. However, she returned a few hours later," the caller hastened to add. "We're back in contact, and I've set one of my best men on her."

The man let out a low curse and lifted his eyes from the laptop.

"Do you have any idea where she went?"

"Unfortunately, no. We don't think she left the city, but there is no way to be sure."

"Where is she now?"

"In her room."

The man sighed and pinched the bridge of his nose.

"I don't like it. Keep her under tighter surveillance. Pull someone else if you need to, but don't lose her again."

"Yes, sir."

The man disconnected the call and set his phone next to the laptop, his lips pressed together grimly. Who was this woman? His people were not clumsy by any means. They knew how to be invisible. Yet she had clearly known she was being watched, and had been able to evade them.

He shifted his eyes to stare out of the small window at the expanse of clouds over the wing. He would be landing in just over an hour, and he had to have something to tell them. Right now he had nothing. He certainly wasn't about to admit that he'd lost someone in Belarus who was probably a clandestine agent for one of the Western powers. He had to give them something, but there was nothing.

He turned his gaze back to the laptop in frustration and reached for the whiskey and soda at his elbow. The Cuban was in hiding, but from what no one knew. He'd had to dispose of the Interpol agent asking questions about the Cellars, which was unfortunate because now they had Interpol investigating his death as a homicide, making Berlin inaccessible at least until they concluded their investigation. An assassin that he'd been assured was killed two months ago had somehow shown up in Zurich three weeks ago, and now a new player was poking around Minsk, asking questions. He frowned.

And she actually had a photo of The Cuban.

That was the most disturbing part of the whole situation. They would want to know how she had a photo, and he had no idea. As far as he was aware, there were no known photos of the arms dealer.

The man drained his glass and pressed the button to summon the steward for a refill. The entire situation was out of control, and the only thing that he knew for sure was that it had all unraveled three weeks ago. That was the catalyst that started this avalanche. It all began with the power outage in Prague. It had seemed like a harmless inconvenience at the time. It had been restored in hours and a system check had revealed that there had been no breach, and nothing was missing. He'd dismissed it for what it appeared to be: a power outage caused by work on an underground power line in the city. But now he knew that that was when everything had begun to slide off the rails.

Just who had managed to get into their server in Prague was a complete mystery. Despite all of his efforts, they hadn't been able to discover the person or organization responsible. He hadn't even been able to determine what they had accessed, but the results spoke for themselves. Someone knew about Les Cinq.

And if he didn't find out who and clean it up, the entire operation was dead, and he'd be dead along with it.

The cold, gray light of dawn was just covering the farm yard when the farmer shuffled out of the house with a yawn. He was dressed in a heavy flannel barn jacket and warm work pants. Stretching, he glanced up at the sky and grunted. The forecast was for sun today. He sincerely hoped they'd got it right. He had a lot to do with the fences in the fields today, and the sun would be much appreciated. The snow was only a dusting now, and the next snowfall was forecast for the end of the week. He wanted to repair the fences before the heavy snow came again.

He blew on his hands and rubbed them together briskly in the cold morning air, then turned to cross the small kitchen garden to the gate. Before he could go out to the fields, the goats and pigs needed tending. He opened the gate and went out, being careful to close it securely behind him before moving towards the barn. He would tend the goats first, then go around to the pigs. By the time he'd finished with them, his wife would have finished preparing breakfast. He would have a quick meal, and then go out to the fields.

Another glance up to the sky and he nodded, his mood lightening. They had been fortunate that they hadn't had very heavy snow as of yet, but he knew that could change overnight. As long as he got the fences repaired before it came, he would be happy. Then he would turn his attention to all the work inside the house that his wife had been asking him to start.

He unlatched the barn door and went inside, leaving the door open to allow what murky light there was in the dawn hours to penetrate inside the door. Bending, he picked up a lantern that sat on the floor just inside and turned it on, holding it up to survey the pen where the goats slept. At the sound of the door, two of them had shook their heads and moved over to the side of the pen closest to him.

"Ah, you're awake, are you?" he asked gruffly, moving towards them.

He hadn't gone three steps when the shadows in the corner shifted. He sucked in his breath and swung his lantern towards the corner in time to watch as a woman emerged. She was dressed in dark pants and jacket with a fur-lined hood pulled up over her head. The shadows played on her face, concealing most of it from his light, and she stopped before the light revealed too much.

"Who the hell are you?" he demanded angrily. "What are you doing in my barn?"

"Just someone looking for information," she said, her voice calm and quiet. "I won't take much of your time. Your billy goats are hungry."

"They are, are they? Did they tell you that?"

Something like a smile crossed her face and she shook her head.

"Why don't you put down the lantern and have a seat on that stool over there?" she asked pleasantly. "There's no reason for you to be uncomfortable on that bad knee."

He blustered, his face turning red.

"How do you know about that? Who are you?"

"It doesn't matter who I am. Please. Sit."

There was an edge of steel in her voice now and he swallowed, looking behind him at the stool.

"I'd rather stand."

"Suit yourself." She studied him for a long moment. "You had a visitor here two weeks ago. A man. Dark hair. Intimidating. What did he want?"

His face went pale and he stared at her, his heart pounding.

"How do you know about that?" he asked, his voice sounding hoarse to his own ears. "I told no one."

"You didn't have to. What did he want?"

His lips tightened and he set the lantern down.

"Who sent you?" he demanded, taking a step towards her in the shadows. "Was it The Cuban? Because if it was, you can tell him that nothing has changed. I will die before I betray my family or my country."

The woman didn't move in the shadows and he took another step towards her.

"It *was* him, wasn't it? Well, he should know better than to

82

The Cuban

send a woman. You'll get nothing from me."

"What did the man want? I won't ask again."

Her voice was like a blade, slicing through the space between them and making him flinch despite himself.

"Ot'ebis."

The word had barely left his mouth when she moved at last. He only had time to gasp in some air before excruciating pain shot up his leg from his arthritic knee. Everything after that was a blur. One minute he was bending to grab his knee in pain, and the next he was falling. It happened so fast that he had no clear recollection of how he came to be laying flat on his back on the barn floor, but the knee pressing into his chest left no doubt as to who was responsible. Before he could make any noise or movement, the razor-sharp tip of a blade was pressing into his neck, breaking the skin and causing an icy streak of fear to go through him. The pressure on his chest increased as the woman leaned more weight onto her knee, and he felt as if he were being buried under pounds of bricks.

"All right!" he gasped. "I can't breathe!"

The pressure lightened on his chest and he sucked in air, his heart pounding against his rib cage. He stared into dark, emotionless eyes and a shudder went through him at the look on her face.

"He wanted to know about an old man!" he exclaimed, terror rolling through him. "That's all. Just some old man who went missing from Minsk."

"When?"

"What?"

"When did the old man go missing?" A note of impatience accompanied increased pressure on the knife tip in his neck and he gasped, sweat beading on his face.

"I don't know. Maybe four months ago."

"Who was he?"

"Nobody. He was nobody. Just an old man who worked in the city." He started to shake his head but froze when the motion drove the knife deeper in. "I don't know what he did!"

The woman stared at him for a long moment, her face an emotionless mask and her eyes dark pools of death. He shuddered again and his heart continued pounding against his chest as she considered him.

"If he was a nobody, why did the man ask after him?" she finally asked softly, her voice skimming over him dangerously.

"I don't know. He didn't say. Just wanted to know about him."

"And what did you tell him?"

"There was nothing to tell. He went missing, but he had no family here, so no one went looking for him."

"And how do you know about this? You don't strike me as someone who follows local gossip."

He stared up at her and swallowed again, his mouth dry.

"He bought milk from me," he told her. "I never got paid for my last delivery. That's how I know he went missing. The milk was still on his step, right where I left it."

"Four months ago?"

The man nodded, exhaling when he felt the knife tip begin to ease out of his neck.

"What was the man's name?"

"Yuri." He watched as she stood up, sliding the knife into a sheath at her waist. "Yuri Morozov."

She stared down at him for a long moment, then reached down a hand. As he hesitated, she shook her head.

"You'll never get up on your own," she told him. "Let me help you to the stool."

"Why would you do that?" he asked, reluctantly taking the offered hand.

"Why wouldn't I?"

He struggled to his feet, pain in his knee making it impossible to put weight on his leg. He grunted as she supported him, guiding him over to the stool. He sank onto it, watching as she went over to a walking stick that leaned against the wall. He kept it there for days when his knee was bad, but how did she know that?

"You would have killed me just now," he said.

She carried the stick over to hand it to him.

"Yes."

"Then why help me now?"

"You told me what I wanted to know." She looked down at him, her eyes emotionless. "You could have saved yourself a lot of pain if you'd simply answered my question from the beginning."

He stared up at her.

"You don't work for The Cuban," he decided. "Who are you?"

"Nobody. Just a ghost."

"You don't look like a ghost to me."

She smiled faintly, and then the smile was gone as quickly as it appeared.

"If you mention me to anyone, I'll come back and make sure you never walk again. Understood?"

He shivered and nodded mutely, then watched as she

The Cuban

disappeared out the door of the barn. Exhaling heavily, he looked over to his goats in the pen. They were all calm, acting as if nothing out of the ordinary had happened, and he frowned. They were a skittish lot, his goats. He turned his eyes back to the door and the frown grew.

Who was she? And why was everyone so interested in old Yuri?

Chapter Twelve

C harlie frowned when his cell phone vibrated on his desk. Glancing at his watch, he reached for it, raising an eyebrow at the secure number displayed. It was after nine o'clock at night, which meant that it was five in the morning where the call was coming from.

"You're up early," he said by way of greeting, sitting back in his chair.

"I haven't gone to bed yet," Viper said. "Are you secure?"

"Yes."

"How quickly can you get me background on someone?"

"It depends on who the someone is."

"Sophia Morozov."

"Who is she?"

"That's what I need to know."

"When did you last sleep?" Charlie asked after a moment's silence.

"What?"

"Sleep. When did you last get any?"

"Are you worried that I'm overdoing it, Charlie?" Viper sounded distinctly amused.

"Worried that you'll be sloppy when you need to be sharp."

"I'll sleep when I've found him."

"You can't push yourself too hard, Viper. This is your first time back out there. I need you on top of your game. If you make a mistake, I lose you both."

"Wow, you don't mince words anymore, do you?"

That drew a smile from him. "Did I ever?"

"I don't remember you being quite so blunt." There was a short silence, then she exhaled audibly in his ear. "I have a long train ride ahead of me. I'll sleep then."

"I know you're running out of time," Charlie said slowly. "Do you at least have a location?"

"Of a sort."

The Cuban

"Of a sort?" he repeated, raising an eyebrow. "What does that mean?"

"I thought you didn't want to know?" she countered. "Are you going to let me do my job, or are you micromanaging these days?"

"You've been fraternizing with Jack for too long," he muttered. "You're right, though. It's best if I don't know. How will I know if you find him?"

"Oh, you'll know. I'm sure of that."

He shook his head, a reluctant smile lighting his eyes. She was just as cryptic as she always had been. As much as he hated to admit it, it was good to have Viper back.

"I'll have a dossier on Sophia Morozov for you in the morning, my time."

"Thank you."

"Viper?"

"Yes?"

"Bring him home."

There was a short, pregnant silence before she replied.

"I intend to."

Plop...plip...plop.

The relentless sound came at irregular intervals, echoing off the slick, brick walls of the small chamber. Just when he thought it had stopped, another drop of water fell into the shallow puddle beneath the spray nozzle attached to a garden hose. It had been draped carelessly over a metal hook in the bricks after his last hose down. As another drip dropped, he wished they'd thrown it on the floor instead. The sound was inordinately loud and distracting, pulling him from his semiconscious state with each plop.

Damon Miles stared through one open eye at the mess below him. The rope that bound his wrists together was looped over a hook in the ceiling and his feet dangled a foot off the ground. Sweat mixed with blood ran down his bare torso, oozing from open lacerations covering his chest and sides. His interrogator had left the room, and Damon tried to focus and remember how long it had been since he'd been left alone. It must have only been minutes, surely. They wouldn't risk leaving him alone for long.

Not that he could do anything to try to escape, he thought bitterly. His body was betraying him. He didn't even have the energy to lift his head, let alone get himself off this damned hook. His neck wouldn't support anything, and his head hung helplessly forward. All he could see was the blood covering him and the floor below his feet, and he was too drained to try to look at the door. He didn't know if it was open or closed. No. There was no fear of him ever escaping this hell hole.

He closed his eye tiredly. He didn't need to see how much blood he'd lost, or how badly they'd carved him up - like a Thanksgiving turkey. Something pulled at his consciousness and he tried to push back the pain long enough to focus on it. Turkeys. Thanksgiving. Had he missed it? It must have passed. How long had he been here?

Damon felt an exhale come from somewhere deep within him. He should know how long he'd been here. The guards had mentioned it again just this morning. Or was it yesterday? He tried to frown as his mind became fuzzy and he felt like he was floating again. Here came the welcome darkness. When it was here, he could rest. He needed to rest.

A long forgotten memory surfaced. Yes. He needed to rest. Without rest, he was dead. He couldn't remember much right now, but he remembered that. It had been drilled into him.

Damon didn't know how long he hung there, suspended between consciousness and darkness, before he slipped into his memories. Suddenly the small, stinking room where he hung faded away, and he was somewhere else. He was underwater, he realized with a start, in a SDV in the Atlantic Ocean. He was watching on a screen as a homing tracker made its way towards them. It was Viper. She was coming to meet him.

Damon jerked, holding on to the memory when it began to fade. There had been blood in the water, he remembered. As she'd got close, he'd seen the blood trailing behind Viper on the thermal imaging as she swam. He left the pod to meet her, ignoring the driver's insistence that he remain inside. As he drew close to her, his heart surged into his throat. She was barely conscious, her eyes closed, and blood was pouring from her neck, torso, and leg. She wouldn't have made it. As it was, he'd reached her just in time. Another minute or two and he would have lost her.

Damon came back to the present with another jerk, the smell of his own sweat and blood filling his nostrils. The pain from his beatings and torture came back in waves, and he swore he felt his heart beating out of his chest.

God, he was tired!

The Cuban

He cracked open the eye that wasn't swollen shut and peered down at his abdomen. Most of the pain seemed to be emanating from his left side, but he couldn't see enough to know how bad the wounds were. The blood covered them. He closed his eye again, willing the darkness to come and take him. He was so tired. If the darkness came, he wouldn't be in pain anymore. He wouldn't be anything anymore. He would simply be at peace.

An image of dark brown eyes, lit with laughter, filled his mind, and Damon could hear Alina's laugh. It was the deep belly-laugh that still surprised him when it happened. It was the laugh of his Jersey Girl, and something that never failed to fill him with warmth and joy. The image expanded and he saw her standing in the sun, gazing over the mountains with the wind blowing wisps of dark hair out from under her battered, well-worn Eagles cap. They had been in South America, high in the mountains, he remembered. He'd met her sensei, and saw where she'd spent two years coming to terms with who, and what, she was. It was the first time she'd truly allowed him to see a part of her that he doubted she even realized was there.

His heart thumped again, and Damon was back in a helicopter, leaning over her in the impossibly small space. They were being lifted to an aircraft carrier where a surgeon was waiting for her. Her skin was almost gray, and the abrasions and lacerations all over her face and neck had looked like something out of a horror film. His heart had felt like it did now, like it could stop at any moment while it pounded out of his chest. He'd spoken in her ear, making sure to speak loud enough for her to hear over the propellers. He'd told her not to leave him. He couldn't live without her. He'd told her not to be a chickenshit, but to fight.

To fight for them.

Damon inhaled painfully and the memory faded as numbness stole over him. He couldn't leave her. She hadn't left him when the darkness came for her. She'd fought until the very end.

The darkness shattered around him as hot, searing pain went into his chest cavity. His heart crashed against his ribs and he gasped, choking as he sucked in a lungful of air. His one eye flew open just in time to watch as two paddles were pulled away from his chest.

"Good! You're back. I'm not finished with you yet."

The bastard had returned to continue. Damon grit his teeth and spit out blood onto the floor. He thought of Alina, lying in the helicopter, and his muscles stiffened. If she wouldn't leave him, he wouldn't leave her. Not yet. Not here. Not now.

"You're not doing very well, but I'm sure you don't need me to tell you that. You're getting tired, and so am I. Tell me what I want to know, and we can both rest."

The man walked around him and then reached out to lift Hawk's chin. He stared into his tormentors face with one eye, noting the smell of fresh cigarette smoke on his breath.

"Tell me about Sophia Morozov."

"Go to hell."

The remains of a room service breakfast sat on a tray as Michael stared at the screen, his brows drawn together in concentration. The silence in the hotel room was broken a moment later when he sucked in his breath suddenly and sat back, the frown on his face disappearing. He rubbed his face with his hands, then reached for his cup of forgotten, cold coffee.

Satisfaction coursed through him. He'd done it! He'd actually figured out the cryptic code from the computer! Somewhere between finishing his last pancake and his coffee growing cold, he'd unraveled the code. Now, he stared at the lists as he drained the coffee from his mug.

The numbers ranged from one to fifteen, and they represented specific prisons or camps across Russia. The names were people who'd been sent to those prisons, or at least the people The Cuban was interested in. Why he had a list of over fifty people imprisoned by the Russians was a mystery. Were they people he'd sent to the Russians for punishment? Were they enemies? Allies? Why was an international arms dealer keeping a meticulous record of who went to what prison camp?

Michael shook his head and stretched before getting up from his chair and walking over to the window. He'd had to get very inventive with how he did it, but he believed he had the locations of at least five of the prisons. The rest were still being run through a cross-checking database of Charlie's. It was comparing the numbers with all known past and present locations of prisons. Everything from known Soviet-era Gulags to present day penal colonies was in the database. It might take some time, but he'd get the rest of the locations. The names, however, were another matter.

It was impossible to discover who they were from only a first name, but someone on that list was important enough to attract another player. He frowned as he looked down into the busy city street below, his mind going back to the shadow he'd seen disappearing into the night. Whoever it was, they had to have been there for this list. He'd been through the rest of the hard-drive. That was the only file accessed in the past three months. It had to be what the other intruder had been looking for as well.

Someone on that list was not only important enough to risk The Cuban's wrath, but also to attract another player who was skilled enough to leave no trace behind.

Exhaling, Michael turned away from the window and went over to the mini fridge for a bottle of water. He'd start running every name on the list against Interpol and CIA and see what he uncovered. While it was a long shot and would generate thousands of hits, it was the only shot he had. They were probably aliases, but somewhere, someone had to know who they were. If they'd managed to get themselves thrown in a Russian prison, records had to exist somewhere. He just had to find them.

Then maybe he'd know who else was interested in this list.

The man burrowed into his fur-lined hood and shifted his weight from one foot to the other. The wind was brutal today despite the bright sun that shone over the city. He pulled one hand out of his pocket and looked at his watch, then shoved it back in and returned his gaze to the front of the hotel. At least he wasn't the only one freezing his butt off out here. There were three others, all placed at points around the block to ensure that the woman wouldn't sneak off again, undetected. He shook his head and pressed his lips together. He still had no idea how she'd done it the other night, but it had caused enough of a flap to make the boss man triple surveillance detail.

A moment later, he straightened up and exhaled as the woman stepped out of the front doors of the hotel. She was dressed in jeans and a black coat that came to her hips. Stepping onto the sidewalk, she settled a pair of large sunglasses on her face, pausing as she glanced up and down the street. It was almost as if she wanted to make sure that they saw her before she turned to her right. As she walked away from him, the man moved out of the alley and jogged across the street, taking advantage of a break in the traffic.

"The woman's on the move." He spoke into the mic concealed beneath his collar. "I'm on her."

"Lucky bastard," a voice replied in his ear bud. "I'm freezing my balls off."

He chuckled and started down the sidewalk after her, keeping a safe distance behind.

"I'll tell you when we're on our way back."

Keeping his eye on the black coat ahead of him, the man rolled his shoulders, glad to be moving. She crossed a side street, striding along the sidewalk confidently. She was heading towards the shopping district, but he would be very surprised if that was her destination. The boss didn't have them watch women who were prone to shopping. He frowned. Actually, the boss usually didn't have them watch women at all. Most of their targets were men. So why was this woman so important? Was she Interpol? She didn't look like Interpol. She didn't look like any kind of law enforcement. He was pretty good at spotting them, and she wasn't raising any red flags. A government operative, then? But she didn't look like one of those, either. She didn't look like anything, but clearly she was something.

The frown sharpened when the woman turned suddenly and disappeared from view. He let out a low curse and closed the distance quickly, jogging through the pedestrians on the sidewalk. A moment later, he reached the alley she'd turned down. He stepped into it, looking around in confusion. It was empty.

He walked down the narrow lane, looking at the ground, searching for some indication of where she'd gone. There hadn't been time for her to reach the other end, which was quite some distance away. The cement beneath his feet was dry, however, with no indication of footprints on the surface.

The man stopped and raised his eyes, looking around the alley thoughtfully. A few feet further down, a metal door was just slightly ajar. His lips tightened and he went towards it. There!

He pushed open the door and stepped through the opening, peering around. He stood in what appeared to be an empty warehouse or storage area. There were no windows, and the only light was what came in from the alley through the door behind him. He took a few steps into the empty space, feeling in his jacket pocket for his flashlight. Before he could find it, a blinding pain shot through his skull, and then everything went black.

Chapter Thirteen

Viper wiped her combat knife on the dead man's leg before sliding it back into the sheath. Looking down at him dispassionately, she pressed her lips together. His name was Karl, and he worked for a local crime boss. Or he had until she killed him.

She turned to leave, ignoring the feeling of hollowness that nagged at her. It had been necessary. The more people she allowed to live after talking to her, the more people that could describe her. She'd made an exception with the farmer, but she couldn't afford to do that every time. Viper had spent four years completely invisible, and she had every intention of remaining a ghost.

Stepping into the alley, she closed the door behind her and turned to stride back to the street. Pulling the hood of her coat up against the brisk wind, she exhaled. She'd known she was being watched and followed the first afternoon at the hotel. When she went to the compound, she'd easily avoided being seen as she mingled with a group of tourists on their way out to a theater production. On her return, she'd entered the front of the lobby without a second thought. It didn't matter if they saw her returning, as long as they didn't know where she'd been.

But she'd had to learn who they were, and why they were watching her every move.

Karl had been reticent at first, but Viper was very persuasive. She'd always been good at getting people to talk, but Mossad had improved her skills considerably. Or rather, had sharpened them, she thought as she blended back into the foot traffic on the city street. She could get the information in half the time now, and usually with much less violence. It was something that she had known would come in very handy, and it just had with Karl. She didn't have time to waste with interrogations at the moment, but she'd needed to know if her mission was compromised. It had been with great relief that she learned that they had no idea who she was, or what she was doing in Minsk. All they knew was that she was looking for The Cuban.

Viper's lips curved humorlessly. They had someone in the hotel, the boy she'd shown his photo to in the restaurant that first day. He was the one who'd told them she was there and asking questions. If not for him, they wouldn't have been involved at all. Of all the people in the hotel, she'd picked the one who was dirty. Typical.

These kinds of mistakes would be made. It was inevitable. After all, she'd been out of the game for a while now. Even so, she was irritated. That piece of bad luck had wasted over an hour of her time.

Time that she didn't have.

Stopping at the corner, Alina raised her hand to flag down a cab. She was behind schedule now and had to move quickly. There could be no more delays or distractions, and that included the other three watching the hotel.

Getting into the back of the cab, she gave the driver the name of the hotel and sat back, turning her gaze out the window. Charlie would be sending the information on Sophia Morozov soon, if he hadn't already, and that was a piece of the puzzle that she needed sooner rather than later. The woman fit into this mess somehow, and she had a feeling that she could be the key to unlocking everything.

Viper lowered her eyes to her watch and her lips tightened. Until then, however, she had a lot of ground to cover, and not much time to do it.

Michael unlocked his door and went into his hotel room, relocking it behind him. After a walk in the brisk wind and lunch in the hotel restaurant, he was ready to get back to work. He'd left the Organization's databases running, comparing the thousands of hits he got from Interpol and CIA to the fifty-odd names on the list, looking for possible matches. He had no idea how many hits he'd get, but he'd be surprised if he didn't get at least one.

Crossing the room, he dropped his room key on the desk next to his laptop and opened the lid, shrugging out of his coat as he entered his password to unlock the machine. As the screen opened, he raised his eyebrows in surprise. The search had finished and he'd got several.

Michael tossed his coat onto the bed behind him and sat down, reaching for his mouse. All the hits were for known aliases, and he settled down to start sifting through them, checking for any known legal names. He really didn't have any idea what he was looking for.

The Cuban

Who would interest an international arms dealer? Why would he have a list of prisoners on a computer in a compound in Belarus? Why was someone else interested in this list?

Michael frowned as he worked, his lips pressed together thoughtfully. He was missing something somewhere. He was sure of it. There had to be much more to this than some prisoners rotting in the Gulag. The very presence of another player the other night was evidence enough of that. Who were they? Had it been another government agent? Or were they working for the criminal underworld? The Russians? He shook his head. If he knew who they were, it would go a long way to helping him figure out what he was missing.

He turned his attention to the names on the screen and began sorting through them, his brows furrowed. None of these people had any connection to either The Cuban or energy corporations. In fact, none of them seemed to have any connection to anything in Eastern Europe at all. Yet there had to be something.

Fifteen minutes later, Michael sucked in his breath and stared at the name before him. Hans Becker. The man was an Austrian businessman who'd disappeared two weeks ago, but Michael wasn't even looking at that. He stared at the name, his mind reeling. He knew that name! He'd seen it before, on a hotel registry in Amsterdam four years ago.

"Son of a bitch!" he breathed, getting up restlessly.

He ran a hand through his hair and circled the room, his eyes going back to the screen. It couldn't be him. It couldn't be the same man. The Hans Becker who signed the registry in Amsterdam was Damon Miles, ex-Navy SEAL, assassin and, as it had transpired, Alina's husband. Michael was almost positive that Damon had used that name after they both disappeared, but he hadn't been able to trace the name past Amsterdam four years ago, and he hadn't seen it since.

Until now.

Michael scowled and stopped pacing, gripping the back of his chair as he stared at the laptop screen. It couldn't be him. The name was common enough. It had to be a different Becker. The SEAL would never have allowed himself to be thrown into a Russian prison. It was just a bizarre coincidence that Damon had used the name four years earlier.

After a deep breath, Michael sat down again and clicked on the name. Interpol was monitoring this Hans Becker for a possible connection to a former Ukrainian general who was suspected of selling military weapons on the black market. They had no actual proof that the Austrian had any dealings with the general, but his name had been

95

flagged in connection with another suspect, resulting in them monitoring his movements. Two weeks ago, all activity on his credit had ceased, and they'd lost his electronic footprint. He had disappeared without a trace. Interpol had flagged him as a low priority, and they didn't seem to be actively pursuing any leads as to his whereabouts.

Michael scratched his chin thoughtfully. If he'd disappeared into one of these Russian prisons, that explained the abrupt lack of any kind of electronic trace. But what would anyone want with a businessman who was mid-level management for a trading firm? More than that, why would The Cuban be interested?

If The Cuban was even interested at all. He let out a frustrated grunt and got up, going to get a bottle of water from the fridge. The more he dug into this, the more he wondered what The Cuban had to do with any of it. He felt like he was going in circles with this, and all these names simply confused the matter further. None of these people had anything to do with arms sales, energy corporations, or financing for either concern. Yet on the surface, it seemed as though something had to connect them to The Cuban. What?

Michael gulped down some water and went back to the desk, staring down at the name. Against everything, he felt that Hans Becker was the key. It made no sense, but his gut was telling him that he was who Michael was looking for. He leaned down and clicked the mouse, pulling up the original list. Hans Becker was being held in #15. He clicked a few more times until he found what he was looking for, then exhaled.

"You've got to be kidding me," he muttered, staring at the corresponding location.

The prison camp was located in Luhansk, Ukraine.

Alina strode across the tarmac towards the small, private jet. The sun was still bright, but it was sinking fast, and a stiff wind whipped around her legs. As she went towards the airplane, a man came towards her, squinting in the bright light and raising a hand to shield his eyes.

"Ms. Molotov!" he called over the wind.

Alina reached out to shake his offered hand as she joined him.

"It's been some time, hasn't it? It's a pleasure to have you onboard again." he said. "We're ready to take off when you are."

The Cuban

"Thank you!" Alina fell into step beside him as they moved towards the airplane. "How close can you get me to the Ukrainian border?"

He looked down at her and scratched his neck.

"There's a military base just twenty miles from the border, but the Russians have full control of it. I don't think you want to go there. The closest I can get you and it be safe is Gomel Airport."

"Gomel it is, then."

He nodded and motioned to a steward waiting at the bottom of the steps.

"You've got it. Paul will take your bag and get you comfortable. We'll be in the air in ten minutes."

"Make it five and I'll throw in some of that vodka you love," Alina said, handing her bag to the steward.

The pilot laughed. "Deal! Wheels up in five, Paul."

Paul nodded and smiled at Alina.

"Let's get you settled, Ms. Molotov."

"Call me Elena," she said, starting up the steps. "I've flown with you enough to be beyond formalities."

"Of course, Elena."

She went up the steps quickly and stepped into the Cessna CJ4. It was one of the smaller private jets that she'd flown on, but she trusted the pilot and crew more than most. They had proven their discretion on more than one occasion, and that was crucial for this trip.

She settled herself into a leather seat and watched as Paul stowed her bag into an overhead compartment opposite from her.

"Once we've taken off, would you like your usual martini?"

"Make it water this time. Thank you."

"Of course. I'll inform the pilot that we're ready to leave."

Alina waited until Paul had disappeared towards the cockpit before she pulled out her phone and swiped the screen. She opened a secure app and sent off a quick message to Charlie, then slid her phone back into her pocket. Leaning back, she inhaled and turned her eyes out the window.

Getting out of the hotel undetected had been easy, thanks to Karl giving up the locations of the other three men watching her. The journey to Minsk National Airport was also uneventful. Getting to the airplane, however, had been more tricky. Avoiding all cameras in the airport was no small feat, and once you added in avoiding both physical security and airport workers, it became even more challenging. But she'd managed to remain invisible for four years, even with Michael O'Reilly relentlessly looking for her, and if she couldn't do it in Belarus, then she had no business being back in the game.

The small airplane began moving and she looked out the window as they turned away from the terminal. Michael was definitely a complication, and one that she was not too happy about. She liked him. She really did. But if he got in her way, he'd get taken down, and that would be a shame. He was one of the few good guys, and her last and only link to her brother.

Dave.

Alina pressed her lips together. She hadn't thought of her brother in months. He'd been killed in Iraq fifteen years ago, and Michael had been with him at the end. Killing Harry had served to finally lay Dave to rest as well, but while she'd finally let go of her brother, she hadn't been able to get rid of Michael quite as easily.

Despite the situation, Alina felt a smile pulling at her lips. She should have known that he wouldn't buy the elaborate ruse they'd sold everyone else. He was a stubborn Irish bastard, that one. They *all* should have known that he wouldn't believe it without a body. Charlie had thought he would accept it eventually, but had finally admitted that they had miscalculated after the Cuba fiasco.

She shook her head now as the little airplane picked up speed and hurtled down the runway. Charlie had warned them off Havana when he realized they were booked into the same hotel Michael was using for his final training op. It had been too late. Somehow Michael had discovered that Raven Woods had a reservation.

And it had been downhill ever since.

In some ways, Alina regretted avoiding him for the past four years. He worked for Charlie. Even if he wanted to expose her continued existence to the world, which she knew he would never do, he was prevented from doing so by his oath of loyalty to his country and the Organization. If any of them revealed the identity of other assets or spies for the Organization, Charlie would have them killed. End of story. They'd all agreed to the terms. Her lips twisted humorlessly. In this case, if Michael exposed Viper or Hawk after all this time, she was fairly confident that Charlie would pull the trigger himself. No. She was in no danger from Michael, and neither was Hawk. Yet she'd continued to avoid him and, deep down inside, she knew why.

She felt guilty for deceiving him; for deceiving them all. It was a dick move four years ago, but at the time it was the only way to keep them all safe. Now that the threats were in the past, there was really no reason to continue the charade, at least where Michael was concerned. But it was easier to stay dead than to say that she was sorry.

went back to digging. "Think maybe it was something about Petrov?"

"I don't know. I don't care, either. I just want to find this guy, take his picture, and get the hell out of here and back to somewhere warm."

The man in the hole stopped digging and gingerly poked at the loose dirt beneath him with one foot.

"I think I've found him."

The other man capped his water bottle and set it down. He picked up the lantern to hold it over the hole in the ground. There, at his friend's feet, a piece of black plastic poked out from the dirt.

"It's the bag," he said, setting down the lantern and joining the other man in the hole. "Come on. Let's pull it out."

"What about the masks?"

"We'll get him out first, then the masks."

The other man nodded and tossed the shovel out of the hole before bending to dig in the loose soil for the rest of the edge of the body bag. The other one began digging with his hands at the other end of the oblong hole they'd created. A few minutes later, they were heaving a body bag out of the grave, sweating and cursing as they struggled with the awkward weight.

"Good thing it's winter," the one gasped as they pushed it onto the ground beside the grave.

"Why?"

"Would you want to do this in the summer?"

The other one grunted and climbed out of the grave.

"Good point. Hand me a mask."

They both secured the masks to their faces and then stared down at the black body bag.

"We're going to hell for this. You know that."

"Why? It's not a blessed grave."

"Doesn't matter. We're disturbing the dead."

"Somehow, I don't think he cares." The man looked at him. "Well?"

"Well what?"

"Open the bag."

"Why do I have to open the bag?"

"Because you're the one who found it."

"That's bullshit. *You* open the bag!"

The man looked down at the bag at their feet and cursed. Crouching down, he looked for the zipper tab.

"You're a chickenshit."

"No, I just have a healthy respect for the deceased. If you

disturb the dead, bad things happen."

The man looked up at him, his fingers pausing on the zipper tab.

"Like what?"

"Like what? I don't know. Bad things! Like zombies eating brains, or vampires sucking blood. Bad things!"

The man scoffed and pulled at the zipper.

"You watch too many bad movies."

He unzipped the body bag and then took a deep breath before gingerly lifting the flap to peer inside. Silence fell over them as he stared into the bag.

"What? Is it bad?" His friend finally demanded, reaching for the lantern. "Are you going to puke?"

The man shook his head and slowly stood up, backing away.

"No, but it's not what I was expecting."

His friend came around and pushed him out of the way, holding up the lantern so that he could see down into the bag.

"What the hell?"

Inside was a rolled up carpet.

"Where's the assassin?"

"Not there."

The two men looked at each other and one pulled off his mask, his face grim.

"Boss isn't going to like this."

"What do we do?"

He shrugged.

"Put it back and go tell him."

"You want to bury a rug again?"

"Would you rather carry it back to the car?"

The other man glowered and bent down to zip up the body bag again.

"What the hell was Petrov thinking?"

"Nothing good. Maybe it's good that he was blown up. It's better than what the boss would do to him now if he was still alive."

Chapter Fourteen

Michael stared out the window at the barren countryside as the train barreled along the tracks. There wasn't much to see. Large swaths of what he presumed in the summer months were rolling meadows were now covered in snow. It looked cold and desolate, and Michael thought of the deep orange and red leaves adorning the streets at home. He sighed. Of all the places that he'd rather not be in late November, Russia topped the list. Yet here he was, speeding towards Moscow where he would change trains to go south.

Getting a seat had been difficult. The war had lowered the number of trains running between Minsk and Moscow, and this one had been fully booked. It would have been another twenty-four before he was able to get a seat at all, but a hefty bribe to an official had ensured his place on the train when, a few minutes before it was due to depart, not all the passengers had boarded. Michael had no idea if the person whose seat he was occupying had tried to board after he had, but there had been no commotion, and the official who pocketed his money had remained behind on the platform.

He didn't know if the documentation the Organization had provided was going to stand up to the scrutiny he would draw moving through Russia and Ukraine, but he had no choice. According to the papers, he was a salesman from Kursk. That was the region most aligned with his accent, which he'd learned from a Russian who was born and raised in that area. Since Russia began the war with Ukraine, he hadn't had to test the documents that, under normal circumstances, would have been beyond doubt. But these days, everything was in doubt in this part of the world, and Michael was not one hundred percent confident that his papers would get him through to Luhansk without question.

Luhansk, Ukraine.

He must be out of his mind. Russia had formally annexed the region in September, but in reality, the area had been under the control of Russian separatists since 2014. Fighting had been ongoing between

Ukraine forces and the separatists for the better part of eight years when Putin made the annexation official. The fighting was still ongoing, only now it was the war between Russia and Ukraine that was at fault.

All of that aside, the entire Donbas region was notoriously dangerous. Ukrainians loyal to Zelensky had been fleeing to Kyiv since the war began, months before Russia officially took over the areas, and they were bringing their stories with them. They said that both Luhansk and Donetsk were run with Soviet-era tactics that were more severe than anything the Kremlin imposed upon the people in Russia. If the separatists who controlled the region even suspected that something might be amiss, people were known to disappear into one of the "cellars," or Gulag-styled prisons that had sprung up throughout Luhansk and Donetsk. Because they were not subject to the oversight of the United Nations Human Rights watchdogs, these prisons were reputed to be some of the most barbaric seen since the end of the Cold War. Those that had survived them described scenes reminiscent of the brutality of the '50's and '60's KGB enforcers.

And that was what #15 was part of.

Yes. He was definitely out of his mind. But if Hans Becker was incarcerated there, then that was where he was going.

Michael looked at his watch and leaned his head back against the seat tiredly. It was a long trip, over 19 hours total. The train from Moscow to Kamenskaia Station, located in Kamensk-Shakhtinsky, Rostov Oblast, was thirteen hours alone. Then, according to his calculations, he would have to drive for another hour and a half to cross over into Luhansk. Flying would have been so much faster, but thanks to the war, Ukrainian airspace remained closed. That left only trains and automobiles.

Pressing his lips together, he shifted his gaze out of the window again. If he could do things his way, he would have called in a favor and had a military airlift ready to go. But Charlie wanted him to have a low profile on this one, and that meant no favors, and certainly no drawing attention to himself with an authorized military flight across war-torn Ukraine. He just hoped that by the time he made it to #15, Hans Becker was still there and, more importantly, still alive.

Michael had no idea how he was going to gain access to what, by all accounts, was most likely a Gulag. Even if he managed it, he didn't know that Becker would be of any use to him at all. He was going all this way on a hunch and, while his gut hadn't led him astray yet, it would be his luck that this would be the one time that it did. A humorless smile twisted his lips. If he got thrown into a hell-hole and

The Cuban

was her black hawk and, while he'd condescended to make Oklahoma his home, he made it clear every time she was home that he was her pet. He'd even learned to tolerate Damon over the past few years.

And so had she.

Alina never thought she could love anyone as deeply as she'd ended up loving her husband. It was almost as if he had become a part of her. Michael had called him her other half once, and she'd felt uncomfortable with that term. Now he was exactly that. When they'd impulsively married, it had been more of an agreeable business arrangement. There had been no mention of love, or of any of the deeper and more sensitive feelings that most couples just loved to gush about. For them, it had been a practical union of assets, with the added bonus of a physical attraction they had both been very tired of denying. They lived their lives in the gray shadows between good and evil, right and wrong, and that's where their marriage had fallen as well.

But in their four years together, that had changed. Now she couldn't imagine a life without Damon, despite the very real fact that she was staring at one now. And yet, in four years, she had never actually told him that she loved him.

Funny, that. She stared at herself, her brows pulled together thoughtfully. Why? Why hadn't she ever actually said the words? It certainly wasn't because she didn't trust him. There was no one on earth that she trusted more. She supposed she simply never thought to tell him she loved him and, to be fair, he hadn't said it either. Was it because they thought they didn't deserve to be so happy together? Or was it simply that too much time had passed and it seemed silly to bring it up now. After all, how did you tell the man you'd shared everything with for four years that you love him? She showed him a million times, every day, and that had always been enough.

But now she wondered if it really was. If Damon died in a Gulag before she could reach him, battered and alone, would he know how much she loved him? As soon as the thought entered her head, she frowned and pushed it aside impatiently. Of course he knew, just as she knew how much she meant to him. They weren't the kind of people to write cute little notes with hearts, or sing love songs to each other. They were very practical, and much preferred to show each other how they felt. Words, as they both knew all too well, were often false and empty. It was the actions that mattered.

And the niggling little voice in the back of her head could shut it. Damon wasn't going to die before she reached him. She wouldn't allow it.

And if he did have the appalling gall to give up before she got there, the people responsible would wish they'd never been born by the time she was finished with them. She'd picked up some new tricks in her retirement, and she wouldn't hesitate to make them beg for death.

Viper looked at her watch again and leaned her head back. Charlie was right. She had to rest and get some sleep. Sleep meant the difference between being sharp and alert, or being dumb and slow. Dumb and slow was a death warrant. She had to sleep.

But as she closed her eyes, her mind refused to cooperate. Every hour that passed was another hour that Damon was fighting to live. Every day that passed, his chances of survival fell dramatically. Of all the places for him be imprisoned, it *had* to be in an old Soviet-era Gulag in Luhansk. The place was a lawless hell-hole run by separatists who delighted in tactics used by the KGB in years past. While she would back Damon against them any day, it was another ballgame entirely when he was their prisoner.

How the hell had he been captured to begin with? Viper's lips tightened. It was a question that had been plaguing her from the beginning. Hawk was far too experienced to make a mistake or give himself away, and Charlie was adamant that no one but himself knew of the current operation, so that ruled out betrayal from within the Organization. What the hell went wrong?

Exhaling, she shifted in her seat and determinedly set the puzzle out of her head. It didn't matter how he ended up there, only that he had. She had the location. She had the resources. And, perhaps more importantly, she had the skill. Wasting time wondering about essentially meaningless and unimportant details wasn't going to get him out; Viper was—and right now Viper needed to rest and recharge.

Then she'd take on the whole damned Russian army if she had to.

The cold stones rushed up to meet Hawk as he fell, thrown into his cell by the meaty guard that had dragged him from the latest round with his tormentor. Grunting as he hit the floor, he listened to the guard back out of the space, waiting for the creaking of the hinges as he pulled the iron door closed. But the sound never came. Frowning, he rolled onto his side and looked at the open door. The guard was standing outside, just out of sight, talking in a low voice with someone. Then a shadow fell across the door and his interrogator entered. Hawk stiffened. Bloody hell. They weren't done with him yet.

The Cuban

"You are a very strong man."

The voice grated on Hawk's nerves and he struggled to sit up, moving so that his back was against the wall. The man stood watching him, seemingly content to save any further comment until Hawk had finished the arduous and painful task of propping himself up.

"I don't think I've ever had one as strong as you," he continued once Hawk had collapsed with his back against the wall. "You've lost the guards quite a lot of money over the past two weeks."

"If they'd asked, I could have...told them...the odds," Hawk muttered, gingerly prodding his ribs. At least two were broken, he was sure of it.

The man was surprised into a laugh.

"You fight until the very end, and then still have the capacity for humor. If you weren't such a bastard, I'd be tempted to like you."

Hawk looked up at him. He'd left his face alone the past two days and the frigid temperature of the stones he laid on had acted as an ice compress, reducing the swelling. He was able to see the man clearly, and he studied him in silence. Why was he here?

"Yes, you are very strong, and stubborn, but we both know your body won't take much more. It will break. No amount of will can prevent that. When that happens, your heart will stop, and even our paddles won't be able to restart it." The man stared down at him almost pensively. "And yet you still refuse to talk. You will die before you tell me what my boss wants to know. Why?"

"To piss you off."

"You subject yourself to this excruciating pain simply to be an asshole?"

Hawk met his gaze steadily and was silent. After a long moment, the man exhaled loudly.

"Well, it's out of my hands now," he said. "Your stubbornness has earned you a reprieve. Someone is looking for you. They're going through great lengths and trouble to find you. There is some belief that they may even be on their way here." The man stopped and looked around the cell. "I very much doubt that, but I follow orders. The decision has been made to suspend my efforts with you. He's hoping that I'll have more luck with the person who is hunting for you. What do you think? Will they be as tough to crack?"

Hawk was aware of those dead, emotionless eyes studying him closely. A twisted flash of amusement went through him. Did the man really expect him to reveal anything at the news that someone was looking for him? After two weeks of unending pain, he should know better. He remained silent and after another lengthy pause, the man shook his head.

"I suppose I'll find out. I look forward to meeting another one like you. Perhaps I'll be more forceful on the first meeting than I was with you." He walked over to stand over him and Hawk was forced to tilt his head back to maintain eye contact. "Is that where I went wrong? Did I start out too easy on you? It's so hard to judge in the beginning. Some men die after one session, and then we never get the information we want. It really is a fine line, isn't it?"

He bent down until his face was inches from Hawk's.

"I'll get you back," he promised in a low voice. "I'll get what I need from your ally, and then I'll have no need to pry information from you. No. I'll be working just for fun. Then you'll wish you weren't such an asshole."

He straightened up.

"Until then, rest and heal. I want a healthy ox so that I can drag it out as long as possible."

He struck out with his boot, kicking Hawk's legs as he turned away. Pain shot up his spine and Hawk felt himself falling sideways against the wall, unable to stop himself. He was too exhausted. It had taken every ounce of energy that he had left simply to pull himself into a sitting position.

As the door swung closed and the sound of the lock snapping into place echoed around the cell, Damon exhaled, his cheek on the cold stones. Once the footsteps had retreated down the corridor and silence fell around him, a smile curved his cracked lips. His eyes slid closed on a whisper, and that whisper warmed him from within as nothing else could.

Viper.

She'd found him. As welcome sleep came to cradle him, for the first time since he landed in this hellhole, Damon was filled with hope...and a hefty dose of confidence.

They had no idea what they were in for.

Chapter Fifteen

V iper strode through the station, a messenger bag hanging across her body and her single travel bag slung over her shoulder. Her eyes moved constantly as she went, scanning every face and noting every camera. Her shoulders were tight and she was alert to every movement made around her, but she walked with a confident and relaxed stride. If anyone chanced to notice the woman walking through the crowded train station, they wouldn't see anything out of the ordinary. She looked like every other passenger trying to catch their train. If her gaze seemed to notice more than most, well, there was a war on, and everyone was more alert and on edge these days.

"Anya!"

A man called out to her, waving gaily over the heads of a throng of passengers. Alina smiled and moved towards him. Dori was right where he said he'd be, waiting for her. He was taller than most and his height would have made it very easy to spot him, even if he hadn't been waving like a loon. But it was his wide smile and warm brown eyes that made her smile grow. It was the face of a friend, and she hadn't seen one of those in days.

"My dear Anya, you are the only woman I know who still looks amazing after being on a train for hours!" He exclaimed as she drew closer. He pushed past a heavyset man dragging a rolling case and the next instant, Alina was engulfed in a welcomed bear hug. "Oh my God, is that a tattoo on your neck? How marvelous!"

"You sound so surprised!"

"I am, my dear. I am!" He bent his head to examine it more closely. "There's a story behind that," he decided. "You must tell me one day. How was your journey?"

"Uneventful, Dori, thank God."

He clucked his tongue and shook his head, turning to lead her through the crowds with an arm around her shoulders.

"It is Yakiv these days, and I'm very glad to hear it. Yesterday one of the trains was derailed by shelling." He led her out a door and

113

into the fresh, crisp morning air. "How long do you have?"

"Not long. My train leaves in forty minutes."

"Oh, that's plenty of time for some coffee and something to eat. There is a cafe across the way. We will go there." He looked down at her, his eyes dancing. "When was the last time you ate?"

Alina made a face.

"Longer than I'll admit to you."

He threw his head back and laughed.

"I should have known. You never change. You must eat to keep up your strength. Did I teach you nothing?" They came to an intersection and he touched her arm. "We cross here. You will have coffee and some pastries."

Alina shot him a look. "Pastries? Do you know me?"

He grinned and winked.

"Hash then. Protein and potatoes. Even you can't complain at that."

A few minutes later, they were seated in a small cafe and he was ordering her breakfast, ignoring any protests she tried to make. When he'd finished, he turned his dark eyes on her and studied her.

"You look tired. Did you sleep on the train?"

"A little."

He shook his head, all laughter gone from his face.

"You will need more than a little for where you're going. Promise me you'll try to sleep on the next train."

"You're a pain in my ass, Yakiv."

He winked.

"I'm just trying to keep you alive, my dear. If anything happens to you, your man will have my balls on a plate."

When she didn't answer, he frowned and his eyes probed hers searchingly.

"He is all right?"

Alina swallowed, her face void of expression.

"I hope so."

He exhaled and let out a low curse.

"Well, now your message makes much more sense." He reached into his coat and pulled a large envelope from an inside pocket. "He's the reason you go to Luhansk?"

"Yes."

He passed her the envelope under the table.

"Here's your delivery. Identities for you and Hawk, as well as enough cash to buy your way out of just about anything."

"There were no problems?" she asked, taking the envelope and

The Cuban

sliding it under her leg on the seat.

"None. Jared sends his regards and requests that you stay alive. He has a new project he'd like you involved in." Dori grinned. "Personally, I would decline. Your talents are wasted in the training room."

She raised an eyebrow, amused.

"Are they?"

"Yes, and you know that. It's why you're here, on your way into a shithole." He fell silent as their coffee arrived, but once the waitress had departed, he continued. "When you reach Kharkiv, you'll be met at the station by Borislav Luchinski. He'll meet you outside. He will be wearing a green camouflage scarf and will respond to the phrase, "Yakiv says you're an asshole."

"Are you serious?"

"Yes. We are not so formal here as your old comrades. They use cute, seemingly random phrases that are all so very boring. We use real words, and the truth."

She chuckled and nodded.

"Anything else I should know?"

"He goes by Boris, and he's a ruthless bastard, but he'll have everything you asked for. Don't ask him how or where he got it. He's very touchy about that. If he tries to throw in something extra, take it. If you decline it, he'll be offended, and believe me when I say he is one person you don't want offended with you."

"Duly noted."

Dori tilted his head and watched as she sipped her coffee.

"Are you sure about this?" he asked after a moment of silence.

"Yes."

When she answered without hesitation, he nodded.

"Very well. Everything Boris has for you has been paid for, so don't fall for any shit."

Alina looked up at that, a quick frown on her face.

"By whom?"

"Who else? Mossad, of course. It is an investment. We're betting on your safe return, so please don't make it awkward. We don't generally enjoy being wrong."

Viper let out a short laugh and reached for her coffee again.

"I'll do my best."

CW Browning

Kharkiv, Ukraine

Viper strode through the station, the hood to her jacket pulled up over her head. Keeping her face turned slightly away from the cameras, she moved through the crowds confident that any playback wouldn't provide an image of her face for recognition. If the Russian separatists controlling Luhansk had any sense, as soon as one of their cellars was breached, they would check all the train stations and bus depots for signs of the perpetrator. While she had no doubt that she wouldn't be recognized, it never hurt to be overly-cautious.

Especially when the world thought you were dead.

Seeing a pair of armed security guards coming towards her, Alina dropped her bag to the floor and crouched down, opening it and appearing to be looking for something. The two men passed her with only a passing, uninterested glance, and once they were well behind her, she closed the bag and stood up, on her way once more.

While one would think that it would be easier to be invisible when one was presumed dead, the reality was that it required just as much work. The reason she and Damon were still presumed dead was because, as far as they were concerned, nothing had changed. They still took all the precautions that they had before, and had added a few more for good measure. Now, she reflected, it was a very good thing that they had. She had never fallen out of the old habits, and she definitely needed them to serve her well here. She was going into enemy territory, where one mistake would cost her not only her life, but Hawk's as well. There was no room to be sloppy.

The exit doors were ahead and she looked down at her watch as she passed the last surveillance camera. Her fellow passengers streamed through the doors with her, and a moment later, she was standing on the sidewalk outside the station. Cabs lined up along the curb, and city traffic poured by on the busy road. Alina cast a sharp gaze along the row of waiting taxis before turning and walking to her left. Boris would not be with a cab.

She was just approaching the intersection when something made her look across the busy road. There, on the other side, was a huge man wearing a black coat. A green camouflage scarf hung around his meaty neck.

He was leaning, arms crossed over a barrel chest, against a rugged black Jeep that looked as if it had seen better days, and Alina

The Cuban

felt a smile pulling at her lips. When she'd requested a four-wheel drive vehicle, she hadn't expected to get her personal make of choice. As she crossed at the intersection, she ran her eyes over the Jeep. It was a Wrangler, a JK, and despite the few dings and scrapes that she could see, it really wasn't in terrible shape. The tires looked new, and the hardtop was in good condition. It would do.

She reached the sidewalk and walked towards it, her dark eyes meeting a questioning glance from the behemoth leaning against it. Although his glance appeared to be uninterested, she was aware of the sharp examination from under his bushy brows. She had the distinct impression that not very much got by Borislav Luchinski.

"Boris?" she asked, stopping on the sidewalk a few feet away.

The man didn't say a word, but stared at her. A dark beard covered his jaw and she noted that he kept it trimmed and manageable. If his eyebrows were anything to go by, the beard had the potential to grow thick and unruly, and Viper found herself wondering why he kept it so neat. Nothing else about him indicated that he was, in any way, a fussy dresser.

They stared at each other silently for a long moment, then she sighed silently.

"Yakiv says you're an asshole," she told him. "Are you?"

He grunted and straightened up, uncrossing his arms.

"Sometimes." His voice was deep and, as he straightened up, Viper felt like she was confronting a bear. "Are you?"

"Sometimes."

Appreciation lit his dark eyes and he walked around the hood to join her on the sidewalk.

"It's nice to meet you, Anya. Your reputation has come ahead of you." He went to the passenger's door and opened it for her. "Yakiv is a fan."

Alina eyed him for a second, then climbed into the Jeep, dropping her bag onto the floor at her feet.

"Yakiv talks too much."

Boris let out a surprised laugh that boomed around them.

"Yes he does," he agreed. "Nice tattoo."

"Thanks."

He nodded and closed the door, circling the hood to climb behind the wheel.

"As you can see, this is the four-wheel drive vehicle that you requested," he said, starting the engine. "It has some dents and scratches, but the engine is good, and so are the tires."

"And the registration?"

117

"Three different ones, as you specified." He pulled away from the curb and into traffic, cutting off a cab and drawing a sharp honk of a horn. "In the glove box is a map. The route to Luhansk is marked out in red for you, with alternate routes in blue and green. I advise you to stick to the marked routes. They are the safest way in, with the least likelihood of any complications or unpleasantness. If you go another way, I cannot guarantee your safe arrival."

"You weren't paid to guarantee my safe arrival," she murmured, opening the glove box and looking at the map inside. "I'll do that."

He grunted and fell silent, weaving through traffic as he put distance between them and the train station. Alina watched the city buildings slide by and wondered who Boris was loyal to. He didn't look like a Mossad agent, although she'd been surprised by them before. Her initial impression had been that he was merely a mercenary, but his attention to detail in trying to ensure her safe passage into Luhansk belied that theory. In general, mercs had no interest in the continued well-being of passing clients.

After about ten minutes, Boris pulled into an alleyway.

"I will show you what your money has bought," he said in explanation at her look. "It is in the back. Better to do it here, where no one can see."

She nodded and he drove halfway down the alley before pulling behind a large, metal dumpster. He shut off the engine and her shoulders relaxed as he reached for his door handle. Climbing out of the Jeep, she was conscious of a sense of relief. This would be the perfect place to dispose of her if he'd been paid off by someone else. If that had been his plan, however, he would have made his move in the vehicle, where any screams would be muffled.

"I was able to get everything on the list," he told her as they met at the back of the Jeep. "A few of the pieces were hard to come by, but I managed it."

"No substitutions?" she asked, shooting him a sharp glance.

"You don't pay for substitutions."

"No." She smiled faintly as he opened the door and pushed up the back windshield. Whoever he was, she liked him. He didn't play around. "You were able to get everything? The Ruger as well?"

Boris opened a fishing tackle box in front of the black tactical crates stacked in the small cargo space. He pulled out a box and handed it to her without a word. Setting the box down, Alina pulled out a brand new Ruger American .45 caliber pistol and one of the magazines. After examining the magazine, she began to disassemble the gun with

The Cuban

quick, sure fingers.

"And the 1911s?"

"In the case at the back with the rest of the small arms."

She nodded and he watched as she examined the slide after removing it.

"No faith, Anya?"

"It's not about faith. It's about never firing a gun I haven't personally inspected."

He grunted, a reluctant gleam of respect in his eyes.

"You'd be amazed how few think that way." He reached for one of the cases and pulled it forward, unlocking it and pushing the lid open. "Here are the accessories. Everything as you requested. You know, it looks like you're going to war."

Viper peered down the inside of the barrel.

"I am," she said shortly before inserting the barrel back into the slide. She reached for the spring. "Are the rest in that other case?"

"Yes. I'll show you."

He closed the open case, relocking it, and lifted it out of the Jeep so that he could reach the largest crate in the back. Alina finished reassembling the Ruger and set it down, watching as he unlocked the lid. He opened it and stepped aside so that she could examine the contents.

"That's some serious gear," he said after a moment of silence.

"I'm a serious person." She finished checking the contents and closed the lid. "The codes?"

"Same for all the cases." He passed her a slip of paper. "You will, of course, want to change them. Do you need me to show you how?"

"No need." She palmed the paper and slid it into her pocket. "Thank you."

He watched as she went into the fishing tackle box and pulled out a box of ammunition for the Ruger.

"The holster is in that box over there," he said helpfully as she began to fill the magazine.

"I have my own. Custom."

He raised a bushy eyebrow in surprise.

"You carry this gun regularly?"

"It's a good gun."

She pushed the magazine into the handle and reached behind her to tuck the Ruger into the holster sewn into the waistband at the back of her jeans. As the familiar weight settled into the small of her back, a wave of relief went through her. She had felt naked without her firearm for the past few days. Traveling through security checkpoints had necessitated being unarmed, something that she never enjoyed and which always made her uncomfortable.

"Yes, but it's a canon."

Viper laughed at that.

"Yes, and it will stop anything coming at me."

Boris studied her for a second, a smile playing around his mouth.

"You are not what I expected," he finally said.

She raised her eyebrows in question and he shrugged.

"You clearly have the respect of Mossad, but you are not one of them. You are too relaxed. They are uptight."

Alina stepped back from the Jeep and pulled the rear windshield down before closing the door.

"I've never seen a benefit to being wound too tight. It tends to cause more problems than are necessary."

"Very true." Boris reached into the inside pocket of his coat and pulled out a padded envelope. "Here. Something extra. No charge."

He handed her the envelope and, as her fingers closed around it, his eyes met hers.

"It is a burn phone. For emergency only. If you get stuck or trapped and need help, call the number programmed into the phone. They can get you anything you need. Use the code word Odesa." He released his hold on the envelope. "The trip to Luhansk will take about five hours. You can find lodging in the Zhovtnevyi district. The address is on the map. Your target is east, near the Donets River."

"What do you know of my target?" she asked sharply, her shoulders stiffening.

"You go to Luhansk, request all of this, and tell me you are going to war," he said with a shrug and a flash of surprisingly white teeth. "It doesn't take a rocket scientist. But don't worry. Your secret is safe with me. I want no part of what you're contemplating."

She stared at him, her face impassive, for a long moment. Her first impression had been correct. Not much got past Boris, and she wasn't sure that she was happy about that. The last thing she needed was an unknown factor knowing her destination. Yet he'd clearly put two and two together, and what could she do about it? She had to go, no matter who found out.

"Who will the phone contact?" she finally asked, breaking her silence.

Boris smiled at her and turned to leave.

The Cuban

"Good luck, Anya," he said over his shoulder.

Alina watched as he went around the dumpster and began to walk away down the alley. She tipped the phone out into her hand and tossed the empty envelope into the dumpster, sliding the phone into her jacket pocket.

A few moments later, the Jeep rolled up to the other end of the alley. Viper stopped and waited for a break in the traffic to pull out. She had everything she needed, as well as something extra.

It was time to go get Hawk.

Chapter Sixteen

Luhansk Oblast

Viper held binoculars to her eyes and watched the armed guards patrolling around the perimeter. She was perched rather precariously in the frozen branches of a massive oak tree some distance from the structure that housed prison #15. Dressed in a white ski suit, she blended with the snow that blanketed the region. Her black hair was covered with the hood of her jacket, and she burrowed deeper into the warmth of the faux fur lining. Of all the times for Hawk to go and get himself captured, it had to be winter in Ukraine.

#15 was situated in what she imagined must have been a Soviet-era factory of some sort. Chimneys rose towards the back of the large, block building, and old, crumbling loading docks stretched across the back of the structure. The building itself was constructed from stone and cement, and it looked as though it could easily withstand quite a bit of damage. It had been built in a time when things were expected to last, and when the threat of war was always uppermost in engineers' minds. She doubted she could put much of a dent in the fortress-like structure with the limited weapons she had available.

Shifting her attention back to the guards, she watched as they patrolled around the outer perimeter. Barbed wire ran along the top of the sturdy stone and cement wall, and she would be willing to bet that it was electrified. Even if she got over the fence, there was no way she was bringing Hawk out the same way. She'd be amazed if he could walk. Climbing a ten foot, barbed wired wall was out of the question. She would have to find another way in — and out.

Viper turned the binoculars to the only opening in the wall. A heavy metal gate provided the only access point into the area. They would have to exit through that gate.

While she studied the gate, a supply truck rattled up to it. As it began to open, she glanced at her watch, timing how long it took. The heavy, ancient metal moved ponderously while the truck idled, waiting. After what seemed like an eternity, but was in fact only thirty seconds, it stopped and two of the guards came out to talk to the driver. After a moment of conversation and examination of papers and a clipboard, the truck was waved through and the gates began their painfully slow journey to close.

Lowering the binoculars, Viper stared at the prison in the distance. She needed a truck, and a reason to gain access to the camp. That was the easy part. Once she had Hawk, getting out would be infinitely more difficult. She couldn't leave the way she came in.

She lifted the binoculars again and studied the perimeter, her lips pressed together. The wall wasn't impenetrable by any means, but getting an injured prisoner out made it almost impossible. She was considering and discarding idea after idea when movement from the supply truck drew her attention. It had pulled up in front of the building and the driver had climbed out, a clipboard in his hand. Something about the way he moved made her click a button on the binoculars and zoom in on his face. Sucking in her breath, she watched as he turned to go to the back of the truck and open the doors.

Her eyes narrowed and she lowered the binoculars, letting out a soft curse. The entire operation, which was already virtually impossible, had just become ten times more complicated.

Michael rubbed his hands together briskly to ward off the cold and glanced at the fireplace. The fire he'd built an hour before was throwing out heat, but the old, abandoned house was drafty and it could only do so much. He shifted on the folding chair he'd bought when he picked up supplies in Luhansk and turned his attention back to the laptop. As cold as it was in the house, he was glad that he'd found it. It saved him from renting a room in a hotel miles away. The more invisible he was, the better all around.

He'd spotted the abandoned house on his way to the prison this morning. It was located about a mile from the compound, buried in some trees. At one time, it had probably belonged to a farmer, but any evidence of crops had long since disappeared. Now it was a dilapidated affair consisting of two rooms and a kitchen. There was no electricity and no water, but the roof was intact and so were the windows. Michael had moved in that afternoon, armed with a folding chair and table, kerosene lamp, and a subzero sleeping bag. Dinner had been canned beans and thick, brown bread that he toasted over the fire. All in all, he would take this over the possibility of being seen in a hotel.

Getting into the prison had been easier than he'd expected, although he admitted to himself that much of it had to do with luck. After he'd surveyed the prison and the wall, he'd gone to the nearest town in search of lunch. He'd found a delivery driver instead.

Michael reached for his water bottle. The driver suffered from an unfortunate accident an hour later. While Michael was confident that his body would never be found, he did feel uncomfortable with the lengths that he'd gone to gain access to the prison. He drank some water, his eyes sliding to the flames in the hearth. He supposed Charlie would say that the ends justified the means, and the spy in him would agree. But the Marine rebelled against the thought of taking a non-combatants life in exchange for a pass into a secure area. He supposed that was why Charlie had his assets, and his spies. The two functions required two different mentalities, and he'd left his killer mentality with the Corps when he discharged.

Yet today it had re-emerged in a frighteningly natural way, almost as if it had never been laid to rest. His lips twisted sardonically and he set the water down. It was unnerving how easily the lines between spy and assassin became blurred when the opportunity presented itself.

Setting the moral and ethical questions aside, Michael turned his attention back to the computer screen. Right or wrong, assuming the identity of the delivery driver had not only gained him access to the prison, but had provided the opportunity to place an electronic device near one of the Wi-Fi hubs in the main offices. The signal enabled him to hack into the closed circuit network, and as long as no one discovered the tiny bug nestled behind a framed photograph of Vladimir Putin, he would have unimpeded access to their entire network. He just had to find his way in.

The silence in the room was interrupted occasionally by the sound of burning wood crackling while Michael worked to hack into the heavily fortified network. Their security was good, but he was better, and after about an hour, he sat back with a grunt of satisfaction.

He was in.

Getting up, he drained his water bottle and turned to toss it into the trash bag he'd hooked over a nail across the room. He stretched a few times, then went to a case of water to pull out another bottle. Now that he was into their system, it would be an easy thing to locate the prisoner logs. Finding out where they were keeping Hans Becker was the easy part. Getting in to see him would be the challenging part.

He rubbed his eyes as he opened a fresh bottle of water and

The Cuban

took a sip. He had absolutely no idea how to do it, and he was contemplating reaching out to Charlie for the assistance of an asset when he shook his head impatiently. There wasn't time. He was here now, and he had to get to Becker while the man was still cognizant. If only half of what he'd heard about these cellars was true, he had very little time before Becker was either dead or mental. He wanted to know everything he knew about The Cuban before that happened.

Going back to the folding table and chair, Michael wondered if he was on a wild goose chase. After all, the only reason he'd come into a Russian-held region of Ukraine, in the middle of a war, was essentially on a hunch. His gut told him that the name couldn't be a coincidence, and so here he was. But what if his gut was wrong and Hans Becker had simply run afoul of the wrong person? What if he had no connection with The Cuban at all?

Then I'm risking everything to walk in there for no good reason, he thought, settling himself into his chair once more. But as his fingers moved over the keys, Michael knew that he had no choice. He'd come this far, and he had to either rule Becker out or confirm that his hunch was correct. If he was right, at the very least Becker would give him another clue to The Cuban. In the best case, he'd be able to give a location or means to make contact. And that possibility alone was worth any price. It would be closer than anyone had been able to get to the arms dealer yet.

Finding the prisoner logs in the system, Michael scanned down the list of folders, looking for Becker. Finding him, he opened it. A second later, he let out a low curse as he stared at the information on the screen. Hans Becker had been moved the day before to a different location. He was no longer there.

Scowling, Michael stared at the notation on the line item. Becker had been transferred to location #9. Bending down, he fished in one of the pockets of his bags until he found the flash drive he'd used in Belarus. A few minutes later, he had the coordinates to prison #9.

It looked like he was going to Donetsk.

London, England

Jack nodded to his driver and got into the back of the SUV, glancing at his watch. He was hungry, but there was no time to stop for lunch. He had a meeting with the Prime Minister in twenty minutes,

125

and then he was on his way to Scotland. Food would have to wait at least until he was on the train up.

"Jeremy, while I'm at Downing Street, will you pop over to the Red Lion and get me something for lunch?" he asked his driver as he settled behind the wheel. "I'll eat it on the train."

"What would you like, sir?"

"Oh, I don't know. Something portable."

Jeremy grinned and nodded, used to his employer's ways.

"Very good, sir."

The phone in his inside pocket began to vibrate and Jack sighed, pulling it out.

"Hello?"

"Good afternoon, sir. I hope I'm not catching you in a meeting."

"No, Rodney. You've caught me between them at the moment."

"Good. I was hoping that I would."

Jack's brows came together. "That sounds rather ominous."

"Well, it's just that we've run into a bit of trouble with Ms. Morozov, sir," the voice said apologetically.

"What kind of trouble?" Jack asked sharply.

"Well, you see, sir," the man on the other end hesitated, then cleared his throat, "she's missing."

"What?!"

"She seems to have...well...disappeared."

Jack pressed his lips together and shifted his gaze out the window, inhaling silently.

"You've had a team watching her, correct?" he finally asked, his voice soft.

"Yes, sir. Around the clock."

"Then how, exactly, could she disappear?"

"We don't know. According to the team leader, she went back to her flat last night, but didn't leave on time for the office this morning. After an hour, he sent in one of the agents. The flat's empty. She's just gone."

"Define gone a bit more clearly, will you?" Jack asked, impatience making its way into his voice. "Has she packed a bag and gone on vacation? Has she left a suicide note and disappeared?"

"No note, sir. That's the first thing I asked as well, given the recent proclivity towards seemingly well-adjusted and happy people suddenly offing themselves. There don't appear to be any clothes missing, and no sign of a struggle or forced entry. Our people say it's as if she vanished."

"I can assure you, humans don't simply vanish," Jack said dryly. "She's given them the slip."

"Yes, sir."

"The question is whether or not she did it voluntarily. What about the security footage?"

"They're sending it to me now."

"Alright. When you know more, let me know. Monitor it yourself, will you? I want to know everything they know as soon as they know it."

"Yes, sir."

"And Rodney? Find out all her normal haunts, where she goes on holiday, where she goes to relax. Check them all."

"Of course."

Jack ended the call and slid the phone back into his pocket, staring out the window, a frown on his face. He'd authorized the surveillance on Sophia Morozov over a month ago when he'd received intelligence that she was a possible target. As a top executive for BenuTec, one of the premier oil and gas companies in Eastern Europe, she fit the profile for all the deceased executives. When one of his agents in Warsaw came across a discarded message indicating that Morozov was proving difficult, the implications were that she would become the next victim. However, despite both Interpol and EU officials warning her that she could be at risk, the woman had refused protective custody. Jack had authorized the surveillance in an attempt to catch at least one of the assassins before they could succeed again. Now it appeared that it had been a wasted exercise.

The Cuban was still out there, and he was still causing havoc.

Three months ago, the international arms dealer had become a priority for MI6 after intelligence surfaced linking him to the deaths of two of the energy executives. However, despite their best efforts, after two months, they were no further ahead than when they began. They were unable to locate The Cuban, let alone put him under surveillance to see just what he was up to. The only thing they had turned up in two months was a name that Jack wasn't even convinced was real: Yasha Novikov. The name had no connection anywhere. There were a few men bearing that name, but none of them were The Cuban. They'd all been cleared after a cursory investigation. And so, after two months, they had absolutely nothing on the mysterious arms dealer.

That's when he'd approached Charlie with the idea that they could work together. Jack was confident that he was in charge of the most skilled and elite spies in the world, but Charlie also had some gems on his side. By combining both of their considerable resources, surely they would hook The Cuban. But Charlie had refused, stating bluntly that it was a problem in Jack's backyard, not his. Jack's lips curved now in amusement. And yet, not even a month later, Viper had been recalled and dispatched; target: The Cuban. Not only that, but Charlie had also pulled one of his other operatives to assist, sending two of his people into Eastern Europe without a moment's hesitation. Amazing what the Americans would do when one of their own was attacked.

The smile faded as quickly as it had come and Jack tapped one finger on the arm rest as he stared at the city buildings sliding by. Charlie had refused to share the lead that his people were following, and while that fact irritated Jack to no end, he supposed he could understand it. The Cuban had proved to be so well concealed and illusive that he had to have people in all the major intelligence agencies. For none of them to be able to find a shred of evidence or any clue to his whereabouts was simply unheard of.

As much as Jack hated to admit that MI6 was compromised, he knew it must be so. He'd launched an internal investigation last month, but so far nothing had turned up. Yet how else could The Cuban always be one step ahead of all of them? Charlie knew it too. When Jack pressed him about the lead Viper was following, Charlie had told him that he didn't want to risk a leak. After that debacle four years ago, Jack could hardly blame him. And so Charlie kept his secrets, and Jack kept his.

And they waited while one of the most intimidating and effective weapons Jack had ever had the pleasure of meeting did her thing.

Jack exhaled silently. While Viper was hunting The Cuban, he had been having his people dig up as much intelligence as they could on all the dead executives. So far, they could find no link that connected any of them to a central source, nor had they uncovered any personal dealings that were suspect in any way. Yet something had to connect them. And now, yet another energy executive had gone inexplicably missing from her flat in the middle of Brussels.

He'd have to tell Charlie about Morozov. He had asked for any information Jack had on her just a few days ago. If Charlie was looking for information, he already knew she was in danger. It was only fair to let him know that she'd joined the list of the missing.

As the SUV pulled around the corner and Jeremy eased to a stop outside #10 Downing Street, Jack reflected that, all in all, it could be worse. Right now, Morozov was simply missing. At least she hadn't committed a questionable suicide like so many of the others. Perhaps they would find that she'd simply slipped out for an assignation with her lover. Perhaps she'd turn up in the next few hours.

As Jack got out of the SUV and buttoned his suit jacket, he sighed imperceptibly. Given the last year, that was very wishful thinking indeed. Sophia Morozov was more than likely dead, and she'd been taken right under the noses of his own people. How the hell was he going to explain that to Charlie?

Michael stretched and looked at his watch. It was just past ten and the dinner he'd had was wearing off. He raised his eyes back to the screen and leaned forward in his chair again. When he'd finished going through this file, he'd stop and toast some more bread. He'd have it with some cheese, and that would have to do until morning when he got on the road.

He turned his attention from his rumbling stomach to the information on his screen. After he'd finished finding out all he could about the location they'd moved Becker to, he'd gone back to the flash drive from the compound outside Minsk. There was a massive amount of information on the drive, and digging through it was time consuming, but he knew it had to be done. Once he was back in friendly territory, he could hook it into his home databases and use algorithms to pull useful data. Until then, however, he had to do it the old-fashioned way.

Michael was still scrolling through memos and financial records ten minutes later when the stillness was broken by an unnatural noise. His head snapped up and Michael listened intently, his heart suddenly pounding. The shifting of the logs on the fire and the occasional creak of the old house settling around him were sounds he'd been hearing for the past four hours, but something else had disturbed the silence. Something more intrusive.

After a second of sitting perfectly still, Michael moved. Pulling the flash drive from the USB port in the laptop, he slid it into his pocket with one hand while he closed the computer with the other. A moment later, he had his Beretta in his hands and was moving silently to the door in the back of the house. While he didn't know what it was that had interrupted him, he knew his pulse was racing and every hair on the back of his neck was standing to attention. Something was wrong. He could feel it.

He grabbed a powerful flashlight from where he'd left it on the floor inside the door and reached for the handle. Stepping out into the silent night, he shivered at the blast of cold air that swirled around him. While the structure wasn't what he'd term warm and cozy, the fire had certainly been doing its share to keep the temperature above freezing in there. He closed the door behind him to try to keep as much of the cold out as possible and switched on the light, shining it over the snow-covered ground. The trees were some distance from the house at the back and he swept the beam over the snow, looking for any disturbance. There were no marks or tracks in the gleaming white carpet, and he turned to move to the corner of the house a few feet away. Whatever he'd heard, it hadn't come from the back.

Michael peered around the corner, shining the light along the side of the house. The night was still and dark, and here, just as in the back, the snow was undisturbed. He began moving along the house, looking out into the trees. Just before the trees were animal tracks. He paused to shine the light over them, but the tracks remained near the trees. Nothing had come towards the house.

He continued to the front, rounding the corner and sweeping the beam over his SUV. It appeared undisturbed and he dropped the light to the ground around it. His tire tracks led from the road, and looped around to return to the road. Nothing marred them, and he looked at the footprints going to the door. There were a few tracks, but he could see at a glance that they were all the same. They were all his.

Michael let out an exhale and adjusted his grip on his pistol, moving behind his SUV to look on the other side. Nothing but smooth snow. Shaking his head, he walked around the SUV to shine the light down the other side of the house. His lips tightened and he moved forward swiftly, his eyes on the ground. Tracks disturbed the snow, going from the trees to within a couple of feet from the house. His fingers tightened on the handle of his gun as he pressed his back against the side of the house. After a moment of staring at the marks in the snow, though, his shoulders relaxed and he exhaled again. They all appeared to be animal tracks. He couldn't make out any human footprints among them.

He sent a searching look out into the trees, shining the light further into the night. The beam slid over something and he swung it back to see two eyes reflecting the light back to him, glowing eerily yellow-green in the darkness. He moved the flashlight again, illuminating four deer in the trees. With a relieved chuckle, Michael flipped on the safety and slid the Beretta back into the holster at his waist. He turned to return to the front door, shaking his head. The deer

The Cuban

must have knocked something over in their explorations.

Michael went back into the house and closed the door, cupping his hands and blowing on them to warm them up. He started towards the fire, then froze as a chill that had nothing to do with cold streaked down his spine. The folding chair that he'd been using at his makeshift desk was gone.

Reaching behind him, he pulled out his Beretta again, flipping off the safety and pointing it straight at a dark figure lounging deep in the gloom on the other side of the room.

The darkness shifted and the figure stood, silent in the corner. Then a whisper of shock went through him as a woman stepped out of the shadows.

"You're a long way from home, gunny."

Chapter Seventeen

Michael stared at the face that had haunted him for over four years, stunned. His breath caught in his throat and his stomach lurched as if it was dropping right out of him. The hair was different, he noted through a clamoring sea of emotions. It was jet black now, and cut short in a straight bob that came to just above her jawline. She looked decidedly French, and he squeezed his eyes shut so that he could refocus. When he opened them, she was still staring back at him with a faint, sardonic curve to her lips. An ornate tattoo crawled up the side of her neck, giving her a distinct bad-girl vibe, but her eyes were the same: a deep rich brown that always seemed to look right through to inside him, just as they were doing now.

"Are you going to lower that gun, or will you force me to go for mine?"

The familiar voice rolled over him, shocking him again, and Michael sucked in a ragged breath, lowering his Beretta. His arms were trembling, and he frowned in response as he pressed the safety and holstered his weapon once again, never taking his eyes from her face.

It was really her. Viper was standing in front of him, alive and in the flesh. She wasn't an apparition. She wasn't a ghost. She was alive.

Fury washed through him, swift and hot, and Michael sucked in his breath again as his entire body tensed. As soon as he did, her lips curved and she was almost betrayed into a smile.

"I was wondering which emotion would win," she murmured. "I'm glad it's the anger."

"You shouldn't be," he bit out, forcing his voice to remain low despite his sudden desire to shout.

The smile emerged and she actually chuckled.

"Oh, I think I can take you, gunny," she said, walking over to stand before the fire, "but go on. Get it out of your system."

Michael stared at her for a tense moment, then turned and wordlessly went across the room to his duffel bag. He crouched down and went into the hidden pocket in the lining. Anger, and something

132

else, made it hard to keep his fingers steady as they closed around two metal discs. When he straightened up and turned towards her again, he was just in time to catch her hand moving away from the small of her back as her shoulders relaxed. Another wave of fury went through him.

"If I was going to kill you, I'd have done it with the Beretta," he snapped.

She shrugged unapologetically, that emotionless mask that he remembered so well fixed on her face.

"Reflex, gunny. Nothing personal."

His eyes narrowed as he advanced across the room towards her.

"Nothing personal?" he repeated. "It wasn't personal when you let us all believe that you'd been blown to smithereens along with that damn yacht?"

"No." Her voice was calm and steady. "That was business."

"Bullshit! Faking your own death? Gutting your best friends? That wasn't business. You could have done your job without destroying everything you left behind."

Michael could hear the anger and harshness in his tone, but he couldn't seem to get a handle on the fury long enough to conceal the emotion.

"Here." He tossed what he'd pulled from his bag at her. "For the next time it's just business."

She caught the metal discs with one hand, her eyes not leaving his. After a moment, she lowered her arm and looked at the dog tags that she'd left behind for him four years before. The mask was firmly in place and he had no idea what she was thinking as her fingers closed over her old, US Navy dog tags. Then Viper raised her eyes to his face once more.

"You're right," she said, surprising him.

"What?"

"I could have done my job without dying." Her dark eyes met his unflinchingly. "But all of you would be dead."

"You don't know that."

"Yes, I do. Harry made all the arrangements. If I survived, no one was getting out alive. It was his final mind fuck. I'd have to live knowing that I'd killed everyone I cared about."

Michael stared at her, his brows coming together sharply. The very assurance in her voice told him that she believed every word she said.

"We found no evidence of anything like that," he said, crossing his arms over his chest and glaring down at her. "Hell, Lina, I *looked* for it. I was convinced you did it to save us, but there was nothing. No one was coming after us."

"You didn't find them because we'd already taken care of it."

They stared at each other for a long moment, then he ran a hand through his hair and turned to pace impatiently around the room.

"Why are you telling me this? If it's true, then it was sanctioned by Charlie and I shouldn't be hearing this."

Silence greeted that and he shot a look over to the fireplace. She was watching him with an unreadable look on her face.

"There's a lot you shouldn't know," she finally said, "but you have a right to know that, at least. I owe you that much."

"Oh really?" He swung around to face her from across the room. "That's it? You owe me so that's my consolation prize? What about Steph and Angie? Will they get one as well?"

"No." Her voice was flat and hard, brooking no argument. "I'm dead, and that's how I'll stay."

He swallowed and tamped down an irresistible urge to bellow at the top of his lungs. He resumed pacing instead.

"So it's just me that gets to know that you sold us a lie."

"Gunny, I never sold *you* anything." The amusement was back in her voice. "You've been stalking me for four years. Don't pretend that you're shocked to see me now."

"Why *am* I seeing you now?" he demanded, stopping again and looking at her. "And what's with the tattoo all over your neck?"

Her eyes gleamed as she gave him an inscrutable look.

"Really? That's your first question? About my tattoo?"

"Actually, the first question was why are you here."

She was laughing at him silently, but she seemed to decide to let his surliness go for the moment.

"Ah. Well, that's the question I'm supposed to be asking you."

"I'm here on business."

"And do you plan on dying while you're here?"

"No, I leave that to the pros like yourself."

Viper let out a short laugh.

"I think I like you pissed off, gunny. You don't hold back." She looked past him at the case of water on the floor. "Are you going to offer me a bottle of water, or is the new, angry Michael opposed to manners?"

Irritation warred with amusement as Michael glared at her for a beat before spinning on his heel to go to the case of water.

"What kind of business?" she asked as he bent down to pull out two bottles. "Is the President in town?"

134

The Cuban

He glanced up at her, a cynical smile twisting his lips.

"Oh, I think you know what kind of business. I know you, Viper. You probably know more about me at this point than I do."

"Fair, but not entirely accurate. I only know what I've picked up along the way. I like to know my opponent."

He walked over to hand her one of the bottles.

"I'm your opponent now? I used to be your friend."

"Anyone who chases me relentlessly over three continents, by definition, becomes my opponent." She took the water and broke the seal. "What gave me away?"

"Havana."

She pursed her lips and shook her head.

"Cuba. Of course. The hotel."

"Raven Woods canceled her reservation."

She drank some water, her brown eyes studying him. When she lowered the bottle, she shrugged.

"She heard that someone she used to know was going to be there at the same time."

"Did Charlie tell you?"

She smiled faintly and looked around before going over to the folding chair. She picked it up and carried it over to the fire, sitting down and crossing her legs.

"Tell me why Charlie sent you to Dachnyi 6," she said conversationally.

Michael felt a flash of frustration go through him and he pressed his lips together. The years had dulled the memories and he'd forgotten just how infuriating it was when Viper knew something that she had no business knowing.

"How the hell do you know about Dachnyi 6?" he asked, not even attempting to deny it.

"I was there. I saw you."

He looked at her, startled.

"That was you! In the office!"

She didn't reply but just looked at him expectantly. He shook his head and leaned against the wall beside the hearth.

"I can't tell you. You know that," he said. "What were you—"

He broke off as an insidious thought took hold, and his eyes narrowed as he studied her.

"You're still working for him," he breathed, the realization hitting him like a gut punch.

"I object to the word 'still', gunny. It makes it seem as though I've been working ever since I left."

"You expect me to believe that you haven't?"

"I don't expect you to believe anything, but it won't stop me from telling you. I *did* leave the fold, but now that you're part of it, I'm sure you understand that you can never really leave." Her lips twisted into a smile that didn't quite reach her eyes; a smile that he remembered well. "It's like the mafia. Once you're in, there's no getting out."

"Did Frankie tell you that?"

Her dark eyes lit with sudden laughter and, in an instant, the cold and ruthless assassin he'd been facing was replaced by Dave's warm and laughing sister.

"Oh Frankie! How *is* he?"

"Still the head of the Jersey Family, not for lack of trying to bring him down." Michael was betrayed into a reluctant smile. "It's funny how he always seems to get tipped off when the Feds are getting too close."

His green eyes met hers and they shared a smile that was over before it really began.

"You're a good man, O'Reilly. Don't ever let anyone tell you otherwise." Viper's mask slid back into place. "Tell me why Charlie sent you to Belarus."

"No."

Her lips twitched at his bluntness and an unholy gleam came into her eyes.

"I'll show you my hand if you show me yours," she offered.

Michael let out a snort.

"You've never shown anyone your hand," he retorted, straightening up from the wall. "Besides, if we're both on the same team, then you must know why I was there."

She studied him in silence for a long moment, then sighed.

"I assume you're on the trail of The Cuban." When he was silent, she raised an eyebrow. "Michael, as you just pointed out, we're on the same team. Tell me what you know and I may be able to help you."

"I don't need your help," he said shortly, walking over to the table and picking up his laptop to slide it into the bag on the floor.

"I wouldn't be so sure of that," she muttered. "What do you know about him?"

He glanced up from the bag and hesitated, then exhaled silently. She was asking what he knew about a man that she already knew about. Sharing information about him wouldn't violate any security terms with the Organization. As long as he didn't discuss his actual operation, it was fine. A reluctant smile pulled at his lips. But of course she knew that. It's why she'd changed the question.

"Not much," he admitted, folding the table and leaning it against the wall. "I don't even have a real name. The man's a ghost. He controls the fastest growing, illegal arms empire and no one can even give a consistent description. He's never been photographed that we know of, and those who have met him personally all give vague and different accounts of what he looks like."

"And the deals that he brokers? Who delivers the merchandise?"

"Associates and people authorized to speak for him." He sat on the floor in front of the fire and stared into the flames morosely. "We've got absolutely nothing."

"Then what did you think you'd find in Dachnyi 6?"

"I got a lead that one of his regular associates, Pedro Merino, was in Zurich overseeing the sale of a shipment of guns. He left suddenly before the exchange was completed and made his way to Belarus."

"You think he was meeting with The Cuban," she stated rather than asked. "Why?"

"He was working on a deal for him, but left mid-exchange. It could only have been his boss. He wouldn't dare to leave early for any other reason."

"And so you went to Belarus hoping to find your target."

Michael glanced at her choice of words.

"I'm not an asset. I don't have targets."

A faint smile crossed her lips.

"My mistake. What did you find instead of your...what do you call them, then?" she asked politely.

"Nothing," he said testily. "I call them by their names."

She looked at him, her eyes gleaming in the firelight, and then she smiled.

"We'll just call him the target. What did you find instead of your target?"

"A computer filled with information. The same thing you found." He tilted his head. "And you still haven't told me why you were there."

She looked surprised.

"I'd have thought it was obvious. I was looking for *my* target."

"The Cuban?" He scowled as he stared at her in consternation. "That's impossible. Charlie would never send you when he wants him alive."

Viper's eyes blazed with unholy amusement.

"You don't think that I can extract someone without killing them?"

"I think that's not what your job is."

She laughed out at that.

"Oh gunny, I've missed you!" she exclaimed, her eyes dancing. "Were you always this much fun?"

"Is this fun?" he asked with a flash of annoyance.

"Well, I certainly think so. And let me assure you, I wasn't expecting to have fun tonight." She sighed and the laughter faded. "You obviously found the list of prisons. What drew you to this one?"

"Hans Becker."

If Michael hadn't been watching her so closely, he would have missed the flash in her eyes. It was fleeting and covered quickly, but he'd hit a nerve.

"Why him?"

"Two reasons. One, I recognized the name, and two, my gut."

She raised an eyebrow, a smile toying with her lips.

"Goodness, how you've grown up. You've really been doing this long enough to trust your gut instinct?"

"Time flies."

"Well, I suppose four years is long enough for anyone," she murmured. "Do you realize that you're pushing the outer limits of your life expectancy with the Organization?"

"Actually, my operational expectancy is six years," he told her. "I'm not an asset. Remember?"

Her lips twisted.

"That's right. I forgot. Well, if you keep coming to places like Luhansk, and chasing down people like Hans Becker, I can guarantee that you won't reach six years. You won't even survive the week." She tilted her head and looked at him curiously. "Why did you recognize the name?"

"I saw it on a hotel registry in Amsterdam four years ago," he said deliberately.

This time there was no evident reaction, but she sighed imperceptibly.

"So it began in Amsterdam," she murmured. "Dammit. He said you were there, but I said it was impossible. You were going into training when we were there. How did you manage it?"

"I didn't. I was there six months later, after I'd been to Sorrento." He frowned. "Where *is* the SEAL? Why are you here alone?"

"We do have our own lives, you know. We're not joined at the hip." She answered a little too quickly and he looked up sharply. "So you're here for a Hans Becker simply because your gut tells you the name can't possibly be a coincidence? Who do you think you'll find?"

"An Austrian businessman who can point me in the direction of The Cuban."

Viper seemed amused by that.

"That's it? You're hoping that he can get you closer to The Cuban?"

"It's the only lead I have."

She studied him for a long moment, then got up restlessly. She rolled her shoulders and stared into the fire for a moment, then turned to pace around the room.

"Well, I can hardly fault you for following it," she finally said, glancing back at him. "I'm doing the same thing, if not for quite the same reason."

She fell silent again and Michael watched her circle the small house restlessly. Her back and shoulders were straight and her whole body hummed with tension. She was on her guard, and for some reason that realization brought with it a rush of irrational irritation.

"Hans Becker *is* an Austrian businessman. You're right about that. At least, that's what the world thinks."

"Thinks? Who is he really, then?"

"He used to be an assassin. He still is, on occasion, but I think you know him best as the SEAL."

Michael sucked in his breath and swung around to stare at her.

"What?" he demanded. "Becker is Damon?"

"Yes." She stopped and turned to face him. "So now you know why I'm here."

"What...how? How did he end up in the hands of the Russians?"

"I don't know."

"Why would they care about him?"

"That I *do* know, but I'm not about to tell you."

Michael got up and ran a hand through his hair, turning to stride a few steps before turning back again.

"He's not there. They've moved him to another prison," he told her.

"I know. He's been transferred to #9."

He gaped at her, unable to stop himself, and she shrugged.

"I had a very enlightening conversation with one of the prison guards this afternoon. He was in the village, stopping for a beer on his way home." She paused and pursed her lips consideringly. "I'm surprised, actually, that he was so talkative. I barely had to do anything to encourage him. At least, not at first."

"I really don't need to hear this."

She shot him a look of amusement.

"Still squeamish? You really should be over that by now. Don't worry. The end was quick." She paused in her pacing, glancing at him in amusement. "How did you get into the prison today? What happened to the real delivery driver?"

Michael felt a flush climbing his neck.

"That's different."

"Whatever lets you sleep at night," she said, a grin pulling at her lips.

Michael watched her pace for a moment, then he shook his head.

"So you're trying to rescue your husband." He stopped and looked at her. "He *is* still your husband?"

"Yes. That hasn't changed."

"Have you been happy?" he asked after a second, his voice quiet.

Alina met his gaze and her face softened.

"Yes. I didn't think it was possible to be so happy."

Relief went through him and Michael nodded, his chest tightening. All these years of chasing them across Europe, Asia, and South America, and that was all he'd ever really wanted to know. He'd wanted to know that she was happy and free, living a life that she deserved.

"I'm glad. I really am."

She smiled and nodded imperceptibly, then resumed pacing.

"I was going to contact Charlie and ask for the help of an asset," Michael heard himself saying slowly. "If we're both after the same thing, we can work together. Lord knows I'd rather have you as the asset than any of the others."

"*Are* we both after the same thing?" she asked, raising her eyebrows. "Damon can't help you with The Cuban. Your trail ends here."

"No, it doesn't. If The Cuban was involved, then he had him thrown into a Gulag for a reason. Damon knows something, and I need to know what it is." Michael picked up his forgotten water and took a long drink. "We'll get him out, I'll debrief him, and then he's all yours."

He capped his water and lifted his eyes to find Viper shaking her head.

The Cuban

"What?"

"You are not debriefing him," she told him, her voice cold. "It's not an option."

"I need to know what he knows," he argued.

"Michael, with every hour that passes, I'm more and more likely to be retrieving a corpse. If, by some miracle, Hawk is still alive when I get to him, I can guarantee that he will be in no condition to answer your questions."

"He was still alive yesterday when they moved him," he pointed out. "If he was dying, they couldn't have moved him."

"I wouldn't put it past them to move a corpse just to capture the person coming for him."

Michael stilled and stared at her, his blood running cold.

"Why do you think they know someone is coming for him?"

"Because the guard told me." She stopped in front of the fire and held out her hands to warm them. "They know I'm coming. Apparently Hawk has proved less than cooperative. They're hoping they'll have more luck with me."

Chapter Eighteen

Michael stared at her, his mind spinning. She was speaking so calmly, as if they were discussing the latest football game.

"Well, that's it. You can't go alone."

"Why not?"

"Are you crazy?" he demanded. "You can't seriously be thinking about going into a trap alone! If they catch you, and they will, they will torture you. Do you understand me? They won't shoot you. They will hang you from your fingernails and slice and dice you until you're in pieces, but still breathing. "

"Why, gunny, if I didn't know better I'd say you were trying to scare me."

"You *should* be scared! These people are serious!"

"So am I." Her voice sliced through the room harshly and Michael felt a chill go through him. "They've done God knows what to Hawk. I'll take my pound of flesh from them."

"Not if they take theirs from you first."

"I won't be captured."

Michael cursed and turned to face the fire, staring into the flames as he tried to get his frustration under control.

"It's impossible. You know that," he said over his shoulder. "You're being stubborn. You can't go into a prison that knows you're coming, and bring someone out with you."

"It's been done before," she said, walking over to pick up her water. "I breached a Taliban camp single-handedly to extract the head of MI6. I think I can take on a handful of Russian thugs."

"Don't underestimate them. The Ruskies are bastards."

He turned his gaze back to the flames as she drank, clamping his teeth together. She hadn't changed at all. She was still the obstinate, headstrong hero that insisted on doing it all herself. God save him from reckless control freaks! He inhaled deeply and turned to face her.

"If you're determined to martyr yourself, so be it. But I'm also going after the SEAL. He has information I need, and I want him out

The Cuban

just as much as you do."

"I highly doubt that," she said dryly.

"It's the height of stupidity to not join forces and pool our resources and respective skill sets," he continued, ignoring her. "You realize that."

"Just stay out of it, Michael. You're a spook. You gather intelligence. Leave the heavy lifting to me."

Michael tamped down a flash of anger. She was baiting him on purpose. Why, he had no idea, but Viper was never nasty without a reason.

"You don't really expect me to do that," he said. "You know me too well. We haven't changed that much over the years."

She pondered him for a moment, her face unreadable, then she seemed to sigh.

"You shouldn't be here, Michael," she said quietly. "You have no idea what you've got yourself into. You don't have to be mixed up in this. Walk away while you still can."

"That's not an option anymore. I have my job to do, just as you do." He exhaled and took a step towards her. "Lina, you don't have to protect me this time around. I'll take care of myself."

Her lips twisted sardonically and lifted her eyes to meet his.

"It's not you I'm trying to protect."

"Then why don't we go together?"

She shook her head and finished her water, recapping the bottle. She tossed it into the trash bag across the room before turning to face him.

"Charlie sent you to find The Cuban. Forget about Hawk and go find your target."

He watched as she turned towards the door.

"You know that's not gonna happen."

"Make it happen," she said shortly. Then, as she reached the door, she paused and glanced back. "And stop trying to find me."

Michael couldn't stop himself from laughing. "You already found me."

The look she gave him was inscrutable.

"This wasn't my choice. You should never have been here." She hesitated, then sighed softly. "Michael, leave the past in the past, for both our sakes."

With that she was gone, the door closing silently behind her.

Light glittered against crystal glasses and sparkled off the diamonds and gems dangling from ears and draped around slender necks. Tinkling, polite conversation swirled around the man as he moved through the party towards the doors leading outside. It was the social event of the year, or so his wife claimed, and it was apparent that no expense had been spared. He was enjoying himself, but as always, he was never unavailable. The vibrating phone in his tuxedo jacket pocket was evidence to that. He pulled it out as he stepped onto a flagged stone terrace flanked with cypress trees draped with twinkling lights.

"Hello?" he answered, nodding and smiling to a couple nearby.

"Good evening, sir. I hope your evening is going well?"

"Very well, thank you."

"Is the lobster as good as everyone says?"

The man chuckled.

"Better," he said. "What news do you have for me?"

"The prisoner has been moved to #9 as requested."

"There were no problems?"

"No. The transfer was smooth and uneventful." The man cleared his throat. "The security has been increased. I've added forty guards and they arrived today. I'm told that the shifting of personnel left #2 short on guards, but I'm sure they will manage for a few days. In any case, everyone is in place and #9 is ready."

"Very good." The man stared out into the night thoughtfully, a warm breeze off the Mediterranean blowing his hair across his forehead. "Has there been any activity at the prisoner's prior location?"

"I think so. One of the regular supply drivers and a guard are missing. They're searching for them."

"Who's in charge at #9? Is it still Golubev?"

"Yes, sir."

"Tell him to be on alert. There can be no doubt that someone is coming for the prisoner."

There was a short silence on the line, and then the caller let out a nervous laugh.

"Who would dare?"

"A dead man."

The man pressed to end the call and slid the phone back into his pocket. Instead of turning to go back into the party, he pulled out a cigarette case and extracted one, then walked across the terrace and

The Cuban

stepped onto the perfectly manicured grass. The extensive lawn had been lit up for the occasion and couples strolled among the trees and sat on the ancient stone benches artfully placed in natural alcoves. He lit his cigarette and walked slowly until he reached a gravel path that went to the left and disappeared behind a hedge. He stood smoking for a moment, his fingers toying with the cigarette nervously.

There was no doubt in his mind that the men he'd sent to the #9 penal colony were more than capable of catching the assassin coming for Hans Becker. He'd personally decided which of the guards to pull from the other prisons. They had been chosen not only for their loyalty and skill, but also for their brutality. If the assassin who had evaded Petrov in Budapest had aspirations of saving Hans Becker, he would run into an opposition that perhaps he wasn't expecting.

The man blew smoke out into the night and watched as it evaporated around him. If it wasn't the assassin from Budapest who was coming, then he would have no need of the extra security. Still, it was always better to be prepared, and now the trap was laid and they were prepared.

Everything was going perfectly according to plan, and yet the man stood in the shadows smoking, his body tense. If something were to go wrong, and the assassin evaded capture, it would be *his* head on the chopping block. He had been told in no uncertain terms that they needed to know what Becker knew. But Becker wasn't talking. He had withstood everything that Dragos had done to him and hadn't said a word. The man would have said it was impossible three weeks ago, yet here they were. His only chance was to catch this stranger who was trying to get to Becker. He had no idea who the assassin was, but he knew they were connected to the woman in Belarus.

The woman. His lips tightened and he sucked on his cigarette. Who was she? She had a photo of The Cuban, which was unbelievable enough. She'd been looking for him, and just when she showed up, one of his best men disappeared. They hadn't found his body yet, but there could be no doubt that he was dead. It was the only thing that would account for his disappearance. Was she an Interpol agent? They had women doing so much now. His lips twisted. Or was she American?

He supposed it didn't matter, really. When she turned up in Minsk, everything had gone to hell. That was all that mattered. Becker had refused to break, one of his men was dead, and now two more were missing from #15. Oh yes. The assassin was definitely going after the prisoner. But why? And who was he? And what did he know?

They had to capture him. Once they had him, he would send Dragos. Becker may not have broken, but the other one would. He was sure of it.

But nothing could go wrong. If it did, Les Cinq would not be kind to him.

Michael stared at the dying flames in the hearth. He was laying in his sleeping bag, zipped up to the neck, wondering what the hell was going on. How had everything suddenly taken such a left turn?

Alina was alive.

The thought kept repeating itself in his mind until he thought he was going mad. It didn't matter that he'd spent the past four years absolutely convinced that she had somehow survived that awful explosion. To walk into this shack and come face to face with her was still a shock. It was one thing to think she was alive, and something completely different to face her in the flesh and have it confirmed.

He frowned. How *had* she survived? He hadn't even asked. How the hell had they managed it? One of the reasons Stephanie had accepted the death as fact was because no one could see any way that she *could* have survived. Yet now he knew that she had.

Anger went through him again, though less intense than it had been earlier. She had played them all, and deep down inside, he'd known it all along. Instead of being relieved and happy, as he'd always thought he would be when he finally caught up with her, he was furious. Furious at her, furious at Charlie, and most of all, furious at himself.

She hadn't shown any remorse. His jaw clamped shut and he glared into the embers, his lips pressed into a thin line. She had been just the same as she was four years ago: withdrawn, sardonic, and glaringly condescending. Her only concession to the hell she put them all through was to tell him that it had been necessary to save their lives. He shook his head, the scowl on his face getting darker. He hadn't found any indication that Harry had arranged any contingency plans for if she survived, and he and Stephanie had both looked. But he also knew that if Harry had left instructions, it would have been just as Alina had said: she and Hawk would have neutralized the threats before they disappeared. And, he admitted now reluctantly, if they had, there would have been no trail for he or Stephanie to find. It would have appeared just as it had: that Alina had died ending a fight that had been started years ago.

The Cuban

Michael flopped onto his back restlessly and stared up at the wooden ceiling. He had to get to The Cuban before Viper. He remembered vividly how she'd been when Harry had gone after Angela, her childhood friend. She had been furious, and Angie had only been a friend. The Cuban had probably thrown her husband into a Gulag. If she got to him first, there would be nothing left, and Michael needed answers. He needed to bring him in alive for Charlie and Jack to question.

Why the hell had Charlie sent Viper after him? He stared at the ceiling chewing his bottom lip thoughtfully. He had to know that she would kill him. Michael mulled over the question for a moment, then his eyes widened. Alina had never actually confirmed that Charlie had sent her after The Cuban! She'd danced around that just as she danced around everything that he wanted to know. In fact, after over an hour of conversation, the only things he knew for sure were that Viper was still alive, and that she was going to try to break her husband out of a Russian hell hole. *He* had been the one to conclude that Charlie had sent her to Dachnyi 6, and she hadn't confirmed or denied it. She had dodged it with misdirection just as she always had in the past. God, he'd forgotten how infuriating that particular trait of hers was!

But if Charlie hadn't sent her, how did she know about Dachnyi 6? Michael shook his head. It didn't matter. She was here, and he had to handle it. He would message Charlie, of course, but it didn't change the situation. He had to reach The Cuban before she did, and he needed her husband's help to do it. The arms dealer had targeted Damon for a reason, whether the SEAL knew why or not. If Michael could figure out why he was so afraid of Damon, then he'd have another clue, and another trail to follow.

And he would have to follow it faster than Viper.

Michael exhaled and reached up to rub his eyes tiredly. Alina complicated things. She would need help getting Damon out of the prison, whether she liked to admit it or not. She couldn't possibly be the same person she was when she went into the Taliban camp. For one thing, she was four years older, and she hadn't been kind to her body. For another, she'd been officially out of the fight for four years. He didn't care if she was moonlighting for Charlie on the side, as she'd inferred. Four years away from this life made you rusty, plain and simple. There was no way she was going to get in, get the SEAL, and get out without being caught—or worse. She needed help, and he needed information from Damon.

Whether either of them liked it or not, they were going to have to work together on this. If he had to get Charlie involved, he would, but she was not going in there alone. He wasn't about to let her get herself killed for real this time out of sheer stubbornness.

Alina tossed her bag into the back of the Jeep and exhaled. Her fireside chat with Michael had taken more out of her than she had expected, and she pressed her lips together in displeasure. Seeing him face to face after all this time was jarring. He'd changed, and yet was still the same. His face had new lines, and there was a hard, cynical twist about his lips that she recognized. This life was a hard one. Eventually, no matter how much you tried to prevent it, it left its mark. It was what Stephanie and Angela had noticed about her, only they hadn't recognized it for what it was. She did.

And she was suddenly furious that Michael had been sucked into this life.

She hadn't been surprised to hear that he'd joined the Organization. He was just the type of person Charlie looked for: ex-military, strong, unwavering, and intelligent. Damon hadn't been surprised either. In fact, he'd said that it was the best thing for the Organization, and for Michael. For a while, she agreed. But after seeing him tonight, she was irrationally upset. He didn't deserve this life. He was a good man.

Viper was just closing the door when a streak of awareness shot down her spine, raising the hairs on the back of her neck. She was parked in a dark alley, away from the center of the city, and the only sound she'd heard was the whisper of the wind swirling between the two buildings. But she knew, beyond any doubt, that someone was there. She reached behind her and pulled out her .45, spinning around and raising it in one fluid motion. Pointing it at the shadows a few feet away, she held it steady as a tall figure emerged from the darkness.

"You have good instincts."

She exhaled silently. She knew that voice.

"Boris. What are you doing here?"

She didn't lower her weapon, keeping it trained on his massive chest.

"I came to help," he said, stopping a couple of feet away. "You can put that away. If I meant you harm, I would have shot you when you walked into the alley."

Alina studied him in the shadows for a long moment before lowering her gun and tucking it back into the holster at her back.

The Cuban

"That's better," he said, visibly relaxing. "I heard that your target has been moved to a different penal colony."

She raised her eyebrows and leaned against the spare tire, crossing her arms over her chest.

"You can't possibly know who my target is. If someone's been moved, what makes you think it's them?"

He shrugged and a smile emerged.

"You requested enough fire power to storm a prison, and directions to one of the towns near a cellar used by the separatists who have taken over these lands. Then, before you can arrive, one of the prisoners is suddenly transferred to a different cellar."

"Coincidence."

"I think not. They do not transfer prisoners. Once you arrive, that is where you stay until you die, or are released. It is quite a compliment. You have forced a change, and that is no small feat, I assure you."

"How do you know someone was moved?"

"Does it matter?" When she stared back at him silently, he sighed. "I pay people to keep me apprised of what goes on in the Gulags. For something so out of the ordinary, there was enough talk to make its way to me."

"And so you came to…do what, exactly?"

"They know you're coming. It is the only reason they would move him. You need my help."

"Why does everyone think I'm incompetent all of a sudden?" she muttered under her breath. "Why would you help me?"

He grinned and nodded to the Jeep.

"I consider you an investment," he said with a flash of teeth. "I like you, Anya. You're different from the others. I don't think you're so concerned with the politics that drive our governments. You follow your own path, and I respect that."

"I'm flattered."

"You should be. It is not praise I give often."

"And how do you think you can help?"

"The villages around #9 are very remote. Any stranger will be noticed, and reported. You cannot just show up and expect to not be seen. I, however, am familiar with the area, and I'm well-known there. I will not arouse suspicion, and neither will a woman with me."

Alina considered him thoughtfully for a moment. He was right. She had planned on remaining in the country where she wouldn't be seen, but that posed challenges as far as food and supplies. She would need both, and the villages were the only places to acquire them.

149

"How do I know you haven't arranged a welcoming committee for me?"

"You don't." He shrugged. "But what would I gain? They have set a trap, and they intend to snare you in it. Whether I hand you to them, or they capture you, their result is the same. They would not pay for your delivery, and I would not do it for free. So, you see, there is no incentive for me to hand you over."

Alina chuckled reluctantly.

"I'm not sure if I should be insulted or grateful, but thank you for being frank."

He nodded in acknowledgement.

"I should mention that I have an ulterior motive," he told her. "My brother died in one of those hell holes two years ago. I welcome any opportunity to kill the bastards."

She studied him in the dim light for a long moment, then unfolded her arms and straightened up.

"And that is something that *I* can respect," she murmured. "If you can get me to the prison, I will be in your debt."

He shook his head.

"No. No debt. No favors. I do not work like that. We go as fellow soldiers."

Alina met his eyes and saw the set of his jaw, then nodded slowly.

"All right."

He nodded briskly and went around her to head towards the passenger's door. Alina locked the tailgate and moved to climb behind the wheel. As Boris' bulk settled into the seat beside her, filling the cab, she glanced at him from under her lashes. She had no idea why he was here, or why he was offering to help. He was telling the truth about his brother, she was sure of that at least, but she didn't trust him as far as she could throw him, Mossad associate or not. He seemed a little too interested in her business, and that was never a good thing. However, he was right. She needed him right now.

She started the engine and rolled down the alley to the street. He would be useful, if only to avoid attention in the village. Beyond that, she would keep an eye on him and play it by ear. Her priority was getting Damon out of hell. If that meant joining forces with a Russian bear, so be it.

Chapter Nineteen

"Another dark corner in a crowded and overpriced pub?" Jack asked, looking down at the man dressed in his usual charcoal gray suit that blended with the shadows around him. "We could be sitting comfortably in my study enjoying a superior sherry."

"I prefer the anonymity of after-work happy hour," Charlie told him with a shrug. "And I'm short on time this evening. I'm on my way to Dubai."

Jack set his pint on the heavy wood table and slid into the booth, looking across the table at him.

"Now that I consider the question, your Viper also preferred to meet in a pub," he said thoughtfully. "Monk's, I believe it was called, in Philadelphia. As I recall, they poured quite a decent pint, for an American bar."

Charlie's eyes gleamed.

"I imagine she took that into consideration when she arranged to meet you there," he murmured. "Her attention to detail has always been one of her strongest traits. She would hardly take you to a dive bar in North Philly."

Jack sipped his beer, then settled back on the seat.

"And how *is* the lovely Maggie doing? Is she making progress?"

"I certainly hope so. She's been at it for six days. If she doesn't have something yet, we're both in trouble."

"You hope so? Don't you keep in touch with your people?"

Charlie smiled faintly.

"We only communicate when it's absolutely necessary. I've found that, by and large, my assets work better without me looking over their shoulder. Viper is no exception. I haven't heard from her since she entered Ukraine."

Jack raised an eyebrow.

"She could be dead, then? Killed by a missile attack for all you know?"

151

"I'd be very surprised if she was foolish enough to get herself killed by a missile."

Jack grunted.

"The way they're lobbing them at each other, it wouldn't surprise me," he muttered. "Even Poland is getting their strays. Very well. How do you think she's progressing, then?"

"I think she'll either have very good news for me soon, or I'll receive word that she's languishing in a Russian Gulag," Charlie said calmly, reaching for his beer. "I'm hoping for the former, of course."

Jack considered him for a moment.

"You have someone watching her? Your other man?"

"No, although I'm sure they've crossed paths by now."

"Then how do you expect to know if she's captured?"

"One of my associates has someone on the ground," Charlie said shortly. "Now, tell me about Sophia Morozov."

"There isn't very much to tell, unfortunately. She disappeared from her flat in Brussels, taken out from right under my people's collective noses. We haven't been able to find any trace of her since. There is one thing that we've discovered, however."

"Oh?"

"Yes. Her father disappeared a few months ago. No one thought much about it, and that includes Ms. Morozov."

"She didn't care that her father disappeared?"

Jack shrugged.

"Didn't care, or kept quiet about it for her own reasons. One of my men came across something. I won't bore you with the whys and hows, but suffice it to say that I now believe that Mr. Morozov didn't disappear. He was arrested, and is currently languishing in a Russian Penal Colony."

"You think it was done to keep her quiet?"

"Or in line."

Charlie frowned thoughtfully.

"What did her father do for a living?"

Jack's smile was humorless.

"He worked for a small energy company based in Minsk."

"And he disappeared into a Gulag. Quite the coincidence. Why did no one report him missing?"

"He requested time off for health reasons and was gone the next day. Everyone thought he'd gone into a hospital in Switzerland. Brochures and information were found in his house."

"And now his daughter has also disappeared."

"Yes. It would be very helpful if we knew where, exactly, The

The Cuban

Cuban was. He's behind this. I'm sure of it."

"The Cuban isn't behind any of the dead executives. Your intelligence was bad."

Jack had been reaching for his beer but with Charlie's words, he stilled and stared at him, his face like granite.

"What makes you think that?" he demanded.

"I don't think. I know." Charlie's voice was steady. "Your agent was fed bad information. The Cuban had nothing to do with the assassinations."

"How do you know that? What have you uncovered?"

"I'm not at liberty to share," Charlie began, then held up a hand placatingly when Jack's face began to take on thunder clouds. "Not yet. It would jeopardize both my people's missions in Ukraine at the moment, not to mention your agent's operation in Warsaw. I assure you that you will have a full report with all the relevant intelligence when it is viable to do so. In the meantime, you have to trust me."

Jack's jaw tightened and he was silent for a long moment, his eyes boring into Charlie's. After a very tense pause, his jaw relaxed and he nodded slowly.

"Very well. I'll accept your word that my intelligence *may* have been compromised. However, The Cuban is still a person of interest for MI6. I trust you *will* advise me when you have him in custody?"

Charlie inclined his head and they were quiet for a moment.

"If you don't believe The Cuban is behind the deaths, then why are you still pursuing him?" Jack asked suddenly. "Why not pull Viper back?"

"I said he wasn't behind the deaths. I do, however, believe that he has information about the deaths. It's that information that I want."

"We've discovered the identity of one of the assassins," Jack told him reluctantly. "His name is Petrov. My man in Warsaw believes that he's responsible for at least three of the assassinations in Russia, perhaps more. We've been unable to locate him, or any trace of him beyond his last known location."

"And where was that?"

"Kherson." Jack reached for his pint. "There was a missile strike a few weeks ago. My man thinks he may have been killed then."

Charlie rose his eyebrows and a smile toyed around his lips.

"How very careless of him," he murmured. When Jack glanced up, his face had returned to its habitually neutral expression. "In any case, it isn't the hired grunts that I'm interested in. I want to know who's paying them."

"And you think The Cuban knows?"

"I think if he doesn't, he knows who does." Charlie looked at his watch and finished his beer. "Tell me, can you still have men in the air in a few hours?"

"Yes."

"Good. They may come in useful after all."

Jack raised an eyebrow and drained his pint, standing with Charlie.

"Do you think Viper will fail?"

"No, I don't." Charlie's voice was firm. "But I also don't think it will be as clean as either of us would like. Have your people ready."

Southeast of Donetsk

Alina drove through the little town, the Jeep clattering over poorly repaired roads. Dawn was just lightening the sky and the town appeared to be still sleeping.

"Turn right up ahead," Boris told her. "Then stay on that road until you reach the edge of the village. The last house on the right is where we will stay."

She glanced at him.

"How do you know it is safe?"

"I've stayed there before. It is rented out by the owner, a woman who lives in another town. When her husband died, she moved to be closer to their children." Boris yawned widely. "I have already paid cash for the house. We have it for one week."

"We won't be here more than a couple of days," she said, turning right. This road was even worse than the last and she grit her teeth as they jostled in and out of a massive crater in the pavement. "When did you rent the house?"

"Yesterday. I wired her the funds."

"Optimistic of you."

Boris grinned.

"No. If you had refused my help, I would have come anyway."

Alina was silent and he looked at her.

"That bothers you?"

"This whole situation bothers me," she replied calmly. "There is nothing to be done about it, however, and so here we are, bouncing over roads worse than where I'm from. And let me tell you, that's saying something."

"The roads are very bad," he agreed. "They are worse than when I was here last. I think we can thank the war for that. There is the house, on the end. Green door."

Alina nodded and rolled past the house, glancing at it. It was a small, two story structure built on a corner lot sometime in the decade after the Second World War. The front garden was small and surrounded by an aging wooden face that looked as though the paint had peeled off many years before. As she turned the corner to drive down to the next street, Boris looked at her questioningly.

"We'll park and walk," she said. "The less I'm seen, the better."

"And you do not think walking across the block will make you seen?"

"I won't be doing it in daylight."

"Ah." He nodded complacently. "Very well. However, I would not advise leaving the crates in the Jeep."

"We'll take them in."

The road that led behind the block didn't have many houses and, spotting an empty lot with an evergreen hedge and ancient oak tree, she shifted into four-wheel drive and pulled off the road. She plowed through the snow as Boris held on to the handle in the ceiling near the door, coming to a stop behind the hedge and beneath the bare branches covered in snow.

"I will brush snow over the tire tracks," Boris said, opening the door and climbing out. "But first, we carry everything in."

"Take care of the tracks first," Alina said, getting out and stretching. "I'll start taking the crates. Is the house locked?"

"The key is in the box next to the back door. The code is 4248."

Alina nodded and opened the back of the Jeep. She slung her bag over her shoulder and reached for one of the black crates. Then, turning, she began the trek to the house on the next block. She wasn't as concerned about the tire tracks as she'd led him to believe. It was a little too neat and tidy that there was a house all ready and waiting for them on the edge of the town. She wanted to go over it before he came in. Boris had proven himself to be a very congenial travel companion over the past four hours, but she'd known many enemies who were charming as well, right up until she put a bullet in their head.

The back of the house came into sight and she glanced back at the Jeep. Boris was busy fashioning a brush out of branches from the hedge. She would have plenty of time. And if she found anything amiss, Boris would wish he'd never tried to involve himself in her affairs.

Michael rubbed his hands together and stepped back from the fireplace, watching as the kindling caught under the logs. This house was much better than the one he'd slept in last night, if two hours could really be called sleep. A nap was more like it. He'd been in the SUV and on the road by three in the morning, and had arrived just as dawn was breaking.

Turning from the fire, Michael picked up his bag and carried it to the single bedroom at the back of the house. The cabin was in the country, between two villages and only a short distance from the prison where they'd moved Hawk. He had no idea who the cabin belonged to, only that Charlie had directed him to it this morning when he messaged him his destination. Clearly he wasn't the first agent to use it, and he was sure that he wouldn't be last. He didn't wonder about the properties around the world that Charlie had in reserve for his people to use. He was simply grateful that they were available. This one was particularly appreciated. It was sparsely furnished, but there was a bed, a couch and a chair. The kitchen appeared to be in working order, and the running water was a welcome bonus. All things considered, he felt as if he was in a four star hotel.

Michael entered the small bedroom and looked around before tossing his bag onto the foot of the bed. A folding table against one wall served as a makeshift desk or dresser, and the small window was flanked by navy blackout curtains. He went over to pull them across the glass, blocking out the gray light of morning. He would sleep for an hour, and then he would get to work.

Viper would wait until nightfall to recon the prison. She wouldn't want to risk being seen in the light of day. None of the assets did. They all preferred the cover of darkness, and shadows where they could conceal themselves. The daylight hours would be his only chance to find a way into the prison before she did. Once he'd found a way in, he could make sure that she got in and out as well.

He turned away from the curtains and went out of the bedroom to check on the fire in the living room. He didn't know why he was bothering trying to help her when she'd been less than appreciative of his offer. The fact that she was just being her normal self as he'd known her before was immaterial. He was irritated by the fact that she refused to even consider working with him, and as he

The Cuban

picked up the poker and nudged the kindling to get a larger blaze going, he frowned. That was the crux of the matter right there. His feelings were hurt, and that realization only served to infuriate him more. After what he'd done to get Angela off that yacht, he supposed he expected that she would acknowledge that he was a good person to have around in a crisis. Apparently that was not the case.

He leaned the poker against the bricks and glowered down into fire. The mess of emotions swirling through him was making him overthink things. It was a simple enough operation. Find a way into the prison, get Hawk, and get out again. It would be easier with the two of them working together, but he had no doubt that he could find a way in. Getting out with a prisoner was another matter, but getting in should be fairly straightforward.

What the hell did she mean when she said that it wasn't him she was trying to protect?

The thought shot into his head and refused to leave, taking his attention away from the problem of breaching a prison. Who else would she be protecting? Not Damon. He was already in the soup. Who, then? And why was she so determined to keep him away from her?

Michael exhaled loudly and turned to drop onto the couch. He stretched out on his back and turned his head, watching the fire. He was exhausted. It was making him emotional and irrational. It had been four years since he saw Alina, and they had both changed. They weren't the same people they were when he said goodbye to her on a little private beach in Georgia. She had a new life with her husband, and he had a new career gathering the intelligence that allowed people like her to do their jobs effectively. They had both turned their backs on who they used to be. Why should he have any part in what, or who, she was now? And vice versa?

Leave the past in the past for both their sakes. That's what she'd said. He rubbed his face and let out a jaw cracking yawn. Easier said than done. Whether either of them liked it or not, they were a part of each other's lives. Dave had made sure of that fifteen years ago. As his eyes drifted closed, Michael knew that his course had been set then, before he'd even met Alina Maschik.

And he wasn't about to simply leave her to her fate.

Chapter Twenty

The woman followed a tall, imposing man dressed in a suit through the marble hall and down a corridor lined with oil paintings, some originals and some copies. Her heels clicked on the floor and she listened to the hushed silence of a house that had no occupants aside from the security and servants. It was a huge house, much too large for the single man who occupied it. There were rumors that he'd bought it for his wife years ago, and when she left him, he'd kept the house out of spite. She couldn't imagine her colleague having that much emotion inside of him, but there was no denying that the house was still his, and he still resided in it when he was in Switzerland.

They reached a door near the end of the corridor and her escort opened it, standing aside silently so that she could enter the study. A large, cheerful fire blazed in the fireplace, and her host was comfortably ensconced in a leather armchair before it. As she entered, he looked up from his contemplation of the deep amber liquid in his glass.

"American bourbon is widely regarded in international circles as being absolute shit," he said as she advanced across the study towards him. "However, I'm quite enjoying this bottle. It was a gift, and it's surprisingly good."

"I prefer vodka myself," she said, glancing at the glass in his hand.

He laughed and waved a hand towards the mini bar located on the other side of the room.

"Of course you do, my dear. Please. Help yourself. I have quite a selection. I'm sure you'll find one to your taste."

She smiled and went over to examine the bottles lined up on shelves built into the wall. Selecting a top end Polish brand, she mixed herself a vodka and tonic while she listened to the fire crackle in the hearth.

"Did everything go as planned in Brussels?" he asked when she turned around and came over with her glass to sit in the chair opposite him.

"Yes. I didn't have any problems at all. I didn't expect to."

"Where do we stand with Becker?"

"He's been transferred to #9. I'm told the move was made without any trouble." She sipped her drink. "If someone was watching, they would have attacked the transport. I think we moved him before they arrived."

He was quiet for a moment, then he leaned his head back against the leather comfortably.

"Why did you move him to a less secure location?" he asked. "#15 is a fortress and virtually impregnable. If he's as important as you say, why move him to a location that is more easily infiltrated?"

"He is immaterial. A nobody. He's not important. What he knows is important," she replied. "If this assassin really is trying to get to him, I wanted to place him in a position that would make it easier for them. I want them to get in so that we can capture them. They obviously know something, and I want to know what it is."

He considered her thoughtfully for a moment, then sipped his bourbon.

"If he isn't anybody, I don't see what the assassin coming for him could know. They can't possibly know anything that will materially affect our plans."

"Perhaps, but I want to be sure." She crossed her legs and gazed into the fire, her eyes reflecting the orange flames. "I don't know who Becker is. Not really. Oh, he's supposedly a mid-level businessman from Austria, but I hardly think that has any bearing on what he was doing in Belarus. I know nothing about him, and what's more, we haven't found out anything since we've had him. The only thing I know for sure about Hans Becker is that he cannot possibly be who he says he is."

"And why is that?"

"His resistance to Dragos' methods would suggest that he is more than a businessman."

"A spy?"

"More likely, but even they break under Dragos." She frowned and lifted her glass to her lips, swallowing a mouthful of vodka and tonic. "He's an enigma. If he's a spy, he's had superior training in withstanding torture."

"Or he's simply a stubborn bastard."

She smiled and glanced at him, amused.

"Or that."

They were quiet for a moment, then he sighed and nodded.

"I quite agree that he isn't who he pretends to be, but do you honestly think that he could have come across anything that would be concerning to us?"

"That's what I hope to find out."

"How did you learn that an assassin is trying to rescue him? And how do we know that it *is* an assassin?"

"The same way that I learned about Becker. They went to visit the farmer in Belarus."

He raised his eyebrows in interest.

"Did they really? And what did the old farmer have to say about it?"

"He couldn't tell us much," she admitted. "He never got a good look at the man's face. He was wearing a balaclava, apparently. He called him a killer, and said that he nearly killed him on the floor of his barn. But when our people examined the barn, there was no sign of a struggle."

"Is he lying?"

"I don't think so. His knee was swollen and there were marks that suggest that blows were made. He's too frightened of us to lie."

The man made a doubtful sound in his throat.

"Do you think that perhaps the farmer has outlived his usefulness to us?" he asked. "He seems to be becoming more of a liability these days. This is the second person who was able to track down his connection to us."

"Agreed. I do think that we can still use him for a little longer, if only as bait until we find out how the connection is being made." She shook her head. "There shouldn't be anything to connect him to us, but obviously someone found something. I'd like to know where the kink in the line is. Once we've straightened it out, the farmer will no longer serve any practical purpose."

He exhaled and reluctantly nodded.

"Very well, but keep a very close watch over him. I'm not happy with the situation. If you haven't found the kink in, let's say three weeks, then we'll tie it off."

She nodded in agreement.

"All right, but I don't anticipate that it will take that long. Once we have both Becker and his associate, the situation will be contained. Dragos will find out how they knew of the farmer. They'll show us the kink themselves."

"If Becker hasn't cracked yet, he won't cave simply because you captured an accomplice. You'll be better served having Dragos concentrate his efforts on this would-be hero come to rescue him. Tell me why you're so convinced it's an assassin? The word of a farmer is hardly compelling evidence."

"Petrov was supposed to have killed an assassin in Budapest before he was unfortunate enough to get himself blown up," she told him. "Something happened to cause some doubt as to whether or not he really had, and so the body was dug up."

"And?"

"And there was no body, only an old rug stuffed into a body bag."

The man frowned sharply.

"And now the belief is that the assassin is the one looking for Becker?"

"That's the theory presented to me, yes."

"And do you believe it?"

She shrugged.

"I think it's unlikely, but it really is immaterial who the person is. They will soon be in our care, and Dragos will learn everything I want to know."

Viper watched through her night vision goggles as Boris moved around the outside of the perimeter, measuring distances and making note of the angles of security cameras and patrols. He was remaining out of sight of the perimeter cameras placed at intervals along the electrified fence, and she pursed her lips together thoughtfully. Who was he? Someone who had been trained to stay out of range of multiple cameras, which was no easy task. Was he a former FSB agent? Whoever he was, Mossad trusted him enough to use as a regular contact for supplies.

She shifted on her frozen perch and watched as Boris slid behind a tree when a pair of guards came into view around the side of a truck parked inside the fence. What was he doing here, really? She didn't believe for one minute that he simply wanted to help a random stranger in an impossible task. There was more to it than that, but what? While his explanation for knowing her target was feasible, she doubted that it was the whole truth. As long as he proved himself useful, she would continue to let this play out, but if she sensed that he was even thinking about something the wrong way, Borislav was done. She didn't care if he was a contractor that Mossad utilized and therefore, for all intents and purposes, an ally. If he posed any kind of threat to Hawk or herself, she'd kill him without a second thought.

After glancing at her watch, Viper turned her attention back to the building that housed prison #9. It wasn't as large as the other one, and the electric fence was hardly the impregnable wall that #15 had surrounding it. This one had more buildings within the perimeter as well, where the other only had the one massive structure. She turned her head and clicked a button on the side of the goggles, bringing one of the smaller buildings into focus. Why would they move Hawk to a less secure location when they knew someone was coming for him? Why not leave him in the fortress? She pressed her lips together grimly, the answer coming as soon as she thought the question. They wanted to make it easy for someone to try to break in. They wanted her to get in.

Be careful what you wish for, she thought. *You might not like what you get.*

In total, there were three buildings in the compound. She studied the smallest building thoughtfully. She knew that it was a storage building. When she'd arrived just as the sun was sinking below the horizon, she'd watched from the trees as a delivery truck unloaded food and supplies through the single door into the structure. There was nothing about it that would make it of any use to her, not unless she wanted to use 20lb bags of rice and flour as a diversion.

She shifted her gaze to the second structure a few yards behind the main building. That one was a mystery. No one had approached it since she'd begun watching the compound over two hours before, but the electronic signature coming from inside indicated that it housed something large. A generator, perhaps? Servers? Whatever it was, it pulled a substantial amount of electricity. There were no cables running from it to the main structure, but she supposed that didn't mean anything. They could be underground. She studied it for a long moment, her lips pressed together. She needed to find out what was inside.

The main building was a single-floored structure made from concrete. It looked reminiscent of a Cold War bunker and, if that was the case, then most of the interior was subterranean. That would make it impossible to plan for, and hell to navigate once she was in. It did, however, explain the smaller footprint above ground.

"Damn Cold War bunkers," she muttered to herself.

The other challenge was the number of enemy combatants. Over the past two hours, she'd counted over forty, and she knew there were more in the bunker that she hadn't seen. She had to assume there

The Cuban

was double the visible amount, which meant she was looking at eighty enemy soldiers to their two - three if Michael insisted on showing up. And she had no doubt that he would.

Viper frowned. Michael. There was another complication. Why the hell had Charlie sent *him*? Of all his spooks, why the gunny? If she didn't know better, she'd think that Charlie was trying to get inside both their heads, but she did know better. Charlie was a lot of things, but a bastard wasn't one of them. He'd always left that to Harry. No. Michael was here for a reason, and probably a good one. And if she was completely honest with herself, she supposed she would rather have him be the one to screw everything up over a stranger. At least she knew he would always have her back. And she trusted him, which was more than she could say for anyone else aside from Hawk. But none of that meant that she was ready to have him anywhere near this insane operation of hers. It would be a miracle if Damon was still alive and, if he wasn't, Michael didn't need to be part of what would come next.

Her lips twisted ruefully as she studied the main building. People didn't react well to Viper. Stephanie certainly hadn't, and neither had Michael's friend, Blake. Her ex-fiancé John had seen that part of her and, surprisingly, had been the only one to handle it with any kind of composure. Everyone else looked at her as if she was an alien launching herself out of someone's stomach. Hawk was the only one who truly understood, and respected, the killer she became when she was working. He wasn't bothered by it because he did the same thing. Theirs was a life that no one could understand if they didn't live it.

And she had always been loathe to allow Michael to see it. He'd caught a glimpse in a clearing in Virginia, but he'd never seen her fully unleashed. At least, not that she was aware of, she amended to herself. She had no idea how much he may have seen on that damn yacht.

Alina never asked herself why it mattered to her what the Marine thought of her, but it did. Perhaps it was because he was like a brother to her own brother all those years ago. Or maybe it was because he had been so sincere when he came back and told her about the day Dave died, and the promise he'd made to him. Michael had never tried to be anything other than her friend and protector, even after he learned that she certainly didn't need anyone to protect her. He was a stubborn, old-fashioned bastard, and there was absolutely no way he was going to sit this one out. Not after finding out for certain that she was alive.

She sighed. Alina knew that now she would never be rid of

him. He would find a way to track her down no matter where she went. For better or worse, she was stuck with the gunny until one, or both of them died.

And all because Charlie had sent him after The Cuban. Why? What did he want Michael to discover? The man was a bloodhound, no doubt. He was a genius at uncovering digital and financial trails. It was Michael who had discovered the money trail that proved Harry was behind her brother's death. Harry had made two mistakes in twelve years, and Michael had found both of them. Was that why he was here? Or was it for another purpose altogether?

Shaking her head, Viper watched as two guards came out of a side door, lighting cigarettes. They weren't dressed in the outdoor clothing of the others she'd seen. They were wearing uniforms and had tasers clipped to their waistbands. Prisoner detail. She studied their faces thoughtfully. If she could get a hold of one of them, they would tell her where Hawk was being kept.

"There are motion sensors in the trees." Boris' voice interrupted her thoughts as her earbud came alive. "They look new, like they were placed here only a few days ago."

"They must run off a Wi-Fi signal," she said, pulling her phone out of her cargo pocket. "I may be able to piggyback it back into their system."

"I already tried," he told her with a short laugh. "I can see it, but it's locked down with a detection wall. If we try to use it, they'll know."

"Well that's no fun. And here I thought we'd caught a break."

"It gets better. The exterior rotating cameras are completely randomized. There's no way to predict where they'll be pointing at any given time. The only way to avoid them is to kill the power."

Viper was silent for a moment, her eyes straying to the second building with the electronic signature. After staring at it thoughtfully, her lips curved into a faint smile.

"Note all the locations of the motion sensors," she told him. "We'll need to avoid them when we're leaving. They won't be a problem when we go in, but it's possible that they might be when we come out."

"Do you have a plan, then?"

"Yes." She tucked her phone back into her pocket and shifted along the branch, preparing to climb down from the superior height afforded by the oak tree. "I'll meet you back at the Jeep. I just want to check one thing more."

The Cuban

"You are too paranoid," Boris said as he opened the door and climbed out of the Jeep. "You insist on parking back here behind this hedge. Why? It creates extra work to wipe away our tracks, and for what?"

"I prefer to not have the Jeep associated with us," Alina said with a shrug. "I'd prefer that no one know we were here at all, but that's not possible in such a small town."

"No, it isn't, but they are no threat. They know I am here. They think I am here with my new girlfriend for a romantic weekend. It is not the first time, and they accept the story. You must learn to relax."

"Why would they think you're here with your girlfriend?" she asked sharply as they used the brushes he'd made earlier to conceal the tire tracks.

"I may have mentioned it this afternoon when I went for food and alcohol. It is better that we do not appear to be hiding. That will only make the curious come looking for answers. This way, they think we are having a nice, cozy weekend together, and they will leave us alone."

"Who comes here for a cozy weekend?" she asked, looking around. "It's not the Riviera."

"No, but it is away from the city. And a couple in love have no need of fancy tourist attractions," he added with a grin.

"Is that why there's subpar wine in the kitchen?"

"All women like wine, even the cheap stuff. I also got vodka if you are opposed to the wine."

"I saw that as well." Alina shook her head, a reluctant smile pulling at her lips. "How many times have you been here?"

"A few times now. My brother used to live here," he said with a shrug. "It is quiet. Good for clearing the head."

They finished brushing the snow back over the tire grooves and started towards the house.

"Well, that explains why the whole town knows you," she murmured.

"And why they will not think twice about you, if they see you." He looked at her as they trudged through the snow. "I told you. It is good that I came."

She didn't answer, her eyes fixed ahead of them.

"Who is he?" he asked suddenly. "This Hans Becker?"

Alina looked at him sharply and he shook his head.

"So many secrets, and no good reason for them. I learned his name when I learned a prisoner had been moved."

"Who he is is nothing to do with you."

"I know, but I'd like to know what kind of mess I've got myself involved in," he replied cheerfully. "If he is, for instance, a terrorist, then I'd like to know before Interpol breaks down my door."

"Rest easy. Interpol won't be breaking down any doors over him."

"Who then?"

Alina didn't answer. She was staring at something through the trees, her brows drawn together into a sudden frown. Seeing it, he followed her gaze and sucked in his breath.

Smoke was pouring out of the chimney of their rental house.

Alina reached behind her swiftly, pulling out her .45 and aiming it at Boris' head. As she did, she found herself staring down the barrel of a Glock 17.

"Who are you?" she demanded, her voice like ice. "Who's in there?"

"You ask me? You are the one with all the secrets!" he snapped back. "Did you bring someone to kill me?"

They stared at each other in charged silence, then Alina's eyes narrowed.

"If I want you dead, I'll do it myself."

After a moment, he lowered his gun.

"I believe you," he said slowly, holstering his weapon when she lowered hers. "Who knows we are here?"

"No one on my end."

"Nor mine."

They turned to consider the smoke.

"I'll go in the front. You take the back," Alina said. "Try not to make it messy. I can't get answers from a corpse."

Chapter Twenty-One

Viper looked around the corner into the small front garden and then moved to the porch. The street was dark and still. As she crossed to the porch, she saw a single set of footprints in the snow leading to the door. Whoever was inside hadn't been worried about covering up their tracks. With a frown, she reached out and twisted the door handle, pushing it open and moving into the living room swiftly, her gun in her hands.

She came to an abrupt stop, her eyes narrowing and her lips tightening.

"I should have known," she muttered, lowering her gun and tucking it into her holster at her back. "You shouldn't have come."

"You knew that I would."

Michael was seated comfortably in the corner near the fire, his legs crossed and his coat draped over his lap. As she put away her weapon, she saw his hands move under the coat. He'd had his Beretta concealed and ready. Smart man.

"Boris, it's all right," she called out, closing the door and unzipping her coat. "How did you find us?" she asked Michael.

"I overheard the big guy in the village earlier. He said he was here with his girlfriend. It didn't take much deduction."

While he was speaking, Boris came in from the kitchen, his Glock still in his hands.

"Who the hell is this?" he demanded of Viper, his eyes on Michael.

"Put the gun away. He isn't a friend, but he's no enemy either."

Out of the corner of her eye, she saw Michael's jaw tighten briefly and felt a flash of remorse at her harsh tone. She pushed the emotion aside quickly. It was in his best interest that Boris not know the depth of their relationship. If he didn't think Michael was important, then it was less likely that Michael would become a target if it turned out that Boris was rotten.

"You can call me Nikita," Michael said, not moving from his seat. "As the lady says, I'm no one to worry about."

167

"No? Then what are you doing here?" Boris asked, reluctantly lowering his gun and sliding it back into his holster.

"I have information about the cellar that I thought you would find useful," Michael said, his eyes shifting from Boris to Alina's face. "I know you like to have all the cards stacked in your favor."

Boris scoffed, looking from Michael to Alina.

"Is he serious?" he demanded. "What can he possibly know that we don't?"

Alina was silent, her eyes on Michael's face. He was far too calm and confident. He'd found something that he knew they had no way of knowing anything about. It was the only reason that he would have come inside to wait so brazenly, knowing that she didn't want him here. He had something they needed.

"You're in already," she stated rather than asked. "How the hell did you do it? You haven't been near the gates all afternoon."

His eyes never left hers, his face impassive.

"I was already in," he replied. "I got into #15 yesterday and their systems are linked. All the cellars are linked on the same network, which is surprisingly sloppy from a security standpoint," he added thoughtfully.

Alina shrugged out of her coat and tossed it over the back of a chair before walking over to the bottle of vodka and glasses on the coffee table.

"Of course you did," she muttered under her breath.

Michael's lips twitched, but before he could say anything, Boris sucked in his breath.

"You hacked into the prison network?" he demanded.

"Yes."

"But how? It is impossible!"

"Clearly not," Alina said, tossing back a shot of vodka. She held up the bottle and looked at Michael questioningly. "Drink? We haven't got Jameson, but the vodka is good."

"No, thanks."

"I'm not surprised that the systems are all connected," Boris said thoughtfully, shrugging out of his coat and nodding when Alina looked at him questioningly, holding up the bottle. "They are arrogant. They would never believe that anyone would attempt to hack into their system, or dare to breach the cellars. They can't really be blamed for that. Until now, no one has tried. At least, not that I'm aware of," he added, sitting on the couch and accepting the glass of vodka Alina handed him. "We're the only two stupid enough to think we can do it."

"It isn't stupid when you know that you can," Alina said,

walking over to stand before the fire. "Stupidity is not taking the shot when you have it."

"Do we have it?" Boris shook his head and sat back on the couch. "I am not so sure. And you," he said, turning his dark eyes onto Michael, "how do you know about this? Did Anya tell you?"

Michael's gaze flicked to Alina's profile but she didn't raise her eyes from the flames in the hearth. After four years, he should have learned how not to blow someone's cover by now.

"She didn't have to," Michael said, turning his gaze back to Boris. "Once I knew she was here, it was obvious."

Boris raised his bushy eyebrows.

"Was it? And what have you to do with it? Why are you hacked into the network of a bunch of hellholes that no one cares about?"

"I'm looking for someone," Michael said shortly.

"Ah yes. Everyone is looking for someone." Boris sipped his vodka. "Me, I am just along for the ride. It turns out that I am something of a knight in shining armor. I can't allow someone to commit suicide without trying to prevent it in some way."

Alina's shoulders shook slightly.

"It's hardly suicide."

"It certainly looks like it," he retorted. "Why *are* we trying to break into a shithole anyway? I know you want to get to your target, but why?"

"The less you know about it, the better off you'll be." Alina finally turned away from the fire, walking over to sit on the other end of the couch. "You're the one who wanted to come."

Boris laughed cheerfully and held his glass up in a silent toast.

"Very true. Here's to the secrets that keep us alive!"

"What have you found out?" Alina asked Michael reluctantly. He grinned.

"Don't sound so enthusiastic," he said. "You two need help if you're going to try the impossible. There's no way you can get anyone out of there on your own. The prison is completely self-contained and off-grid. That's why they moved him to that location. On the surface, it looks like an easier compound to breach, but in reality," he shook his head, "it's worse."

"Worse how?" Boris asked.

"All the communication and electrical power comes from an offsite power hub. What that means is that you can't cut the power from inside the compound. Well, not unless you're willing to burrow thirty feet down to the cables. In addition, the prison itself has a massive backup generator that will run emergency power for up to twenty-four hours should a storm blow something at that power hub. So, even if you did manage to kill the power at the hub, you're still out of luck. But the odds of you even getting that far aren't good. You can't access the power hub without military clearance, and even if you managed to hop a ride in, only two people have access to the command tower where you can kill the power."

"So we're stuck with the power."

"Yes. That brings me to the surveillance. You can't hide because half of the security cameras are completely randomized, which means..."

"We don't know where they'll be pointing to avoid them," Alina finished. She flashed a look of amusement at Boris. "So I've been told."

"The power hub controls everything inside that fence. Even if you find a way in, once you're there you'll be facing over seventy heavily armed guards, all of whom are ex-soldiers."

"Seventy?" Boris scowled. "That's an absurd amount."

"Forty of them arrived yesterday according to the logs," Michael told him. "They're expecting you."

"And the building itself?" Alina asked.

"The bunker is subterranean." Michael shook his head. "I have a rough layout, but there are too many places to be ambushed, and with that many guards, they'll have the manpower to do it. Without knowing exactly where your target is, you won't make it past the first level. And even if you *do* know where your target is, two people are not enough."

"He is right," Boris said, coming to Michael's support unexpectedly. "Thirty guards we could have managed. Seventy is too many."

Alina was silent for a long moment, her lips pressed together grimly.

"You're right," she finally agreed. "We can't handle seventy."

She got up and began to pace around the living room, deep in thought. The two men watched her for a moment, then Michael looked at Boris.

"I'll take that drink now," he said.

Boris nodded glumly.

"I'll have another and join you," he said, leaning over to pick up the bottle. "What are you doing?" he asked over his shoulder.

"She's thinking," Michael said, getting up and draping his coat over the back of the chair. "Better to leave her to it."

Alina's lips twitched and she noted that there was no sign of his Beretta when he stood up. Amusement went through her again. He had certainly learned a few tricks since she'd last seen him.

"There is much to think about," Boris said behind her, pouring vodka into a glass and handing it to Michael. "I don't say it's impossible, but it's damn near it."

"Nothing is impossible," Alina said, her voice steady. "There's always a way."

"Not for only two people," Michael said, sipping the clear liquid. "Why don't you take me up on my offer? You need all the assistance you can get."

"*Are* you offering to help?" Boris asked, looking up at him. "Why?"

"Why did you?" Michael countered.

Boris chuckled and set the bottle down, sitting back with his refreshed drink.

"I told you. I find I have a hero lurking inside me somewhere."

"Nikita was born a hero," Alina muttered behind them. "God save me from the lot of you."

"I think you have that backwards," Michael said. "We're trying to save *you* from meeting God."

"Ha!" Boris slapped his leg. "I like you, Nikita. You have a way with words. Why were you born a hero? Were you born into a military life?"

"Something like that."

"As was I. My father was a General. He was a bastard, but he taught me well."

"And now here we are."

Boris toasted with his glass.

"To the thankless task of being heroes."

Silence fell in the room as Alina paced back and forth, lost in thought. Michael stood before the fire, gazing into the flames with his lips pressed together while Boris pulled out a pocket knife and began cleaning under his nails with the blade tip. The heat from the fire had settled into the room, making it cozy and comfortable, but Alina barely noticed as she considered all the possibilities open to her. Scenario after scenario was discarded for one reason or another, and it was with extreme reluctance that she accepted that she *would* need Michael's help. Not only did she need a third person, but it had to be someone she could trust, not with her life, but with the life of the one person who meant more to her than anything.

She didn't want him involved. She didn't want him to know anything about the operation that he'd stumbled into, but there was no help for it now. Her brows drew together into a frown. Charlie had made sure of that the second he sent Michael after The Cuban.

It was some time later that she hit on an idea. She stopped mid-step and pursed her lips thoughtfully. It was an insane idea, but if they could do it, it would virtually ensure that they would be facing much better odds inside the prison.

"You're right," she said, turning to face Michael. "We can't do it with just the two of us. If you're still willing to help, I'd appreciate having you."

Michael raised his eyebrows in surprise, but nodded briskly.

"Good. Then we need to work fast, and we need a good plan." She smiled. "I have a plan."

"But is it a good one?" Boris asked, tilting his head back to look up at her.

"That cell phone you gave me," she said. "Can they really get me anything I need?"

"Yes."

Her smile grew.

"Then I have a good plan."

The mournful sound of a violin filled the small office, blocking out the ambient noise from outside. At the desk, a man was hunched over a machine, carefully packing loose tobacco into a long groove that would force it into an empty paper tube. A can of soda was open at his elbow, and he hummed along with the symphony while he rolled his cigarettes. When a knock fell on the door, he glanced up, then sighed.

"Enter!"

A senior guard came in, closing the door behind him and standing to attention in front of the desk. The man waved his hand impatiently.

"Yes, yes, what is it?"

"I apologize for interrupting you, sir. There is a problem with the new prisoner."

The man's hands stilled and he looked up sharply.

"What kind of problem?"

"A medical problem, sir. I believe that the doctor should be called to see him."

The man picked up a remote, stopping the music, and sat back in his chair, tossing the remote back onto the desk.

The Cuban

"What is the matter with him?"

"He's been running a fever since this morning. The wounds on his torso are looking bad. I think he's developed an infection." The guard cleared his throat. "I wouldn't mention it, sir, but you said that he is a high priority prisoner. As such, I thought you'd want to know."

The warden studied him for a long moment, then nodded.

"You did well to bring it to my attention," he said. "I will send the doctor down. Is he conscious?"

"Yes, but he's not making any sense. He's babbling."

"What's he saying?"

"Nothing that we can make out. Just a bunch of words and nonsense, a lot of it in German, I think. I caught something about snakes." The guard shrugged apologetically. "He is delirious."

"Very well. Return to your post and wait for the doctor."

The guard nodded and turned to leave. As soon as the door closed behind him, the warden rubbed his eyes and leaned forward. He picked up the telephone and dialed a number, drumming his fingers on the desk while he waited for it to ring on the other end. Of all the prisoners, it had to be that one that fell ill. He'd just arrived!

"Yes?"

The call connected and the warden cleared his throat.

"It's Golubev, the warden at #9," he said. "We have a small development with the prisoner."

"What is it?"

"The guard believes that he's developed an infection from his wounds. I'm calling the doctor to take a look. What do you want me to do?"

There was a brief silence, then the voice on the other end spoke.

"You're doing it. Get him medical attention. Under no circumstances can he die, do you understand?"

"Yes, sir."

"Good. If we lose him, we lose any opportunity to learn what he knows. In addition, if it gets out that he's dead, then we also lose our trap."

"I understand."

"How the hell did this happen? He was in relatively good health when he left #15."

The warden cleared his throat uncomfortably.

"When he arrived yesterday, he was barely conscious and all the wounds on his torso were torn open and bleeding through his shirt," he said. "One of the escorting guards had a broken nose, and

173

another had a broken wrist. They claimed that he tried to escape."

There was a longer silence this time, then a snort of disbelief.

"Escape? I watched the video of his departure from #15. He could barely lift his head without assistance when he was carried out to the transport. If he tried to escape, I'm Vladimir Putin. Where are the guards who escorted him? Are they still with you?"

"Yes, sir. They're remaining here as part of the added security detail."

"Place them in confinement immediately. If the prisoner dies because of their interference, they're to be held directly responsible. Do you understand?"

"Yes, sir. I'll see to it personally."

"Good. Keep me informed of his condition."

"Of course."

The warden hung up, swallowed, and wiped the sweat off his forehead. Then he pushed his chair back and stood up. He would get the doctor first, then see to the guards. His cigarette case would have to wait a little longer. Any more delay in getting the prisoner treatment could result in all of them being held responsible.

As he hurried out of his office, the warden swallowed again and sent up a quick prayer to whatever god was listening. The prisoner must survive, or his life wouldn't be worth living anymore.

Chapter Twenty-Two

Alina stared back at the two men who were gazing at her as if she'd suddenly sprouted two more heads, complete with horns. Michael had moved to the couch with Boris while she stood in front of the fire, outlining her plan. Judging by the looks on their faces, they didn't think it was such a good one. She waited patiently for the arguments to begin.

After a full minute of silence, Boris suddenly started laughing, his shoulders shaking.

"It's so insane that it just might work," he chortled.

Michael glanced at him in disgust and shook his head.

"It's not just insane, it's suicidal," he muttered. "You both have a death wish, don't you?"

Alina's lips curved in amusement.

"You really need to stop thinking like a desk jockey and start thinking like the soldier that you are, Nikita," she told him. "Stop being a pussy."

"What you propose is nothing like a military operation," he retorted. "It's a disaster waiting to happen. It'll be FUBAR before we even get out that door!"

"She's right, comrade. Stop being a pussy," Boris said, slapping him on his shoulder. "With some tweaks and planning, it is a good plan. And fun!"

"Fun?" Michael sputtered, looking at his empty glass. "How much vodka have you had?"

"Not enough, and yes, fun. There is nothing like a good fight to know you're alive, eh?"

"Or make you dead."

Alina laughed at that, unable to stop herself.

"You won't get dead," she assured him. "I won't allow it."

Michael opened his mouth, then thought better of whatever it was that he was going to say. He snapped his jaw closed and leaned forward to refill his glass from the bottle on the table instead.

"What about timing?" Boris asked, getting down to business.

175

"When do we go?"

"A large portion of the guards will have to leave the compound to deal with the threat," she told them. "They won't want to risk gambling on the idea that the threat isn't real. The warden will have to commit a large number of men to confirm the situation. The ones left behind will be in chaos."

"They will also be on alert," Michael pointed out. "They know you're coming. They'll know that they're vulnerable."

"Exactly!" Alina pointed at him. "And that's why we'll strike quickly, before they even know what's happening."

"Catch them before they can organize themselves," Boris said with a nod, taking the bottle of vodka from Michael. "The left hand will not be talking to the right. We will catch them with their pants down."

"The generator in the compound will provide emergency power. How long did you say, Nikita?"

"About twenty-four hours. There's something about that, though. It's strange, really. The backup power will only run emergency lighting and medical equipment in the actual prison. The rest of the power goes to supplying the servers."

"What's so strange about that?" Boris asked.

"It maintains the servers, but the power to the computers isn't fed. In other words, the generator protects the information stored on the servers, but the computers in the prison go out with everything else."

"So they won't be able to access anything?" Alina asked.

"No. It's very strange. They'll have partial lighting and power to the infirmary, but no phones, computers, satellite, nothing like that."

"Why the hell would they do that?" she asked with a frown, turning her gaze to Boris. "Any idea?"

He shrugged.

"My only suggestion is that they don't think it will ever happen," he said, shaking his head. "Or perhaps the generator is so old that it can't handle all the electronics we have now, so they created the system to protect what was most important."

"The records." Alina pursed her lips thoughtfully. "It's possible, I suppose, if the generators are relics from the Cold War."

"Whatever the reason, it will only help us," Michael said after a moment. "Everything will be down."

"Cell phones?" Boris asked. "The power outage will not affect them."

"No, but the cell towers will," Alina said. "There are two

within range of the compound. We're going to blow both of them."

Michael raised his eyebrows.

"We are?"

"Yes. We'll set remote charges on a timer and they'll go at the same exact time that we kill the power at the plant."

"*If* we can kill the power at the plant." Michael took a sip of vodka and shook his head. "This whole thing hinges on a power outage that we don't know for sure we can pull off."

"It will happen," Boris said with a nod. "That might be the only thing that I can say with certainty *will* work."

"All right." Michael set down his glass and stood up, stretching restlessly. "Let's say that we're able to kill both the power and the cell towers. What about the regular telephones? Surely the warden will know enough to take a telephone and plug it directly into the servers?"

"That only works if they're running VOIP," Alina pointed out, "and they're not. They have landlines."

"How do you know?"

Alina gave him a long forgotten look that used to make him feel like a silly school boy, and he grinned ruefully.

"Never mind."

"With everything down, telephones, cell signal, power, computers, they will be completely cut off from everything," Boris said.

"Yes."

"For how long?"

"However long it takes for the Oblast to restore power."

Boris grinned and chuckled. "That could be weeks."

"Yes, but we won't have weeks. We'll have, at most, half an hour." Alina rolled her shoulders and went over to sit in the chair abandoned by Michael. "It takes ten minutes to get to the power plant from the compound. Once the contingent of men arrive and see that it is exactly what it appears and not a takeover threat, they will return to the compound. We have to be gone before then."

They were quiet for a moment, then Michael shook his head.

"What makes you so sure that they'll fall for it?" he asked. "What if they know it's a diversion and leave all the guards in place?"

"You really are a pessimist, aren't you?" Boris demanded, drawing a laugh from Alina. "You have nothing good to say."

"I prefer to examine all the possibilities before I commit myself to the probability of being shot to death."

"And that's fair," Alina said. "The warden won't be in a position to gamble. Even if he thinks that it's a diversion, he will have to confirm it. He knows that an assassin is coming for his new inmate.

He'll be expecting something, and that's why he will have to send the guards. He'll have to make sure that the assassin is not in control of the power plant."

Michael raised his eyebrows in sudden understanding.

"You're using their advance knowledge against them," he exclaimed. "They don't know what to expect, so they have to expect anything, even a takeover of their sole source of power."

"Exactly. I know if I was trying to protect someone, and I lost power and was cut off from all communication, the first place I'd look is the power plant."

"That's…not something I would have considered," he admitted. He nodded reluctantly. "That might actually work."

"Anya, I've liked you since we met," Boris told her with a grin. "Now I know why. You have got some serious balls on you. I must remember to tell our mutual acquaintance that he did not do you justice when he said you were dangerous. You are lethal, and I love it."

Alina smiled faintly, watching as he leaned across the couch to grab her empty glass.

"Here. You have a drink. You've earned it," he said, pouring some vodka into the glass. "We'll need more fire power than what we have. I know the perfect explosive to handle the towers, and we will need more ammunition."

Alina looked at her watch, then got up to take the glass from him.

"You have nineteen hours," she told him. "We go tomorrow night."

"Why so soon? We need to make arrangements."

"Becker may not be alive if we wait any longer. We go tomorrow night, with or without the extra fire power."

Her voice was steel and brooked no argument. After a moment of thought, he nodded, tossing back the rest of his drink. He stood up, pulling a phone out of his pocket.

"I will make some calls," he said. "I'll get what we need in time."

Alina watched as he walked out of the room, his phone pressed to his ear. She had no doubt that he would procure the extra gear. The question was how much it was going to cost her, not in cash, but in exposure.

"What about the extraction?" Michael pulled her attention back and she turned her gaze to his. "Once we have him, and we get away from the prison, how do we get out of Ukraine?"

"I'll take care of it."

The Cuban

He looked skeptical, but wisely let it go.

"What can I do?" he asked instead.

"How are you with viruses?" she asked, lifting her glass to her lips.

He raised his eyebrows. "Define virus."

"I want you to infect the network with a virus that will cause havoc to their system. The more chaos we can manufacture tomorrow, the better. Let's get them off kilter before the fun even begins."

Michael grinned.

"I'm on it."

Alina stood in the back door, watching as Boris disappeared into the night. It was past midnight and he was leaving to get what they needed. True to his word, he'd been able to locate and arrange pickup in order to have the extra weapons in time. As he'd gone out the door, he'd said that he would be back by lunch.

She closed the door and locked it, turning to go back into the living room where the fire was dying down but still throwing out warmth. Michael had left earlier, promising to return in the morning. He would be working through the night to insert a virus into the network that would, hopefully, hamper all the prisons linked into the system as well as their own.

Everything was in motion.

She went over to the bottle on the table and picked it up. Between them, Michael and Boris had managed to drink half the bottle, and yet neither of them were remotely affected by the alcohol. Not such a surprise with Boris. He was Slavic, after all. She hadn't been able to determine which country he hailed from, but he was definitely from this part of the world.

Pouring herself a drink, she shook her head. Four days ago, she would never have thought she'd be in a house in Donetsk with two men drinking vodka as if it were water. And what two men! One was a complete mystery, a helpful ally who was certainly keeping secrets of his own, and the other was an old family friend that she never thought to lay eyes on again.

Carrying her drink over to the front window, she pulled the blackout curtain back and looked out into the night. Her gaze went over the street searchingly. It was dark and quiet. There had been no

179

evidence of surveillance, or even of curious townspeople looking to see who was in the house at the end of the street. Everything had been quiet since they arrived, and she reluctantly admitted that Boris had been right. They weren't curious because they thought they knew the answer to who was renting the little house at the edge of their town, and no one else knew they were here. She was perfectly content that she was safe. For now.

Alina sipped the vodka, staring at the moonlight glittering on the snow. Whoever Boris was and whatever he was doing here, he hadn't blown her location. Yet. It was possible that he was simply a Mossad contact helping out someone that he thought could be useful. She had done it herself enough times. Yet she really didn't think that was the case. No. Boris was here for a reason. But why? Was he also looking for The Cuban? Was everyone looking for the notorious arms dealer? She shook her head impatiently. Until Boris said or did something to give away his purpose for being here, it was a waste of time thinking about it. She would be better served keeping her attention on the mission right now.

Glancing at her watch, Alina took another sip of her drink. If everything went according to plan, at this time tomorrow night, she would have Hawk back. Dead or alive, at least he would be out of there. Her lips tightened and she turned away from the window, carrying her glass to set it down on the table. She had to believe that he was not only still alive, but also mentally competent. She was well acquainted with the ways of torture, and the damage they could, and did, inflict on the human body and brain. Not knowing what had happened to him was the worst part of all of this, she admitted to herself. It would almost have been better if he'd been captured and killed immediately. At least then she wouldn't be living with this knot of dread deep in her gut.

But then there would also be no hope of getting him back.

They had known, of course, that this could happen. It could happen to either one of them, at any time. It was a reality that they had both lived with since joining the Organization. Yet, somehow, she'd managed to convince herself that Hawk was invincible. They had been through so much together, survived so much over the years, that it seemed unreal that this was happening now. But it was, and every minute that passed was another minute that could be the last one.

Alina went into the kitchen and took a bottle of water out of the refrigerator, breaking the seal and drinking. She needed both Michael and Boris to pull this off. While she had no doubt that she could have come up with something on her own, it would have taken much longer, and been much more involved. Because both men had insisted on becoming involved, each for their own reasons, she now had the chance to save Damon before anything more happened to him. She would have been a fool to turn down their help, and Viper had never once been accused of being a fool.

Turning to go back to the living room, Alina rubbed her neck tiredly. Even with Boris and Michael, the entire operation was going to be dicey. They had perhaps a sixty percent chance of pulling this off without a hitch. Getting in and getting to Hawk wasn't her main concern. While challenging, the chaos they would create would facilitate that portion of the plan. No. The real test would be getting out again, and then making it out of Donetsk. Once they were away from the region, the closest relatively safe extraction point was in Ukraine territory still held by the Ukrainian forces. However, the window to get there would close rapidly once they were out of the prison. In fact, she didn't think it would be viable to use Ukraine at all after a few hours.

Swallowing more water, Alina sat down on the couch and stared into the dying flames. They would have to get into Ukraine and to the extraction point within two hours, and the transport would have to be waiting for them so they could leave immediately. It was the only way they would get away. As soon as the people who put Hawk there knew he was gone, they would shut down all routes to safety. Not only that, but she had no doubt that they also had people in Ukraine. They wouldn't be safe until they were out of the country altogether.

Pulling her phone from her pocket, Alina dialed a number from memory and waited while the call was routed through layers of security. When the answering service finally connected, she breathed a small sigh of relief.

"Access code 49721," she said.

There was a brief pause and then a click as the call began another journey through layers of security. She picked up her water and took another sip while she waited, her eyes on the fire. When it finally connected again, a woman's voice asked who was calling. A smile crossed her lips as Alina set down her water bottle.

"Tell him it's Maggie." Alina stood in the back door, watching as Boris disappeared into the night. It was past midnight and he was leaving to get what they needed. True to his word, he'd been able to arrange pickup of the extra weapons in time for them to go tomorrow night. As he'd gone out the door, he'd said that he would be back by lunch.

She closed the door and locked it, turning to go back into the living room where the fire was dying down but still throwing out warmth. Michael had left earlier, promising to return in the morning. He would be working through the night to insert a virus into the network that would, hopefully, hamper all the prisons linked into the system as well as their own.

Everything was in motion.

She went over to the bottle on the table and picked it up. Between them, Michael and Boris had managed to drink half the bottle, and yet neither of them were remotely affected by the alcohol. Not such a surprise with Boris; he was Slavic, after all. She hadn't been able to determine which country he hailed from, but he was definitely from this part of the world.

Pouring herself a drink, she shook her head. Four days ago, she would never have thought she'd be in a house in Donetsk with two men drinking vodka as if it were water. And what two men! One was a complete mystery, a helpful ally who was certainly keeping secrets of his own, and the other was an old family friend that she never thought to lay eyes on again.

Carrying her drink over to the front window, she pulled the blackout curtain back and looked out into the night. Her gaze went over the street searchingly. It was dark and quiet. There had been no evidence of surveillance, or even of curious townspeople looking to see who was in the house at the end of the street. Everything had been quiet since they arrived, and she reluctantly admitted that Boris had been right. They weren't curious because they thought they knew the answer to who was renting the little house at the edge of their town, and no one else knew they were here. She was perfectly content that she was safe. For now.

Alina sipped the vodka, staring at the moonlight glittering on the snow. Whoever Boris was and whatever he was doing here, he hadn't blown her location. Yet. It was possible that he was simply a Mossad contact helping out someone that he thought could be useful. She had done it herself enough times. Yet she really didn't think that was the case. No. Boris was here for a reason. But why? Was he also looking for The Cuban? Was everyone looking for the notorious arms dealer? She shook her head impatiently. Until Boris said or did something to give away his purpose for being here, it was a waste of time thinking about it. She would be better served keeping her attention on the mission right now.

Glancing at her watch, Alina took another sip of her drink. If everything went according to plan, at this time tomorrow night, she would have Hawk back. Dead or alive, at least he would be out of there. Her lips tightened and she turned away from the window, carrying her glass to set it down on the table. She had to believe that he was not only still alive, but also mentally competent. She was well acquainted with the various methods of torture, and the damage it could, and did, inflict on the human body and brain. Not knowing what had happened to him was the worst part of all of this, she admitted to herself. It would almost have been better if he'd been captured and killed immediately. At least then she wouldn't be living with this knot of dread deep in her gut.

But then there would also be no hope of getting him back.

They had known, of course, that this could happen. It could happen to either one of them, at any time. It was a reality that they had both lived with since joining the Organization. Yet, somehow, she'd managed to convince herself that Hawk was invincible. They had been through so much together, survived so much over the years, that it seemed unreal that this was happening now. But it was, and every minute that passed was another minute that could be the last one.

Alina went into the kitchen and took a bottle of water out of the refrigerator, breaking the seal and drinking. She needed both Michael and Boris to pull this off. While she had no doubt that she could have come up with something on her own, it would have taken much longer, and been much more involved. Because both men had insisted on being part of it, each for their own reasons, she now had the chance to save Damon before anything more happened to him. She would have been a fool to turn down their help, and Viper had never once been accused of being a fool.

Turning to go back to the living room, Alina rubbed her neck tiredly. Even with Boris and Michael, the entire operation was going to be dicey. They had perhaps a sixty percent chance of pulling this off without a hitch. Getting in and getting to Hawk wasn't her main concern. While challenging, the chaos they would create would facilitate that portion of the plan. No. The real test would be getting out again, and then making it out of Donetsk. Once they were away from the region, the closest relatively safe extraction point was in Ukraine territory still held by the Ukrainian forces. However, the window to get there would close rapidly once they were out of the prison. In fact, she didn't think it would be viable to use Ukraine at all after a few hours, and then they really would be up the creek.

Swallowing more water, Alina sat down on the couch and stared into the dying flames. They would have to get into Ukraine and to the extraction point within two hours, and the transport would have to be waiting for them so they could leave immediately. It was the only chance they had to get away. As soon as the people who put Hawk there knew he was gone, they would shut down all routes to safety. Not only that, but she had no doubt that they also had people in Ukraine. They wouldn't be safe until they were out of the country altogether.

Pulling her phone from her pocket, Alina dialed a number from memory and waited while the call was routed through layers of security. When the answering service finally connected, she breathed a small sigh of relief.

"Access code 49721," she said.

There was a brief pause and then a click as the call began another journey through layers of security. She picked up her water and took another sip while she waited, her eyes on the fire. When it finally connected again, a woman's voice asked who was calling. A smile crossed her lips as Alina set down her water bottle.

"Tell him it's Maggie."

Jack looked up in surprise as his cell phone vibrated on the desk. He glanced at the time and frowned. Who on earth was calling this late?

"Hello?"

"I'm sorry to disturb you, sir, but I have a field call on the line. Access code 49721," a woman told him apologetically. "She said her name is Maggie."

Jack sat back in his chair, setting down his pen, a smile crossing his face.

"Very well. Put her through."

"Very good, sir."

A moment later, a faint click told him that the call had been connected.

"Hello, Jack," a familiar voice said cheerfully. "I'm sorry about the time. I haven't interrupted anything fun, have I?"

Jack felt a chuckle well up inside him.

"Only paperwork, more's the pity," he said.

"Working at this time of night? Don't they say that all work and no play makes Jack a dull boy?"

"Yes, well, they also say that there's no rest for the wicked, which accounts for both of us working at this time of night."

Viper chuckled.

"Touché," she murmured.

"While it's always a pleasure to hear from you, Maggie, I don't

184

imagine that this is a social call."

"Unfortunately, no."

"I thought not. What can I do for you?"

"I need an extraction for four people. Charlie said that I should contact you if it became necessary."

"And it's become necessary?"

"Yes."

"When?"

"In...twenty-two hours, give or take a few minutes."

"Where?"

"Eastern Ukraine, as close to Donetsk as you can get."

He raised his eyebrows, betrayed into a low exclamation.

"What the hell are you doing there?"

"I don't think you want to know," she said, a trace of amusement in her voice.

Jack rubbed his eyes tiredly.

"No, I don't suppose I do," he agreed. "It will be a tight window."

"I know. Just let me know where to go, and I'll make it happen on my end."

Jack looked at his watch.

"I'll have to call you back. Is this number a good one to reach you on?"

"Yes."

"Let me see what I can arrange. I'll be back to you within the hour."

"Jack?"

"Yes?"

"Thank you."

He smiled faintly.

"Just stay by the phone."

Chapter Twenty-Three

M ichael shifted and lowered his eye to the scope, making an adjustment. It was after midnight and the darkness was still and cold around him. He was settled beneath tall pine trees on an incline overlooking the road that led to the prison. Dressed in a white ski suit, he blended with the snow around him, but there was no one around to take notice. The entire area was silent and desolate.

He finished making his adjustments to his rifle and lifted his head, glancing at his watch. It wouldn't be long now. The sky was clear and there was no wind—perfect conditions for an already easy mark. If only tomorrow night could be as straightforward.

A few minutes later, headlights became visible in the vast darkness. He lowered his head again, watching through his scope as the pinpoints of light grew larger and the dark silhouette of a truck took form. Good. They were right on time.

Michael watched as the vehicle grew closer. For someone who prided himself on the fact that he was not like Viper, he was certainly acting like her. He shook his head as he slid his finger over the trigger. At this rate, he might as well just accept that his role right now required him to be more of an asset than the spy that Charlie had trained him to be. Viper would be proud, but he certainly wasn't. This wasn't who he was. In fact, he was beginning to wonder what the hell he was doing here at all.

Exhaling, Michael squeezed the trigger, sending a round into the front right tire of the truck. The vehicle pulled violently to the right when the driver lost control, and as it careened off the road and into the banked snow alongside, Michael squeezed the trigger again, twice in rapid succession. His shots were true and he watched through the scope as his bullets went through the foreheads of both the driver and passenger.

Before the truck had come to a complete stop, he had his rifle off his mount and was disassembling it with quick, sure fingers. He had to move quickly, and a moment later, he was making way down the incline to the wrecked truck. It was going to take a few hours to get this mess cleaned up alone. He would move the truck out of sight of the road, then take care of the tracks. There could be no trace of the wreck or the dead men. That was crucial.

He reached the truck and opened the driver's door, pulling the dead man out before climbing behind the wheel. The engine was still running and he reversed out of the snow bank before pulling back onto the road. The right tire made steering difficult, but not impossible, and a minute later he was pulling down a lane a few yards away. Steering into the darkness of the trees, he killed the engine and glanced at the dead passenger next to him.

"Sorry man," he muttered. "Nothing personal."

He climbed out of the cab and turned to go back to where he'd left the driver next to the road. Any disquiet that he felt in killing two men in cold blood was offset by the fact that they were, when all was said and done, the enemy. He wondered if that was how all the assets justified it, or if they were just bastards. Shoving his gloved hands into his pockets as he trudged through the snow, Michael shook his head. No. Viper wasn't a bastard, and neither was Hawk. They did what they were trained to do, and they did what no one else could. He'd seen glimpses of the toll it had taken on Alina. They weren't immune to what they did, but they did it because it had to be done.

Just as this had to be done.

Alina inserted the cleaning wand into the long barrel, gently sweeping it around the cylinder. Her rifle was in pieces on the table in front of her as she cleaned it thoroughly. It didn't need cleaning, but the act calmed her nerves and allowed her time to think while she awaited Jack's call.

She wasn't happy about leaving so many things to Boris and Michael, but it was the best way to be efficient and move with the speed that they needed. And the speed was paramount to the entire operation. They would have to move quickly before any of the guards left at the compound had any idea what was happening. She knew Michael could do his part. He'd proven himself in the past. She was taking a huge risk with Boris. He was the unknown factor. If he couldn't do his part, then they were going to end up in a shit show the likes of which she didn't want to consider.

Her phone rang, pulling her from her thoughts, and Alina set down the barrel before reaching for it. She glanced at the screen and smiled, picking up.

"Do you have good news for me?" she asked.

"Of course I do," Jack replied. "Were you worried?"

"I never worry." She stood up and walked over to pick up a poker, stirring the dying embers in the fireplace. "Where am I going?"

"We can extract you from Kopani, in the Dnipropetrovsk Oblast. It's a rural village about halfway between Donetsk and Dnipro. That's as close as we can get, I'm afraid."

"How close is it?"

"My best estimate is about an hour from the border with Donetsk, depending on where you are. I'll send the coordinates. The helicopter will be there at 2240."

"Roger that."

"Will you be able to make it?"

"We'll be there," she assured him, leaning the poker back against the bricks.

"Do me a favor this time, will you?" he asked.

"What's that?"

"Bring yourself back in one piece? If I end up with a walking corpse like I did the last time, I'll refuse any more extractions. It's too draining on my people."

Alina let out a short laugh.

"Don't worry. If I'm going to die, it will happen long before Kopani."

"Why don't we make sure that it doesn't happen at all? I'd hate to see Charlie lose you on your first charge back into the fray," Jack said dryly.

"Rest easy, Jack. I have no intention of dying this week."

"No one ever does, Maggie."

Alina looked up from her laptop at the sound of tapping coming from the back door. She frowned and stood up, pulling the .45 from the holster in her back as she moved towards the kitchen. Early morning sun poured through the window above the sink and she relaxed when she saw Michael peering through the small panes of glass in the door.

"You're early," she said, opening the door.

The Cuban

"I've been up for hours," he replied, stepping into the kitchen. He had a large bag in one hand and a huge Yeti thermos in the other. "Don't tell me you've just got up."

She shook her head, tucking her gun back into its holster. "Hardly."

"Well, I come with caffeine." He held up the thermos. "I thought you'd appreciate real coffee."

Alina raised her eyebrows as he set it down on the counter, tossing his bag onto the small kitchen table.

"Coffee? From where?"

He glanced at her in surprise.

"I travel with my own. Don't you?"

She shook her head, a bemused smile pulling at her lips. "No."

"That surprises me." He started opening cabinet doors, looking for mugs. "You were always so picky about your coffee."

"I still am," she admitted. "It just never occurred to me to bring it with me."

"Huh. So what have you been drinking?"

"Since I've been here? Nothing. Boris brought energy drinks yesterday, but that's about the extent of it."

Michael made a face and poured steaming black coffee into a mug, handing it to her.

"No wonder you're so pissy these days."

"Not wanting you here doesn't constitute being pissy," she said, lifting the mug to her lips. The coffee was piping hot, strong, and absolutely delicious. "Mmm. That's good coffee."

He grinned and poured his own cup before sealing the thermos again.

"I know. Where are we with the weapons? Did Boris have any luck?"

"Yes." She turned to walk back into the living room. "He left last night to pick them up. He just called a few minutes ago. He's on the way back. He'll be here in two hours."

"Who is he, exactly?" he asked, following her. He watched as she closed her laptop on the coffee table. "Where did you pick him up?"

"I didn't. He's a supplier. He provided my gear when I arrived." She sat down and glanced at him, hesitating, then she sighed. "He's one of Mossad's contacts. They arranged the gear, he delivered it."

"And you just brought him along for company?" he asked

incredulously.

"Of course not. He found me after they transferred Hawk. He'd put two and two together and said that I needed his help. As it turns out, he was right. The only reason I'm not drawing any attention in this town is because they know him, and this isn't the first time he's stayed in this house."

Michael scowled.

"How did he even know what you were doing?"

She shook her head. "I don't know. He says it didn't take much to figure it out, but I don't think that's entirely true. I haven't been able to figure out what his real game is, but I will."

"Do you trust him?"

Alina laughed mirthlessly.

"No, but there's no denying that he's useful."

Michael sipped his coffee, watching her over the rim.

"This a huge risk you're taking, then."

"Not as huge as you think. If he even sneezes wrong, I'll put a bullet in his skull."

Michael made a face, but let the comment pass.

"I have something that I think will help tonight," he said, setting down his mug and going back out to the kitchen. He returned a moment later with his bag. "Even with all the chaos we're creating, I'm worried about getting into the prison. This will make it easier."

He unzipped the bag and pulled out two guards' jackets. He tossed them over the back of the couch and pulled out the matching pants and shirts.

"Guard uniforms?" Alina picked up one of the jackets. "My, my, you *have* been busy."

"It will be easier for us to get in if we're wearing these."

She looked at him thoughtfully.

"But even with these, you and Boris are still strangers. They'll buy you a few seconds, but not much more."

Michael grinned at her.

"That's where you're wrong. The warden is expecting two new guards to arrive this evening. They're being sent to aid in the security effort. He received the orders this morning from within the network."

"Now there's the gunny I know and love," Alina said with a grin. "Good thinking. How did you get the uniforms?"

"Some of the guards who live locally go home at the end of their shift. I stopped two of them last night."

She looked at him sharply, the smile gone.

"You didn't leave a mess?"

The Cuban

He frowned. "Of course not. I was trained by the same people who trained you, remember?"

She relaxed and smiled ruefully.

"Sorry. I'm still getting used to that." She drank some more coffee, taking a second to savor it. "Did you get the viruses inserted?"

"Yes." He zipped up his bag and picked up his mug again. He looked at his watch. "They should already be causing havoc everywhere. While I was doing that, I had another look around for any indication of where they're keeping the SEAL. There's nothing in #9's logs to say where he is."

"He *is* there, though?"

"Yes. He went through their intake process. They just haven't logged where he is inside. Right now, we're blind. I'm going to keep checking throughout the day to see if they update their logs, but if the viruses do their job, it's doubtful they'll get much data entered today. When Boris and I get in there tonight, we'll have no idea where to go."

Alina looked at him, a faint smile on her face.

"The two new guards should be able to discover one inmate's location easily enough," she said, her voice even. "And if they can't, I'll have to question what the hell you learned in your four years under Charlie."

Golubev looked up from his breakfast of scrambled eggs and diced potatoes as the resident doctor sat down across from him at the table in the cafeteria.

"Good morning, comrade," he said cheerfully. "How is your patient this morning? Do you have a diagnosis?"

"He is suffering from a staph infection, most likely from the lacerations on his torso. Some of them are very deep and, though they've begun to close, they've become infected," the doctor told him.

The warden eyed the single cup of coffee that the doctor had brought to the table with him.

"You are not eating?"

"I ate earlier. The coffee is all I need."

He grunted and went back to his substantial breakfast.

"So it is a simple infection?"

"There is nothing simple about a staph infection, and this one is quite severe." The doctor shook his head. "I've placed him in the infirmary and have started an IV of antibiotic."

191

"How long will that last?"

"It could be hours, or it could be days before we see improvement," the doctor said with a shrug. "As I've said, it's a severe case. I've put him on the strongest antibiotic that we have here, but it all depends on how quickly the patient responds to the treatment."

"The prisoner cannot remain in the infirmary for more than a few hours," the warden said, wiping his mouth and reaching for his coffee. "I need him back in his cell where he is contained and protected."

The doctor frowned and shook his head.

"That's not possible. He must remain on the IV and his vital signs must be monitored. We cannot move that equipment into a cell."

"I cannot confine him in the infirmary," Golubev argued. "There are too many entrances and exits." He lowered his voice. "This man is a high priority inmate. He must be kept in solitary confinement and guarded at all times. Someone is coming, an assassin they say, to try to rescue him. I am tasked with the job of catching the assassin and making sure that the prisoner remains in our custody. Do you see? It simply isn't possible to keep him in the infirmary. It would be like handing him over with our compliments!"

The doctor was quiet for a moment, his lips pressed together, then he shook his head.

"Let me explain it to you this way," he said finally. "If I stop the treatment in a few hours, and his body has already begun to respond, in all likelihood, he will get worse. The infection will rebound stronger than before."

The warden exhaled loudly, considering the doctor over the rim of his coffee mug.

"Is it life threatening, this infection?"

"Absolutely. With the severity, it could easily spread to his blood and turn into sepsis, and then yes, he would likely die."

Golubev grunted and picked up his fork again.

"You leave me no choice then," he muttered. "Very well. Keep him. But as soon as he is out of danger, he is to be moved back to his cell. I'll have two guards moved to outside the infirmary, and make sure no one is admitted while he is there."

The doctor nodded, finishing his coffee and standing.

"You've made a wise choice," he told him, looking down at him. "This is your only hope of saving his life and, if he is such a high priority, I'm sure that you cannot afford to have a corpse on your hands."

The warden nodded and watched as the doctor left the

The Cuban

cafeteria. He'd known the good doctor for years, and trusted his skills. If he said this was necessary, then he had no choice.

The inmate had to remain healthy, or there would be hell to pay.

Chapter Twenty-Four

When the back door into the kitchen crashed open, Alina motioned for Michael to remain in his seat as he started up with his Beretta in his hands.

"It's only Boris," she said, standing. "He called to say he was back."

Michael relaxed and put his gun away, settling back into his chair.

"I am back!" Boris' voice boomed out of the kitchen. "And I have toys."

Alina went to the door of the kitchen. There was a black crate on the kitchen floor and Boris was in the process of heaving a larger, and by the looks of it, much heavier one through the door.

"Good Lord, what did you get?" she demanded, eyeing the crates. "There are only three of us. We can only fire so many guns at once."

Boris grunted as he thumped the larger crate down onto the floor, straightening up to stretch his back.

"It is always better to be prepared," he told her, closing the door and unzipping his coat. "It's snowing again."

He took off his coat and shook the snow off of it before hanging it on the back of a kitchen chair.

"Prepared for what? Armageddon?" Michael asked from the door, eyeing the crates.

"No, for storming a Russian penal colony." Boris shook his head. "I don't think you two realize what we're up against. It is better to have weapons we don't have to use than to be caught without ones that could mean the difference between failure and success."

"That's true enough," Alina admitted, walking over to the smaller crate. "Are you going to show us?"

He grinned and unlocked both cases.

"I think you will be pleased," he told her as she opened the smaller one. "Oh, those are thermal suits to wear over our clothes," he said when she lifted out a white ski suit. "Necessary for blending with

194

the snow."

"I have one already."

"Yes, but not like these." Boris took it from her and unzipped the jacket. "These are reversible. You can reverse it to black. Handy, no?"

Alina smiled at his enthusiasm and nodded reluctantly.

"Very handy."

"We have more ammunition, and I was able to get all the charges and explosives I wanted for the cell towers and the fence." Boris opened the large crate. "This is something extra, and I didn't think I would be able to get it, but here it is."

Alina looked into the crate and a laugh bubbled up inside her.

"A rocket launcher?!" Michael exclaimed from behind her. "Are you out of your mind?"

Boris frowned and looked at him.

"No. Why?"

"You don't think that's overkill?" Michael asked, his eyebrows in his forehead. "A rocket launcher? Do you plan on bringing down a jet?"

Alina laughed at the look on Michael's face and clapped him on his shoulder.

"We may not end up needing it," she said, "but you have to admit that it's a fun thing to have."

"Fun isn't the word that I would use."

Boris looked at Michael for a moment, his bushy brows knit together in thought.

"Are you Interpol?" he demanded. "You act like the western police."

Alina bit back another laugh.

"No, he's just grumpy today. Ignore him."

Boris made a sound suspiciously like a harumph, but closed the cases with a shrug.

"The rest is extra ammunition and explosives," he said. "We have enough here to blow our way in if everything else fails."

"Nothing will fail," Alina said, turning to go back into the living room. "But as you say, it's best to be prepared."

Boris followed her and Michael, rubbing his hands together to get them warm.

"My associate told me something interesting while I was loading the Jeep," he said, walking over to the radiator near the window and holding his hands over its warmth. "There is talk in Kyiv that a Western assassin has disappeared and the men in power are concerned that it will reflect poorly on Ukraine."

A chill went down Alina's spine and her eyes narrowed as she stared at the back of Boris' head. Michael glanced at her sharply, then moved to sit on the couch.

"Why would the Ukrainian government be concerned if an assassin disappeared?" he asked, his voice even. "It's hardly something that would affect them."

"They say the assassin disappeared while he was on Ukrainian soil."

"I still don't see why that would be problematic. People disappear every day."

"According to the story I got, the assassin was pursuing The Cuban," Boris said calmly, turning around and looking at them. "You know who that is?"

"Of course," Michael replied. "He's an international arms dealer. So what? I'm sure he's made several enemies in his business dealings."

"No doubt. However, The Cuban has been providing weapons to the Ukraine army to help in their struggle against the Russian forces," Boris told them. "If an assassin was going to kill him, it would be in Ukraine's best interest to eliminate the threat."

Alina looked up, her face impassive.

"Is that what they did?" she asked, her voice soft.

Boris studied her for a moment, then shook his head.

"No. From all accounts, they know nothing about the disappearance, and no body has been found. The concern, of course, is that the western power that controls this person will presume that Ukraine was responsible for his disappearance."

"If the person is an assassin, I very much doubt that any power will claim responsibility for him at all," Alina said calmly. "I think whoever the men in power are that have these concerns should relax and focus on the more immediate threat of the war they're fighting."

Boris smiled faintly.

"You're probably right," he agreed easily, walking over to perch on the arm of the couch. "Tell me, though. This Hans Becker, who we are going to break out of a prison tonight, is he the missing assassin?"

The Cuban
Dubai

Charlie walked among the throngs of shoppers in the market, his eyes moving behind the sunglasses perched on his nose more out of habit than from wariness. His perpetual gray suit that Viper had teased him about had been replaced with cream linen pants and a relaxed, short-sleeved, navy shirt, allowing him to blend in with the other travelers and natives alike. While he wasn't hiding by any stretch of the imagination, he was also not trying to draw attention to himself in the busy outdoor market.

He stopped at a vendor selling an astounding variety of loose tea and considered the offerings, nodding to the man behind the table amiably.

"You are looking for something specific?" the vendor asked in heavily accented English.

Charlie waved a hand and smiled.

"I always end up with the hibiscus, but I feel as though I should broaden my horizons," he said in Arabic. "What would you suggest?"

"I have a very aromatic Morrocan green tea here that you might like," the man replied, relaxing at the use of his native tongue. "It is delicious with fresh mint."

"That does sound delightful." Charlie pretended to consider, shifting his gaze between the green and the hibiscus. "Oh, what the hell. I'll take both."

The vendor smiled and reached for a bag.

"You will not be disappointed," he assured him, scooping the green tea leaves into the bag.

Charlie was watching him when a man joined him at the table, also perusing the tea selection.

"I have the parcel, but there was a problem," the newcomer said in a low voice. "The courier proved to be difficult."

"How difficult?" he asked, glancing at him.

"He's dead. He jumped out of a fifth story window. The local police are treating it as a suicide." The newcomer smiled at the vendor, watching as he scooped hibiscus tea into a second bag for Charlie. "Well, they can hardly do anything else, can they? Witnesses saw him throw himself over the balustrade."

The vendor handed Charlie the two bags of tea and he passed him some money, thanking him for his recommendation.

"Suicides appear to be the trending theme this year," he murmured to the newcomer.

He began to turn away and the man slipped a thumb drive into his palm.

"At least I got this before he took his swan dive," he said.

Charlie nodded and smiled at him.

"I highly recommend the hibiscus," he said, raising his voice. "It's delicious iced with a squeeze of lemon."

"Thank you. I will try it."

Charlie melted back into the throng of shoppers walking through the market, holding his tea in one hand while his other slid the thumb drive into his pocket. He moved through the crowd, a small frown creasing his brow.

The courier that was relieved of his package had preferred to die rather than admit failure to his handlers. He'd thrown himself out of a window to avoid facing them. That kind of fear was rare, and incredibly dangerous. It was virtually impossible for his people to combat that kind of sheer terror and will. No amount of bribery or coercion would be effective. He'd seen it before, and it almost always led to an excess of fatalities—on both sides.

So it was just as he'd suspected all along. This wasn't simply a case of a Russian oligarch consolidating his power by replacing executives with ones loyal to him. This was something more. This enemy was ruthless, and they ran their business with inflexible expectations that must be adhered to, or punishment would be swift. The suicides and body counts connected to them were piling up, and now here was another one. And he was no closer to uncovering their identity now than he had been nine months ago.

It wasn't for lack of trying. Their attempts to infiltrate the network had failed, just as their attempts to draw them out had. Whoever was behind it all was incredibly well-connected and well-funded, not to mention efficient. They had even managed to capture Hawk, something that was as incredible as it was foolish.

The frown on his face eased and Charlie felt a prosaic flash of amusement go through him. They had no idea what a Pandora's box they had opened the second they decided to keep Hawk alive and throw him into a Gulag. It would have been better for them if they had killed him outright, but of course they had no concept of the bear they had unwittingly poked. It wasn't only Viper they would have to contend with, either. If Hawk came out of it alive and in one piece, he was a force of his own. The two together? Well, Charlie was just thankful that they were with him. They were a ferocious weapon that he hesitated to wield, but now he admitted that it was out of his hands. They would go after this enemy and, he reluctantly acknowledged, they

The Cuban

just might be the only ones who could get to the bastards. After all, it was what he'd trained them to do.

The problem would be directing them through the avenues that would be least likely to cause far-reaching, international chaos. Charlie's lips twisted briefly. O'Reilly would help there. It was one of the reasons why he'd sent him after The Cuban. He would act as a calming force in the storm, and Charlie was well aware that he was probably one of the only men Viper would listen to. However, if anything happened to Hawk, Charlie wasn't sure that even the gunny would be able to control her.

As he exited the market and turned to make his way back to his hotel, he pressed his lips together grimly. This enemy, whoever they were, had to be stopped. That was quite clear to all the Western powers, and he'd been told that his section was expected to take care of it. But until he discovered who they were, all he could do was move his players into position and then watch, trying to unravel what their goal was. The attack on Hawk was unfortunate, and it had significantly shortened the amount of time that he had. While he had unlimited patience to wait until they made a mistake, Viper did not.

The Cuban was the key, and he was running out of time.

The silence in the room was thick and Alina felt Michael look at her sharply from the couch. She suppressed a sigh and sat down in the chair near the fireplace, meeting Boris' gaze across the room. Boris she could lie to, but Michael was another story. He didn't know how or why Hawk had ended up in the prison, only that he believed The Cuban was responsible, and that was just how she wanted it. Unfortunately, she knew that was about to change. Michael knew her too well, and knew too much about what she and Hawk had done for years. If he didn't already suspect the truth, he would by the time this conversation was over.

"Anya? Is Becker an assassin that was after The Cuban?" Michael asked as the silence in the room grew.

Alina never took her eyes from Boris' face, a faint smile toying with her lips. She couldn't help the conclusions Michael would come to, but she could certainly make sure Boris didn't know the truth.

"I don't know what Becker was doing," she finally said with a shrug, her voice even. "All I know is that he was thrown into a Gulag and I'm here to get him out."

"That's it? That's all you know?" Boris asked, raising an eyebrow skeptically. "Forgive me, but I find that hard to believe. An intelligent operative such as yourself would know much more than that about a target."

"Normally, yes," she admitted with the flash of a smile that didn't quite reach her eyes. "In this case, however, no. I don't know how it works in your business, Boris, but mine is very compartmentalized. It was determined that I didn't need to know why Becker is here, only that he is, and my job is to get him out. Nothing more, nothing less."

His gaze bore into hers for a long moment, then he exhaled and nodded.

"Very well. Hell, it is probably all nonsense anyway. Rumors have a way of growing until even the most far-fetched stories are considered truth."

Alina was uncomfortably aware of Michael staring into the cold fireplace, his face impassive. She didn't like this new spy that Charlie had manufactured. She couldn't read him as easily as the old gunnery sergeant who had promised to look out for her all those years ago. She supposed it was unrealistic for her to hope that he wouldn't work out the truth, but she did nonetheless. Right now, he could still walk away from this. If he stumbled on the truth, he would be as embedded in the mire as she was herself.

"What are these?" Boris asked suddenly, pausing on his way to the kitchen. He was staring at the uniforms still draped over the back of the couch. "These are guard uniforms!"

"Yes. Nikita managed to obtain them last night. The warden is expecting two new guards this evening."

"How did you…no, don't tell me. It's best that I not know," Boris said, picking up one of the jackets and examining it. "This is good. If we can walk in and find out where they're keeping Becker without raising any questions, then half the battle is won."

"Half the battle will be won once you're out again," Alina said, getting up and walking over to the coffee table and her bottle of water. "We still have to get into Ukraine. The prison is only part of the operation."

"Bah. The rest is child's play," Boris said with a grin. "Everything is arranged just as you requested for the power outage. If anything was going to give us trouble, it would have been that."

Alina raised her eyebrows.

"I thought you said that they could get me anything I need?"

"I wasn't expecting that your need would be so, shall we say,

200

unusual?"

She grinned and uncapped her water bottle.

"If you knew me, you'd know that's not so unusual," she said, lifting the water to her lips.

"And that is why I wish I could know you more," he said cheerfully. "You're fun. Kickoff, as the Americans say, is at seven-thirty."

"What's the plan to get out of Donetsk?" Michael asked, stretching. "Have you two figured that out yet?"

"I arranged that as well. A helicopter will take us as far as Voskreshenka, where I can have a vehicle waiting for us."

"Can have?" Alina looked at him sharply. "It's not arranged?"

"Not yet. I wanted to be sure that Voskreshenka was acceptable."

"Is there another choice?"

"Not really. That is as far as our pilot can go."

"Then it will have to be acceptable," she said wryly. "Make the call and get the transport."

"How the hell is a chopper going to get us out?" Michael asked. "The Russians will shoot it out of the air!"

"No, they won't. It's one of theirs," Boris said with a grin. "I'm calling in a long-overdue favor."

"The Russians are going to fly us out?"

"Yes, but they are not bad Russians. They are just men doing their job to provide for their families, and to avoid the Gulag."

Alina grinned at the look on Michael's face.

"Don't worry, Nikita. If anything goes sour, we'll handle it."

Boris frowned.

"Nothing will go wrong. These are good men. I trust them."

"Yes, but I don't trust you, so forgive me if I think defensively."

Silence fell, but instead of being offended, Boris chuckled.

"And this after all these toys I've managed to get," he said mournfully, his eyes dancing. "Ah well. It is the way of the game. I understand."

"Don't take it personally, Boris," Michael told him. "She doesn't trust me either."

"If the helicopter will get us to Voskreshenka, we can make it to the extraction point from there easily with a fast vehicle," Alina said, looking up from the map on her phone. "It will need to be a fairly large one. We don't know what kind of condition Becker will be in. We have to assume he will need space to lie down."

"I'll see what I can get," Boris said with a nod. "It shouldn't be a problem. Where is the extraction point?"

Alina shook her head, sliding her phone back into her pocket.

"That's need to know, and you don't," she said. "If either of you are caught, I can't run the risk of them learning the location before I get Becker away. Sorry."

"So we don't know?" Michael asked, startled. "That's how it is?"

"That's how it is."

"That is probably a very good thing," Boris said, heading towards the kitchen. "She is right. If we are caught, they will waste no time in making us talk. I, for one, will not swear that I can remain silent under the kind of torture that they will inflict."

Alina looked at Michael as Boris disappeared into the kitchen, the expression on her face unyielding.

"Nothing personal," she said with a shrug. "There's too much at stake."

"And if you're caught?"

The look that crossed her face was chilling.

"If I'm caught, we're all dead anyway."

Chapter Twenty-Five

Michael finished buttoning the uniform shirt and looked at himself in the mirror hanging over an ancient, cheap dresser in one of the upstairs bedrooms. The shirt was tight across his shoulders, but the jacket would conceal that fact. The pants, however, were too big. Holding them up with one hand, he turned to rummage around in his bag, looking for a belt.

He was still smarting over his own stupidity regarding the reason the SEAL had ended up in a Russian prison. Why the hell hadn't he considered the blatantly obvious fact that he had been sent to assassinate The Cuban? And how had a gorilla sporting the questionable nom de plume of Boris figure it out first?

Michael pulled out a brown leather belt and began feeding it through the loops on the pants, his lips pressed together in a grim line. It was so obvious. He knew what Hawk was, and how good he was at his job. It should have been his first thought the instant Alina told him Hans Becker was Damon Miles. And yet, it wasn't. In fact, he'd hardly given any thought to why the SEAL had ended up in a Gulag, focusing instead on what he might know about The Cuban. If he was sent to kill him, then Alina's husband knew everything there was to know about the arms dealer. He let out a muffled expletive.

And that meant that Viper knew a hell of a lot more than she was saying as well.

It all made sense now. Hawk was sent to eliminate The Cuban, and Viper was sent to rescue him. Michael's head snapped up, his eyes widening. Had she also been sent to finish what Hawk had begun? Was her next target The Cuban, not out of revenge for Hawk's imprisonment, but because Charlie wanted The Cuban dead?

Then why send him? He shook his head. It didn't make any sense to send him after The Cuban if he'd already dispatched not one, but two of his best assets. Then again, nothing made any sense to him anymore. It made no sense that he was trying to help a woman who clearly wanted nothing to do with him or their past, or why he was dressing in a uniform he'd taken off a corpse that he'd shot the night before. Nothing was as it should be. This wasn't even his job, yet here he was preparing to go into battle with a sketchy Russian on one side and a ruthless assassin on the other.

A sudden laugh went through him, making his shoulders shake. When he boarded the flight in Philly, he hadn't known where he was going, but he certainly would never have guessed that this was where he would end up.

He finished doing up the belt buckle and grimaced at the bunched waistband. Hopefully the jacket would cover that as well. Michael was just reaching for the jacket in question when the door opened unceremoniously and Boris came in.

"I don't think this fits," he announced.

Michael turned to look and his eyes widened before he began laughing. Boris had put on the other guard uniform, but the results were less than spectacular. The uniform shirt was impossibly taut across his barrel chest. He'd somehow managed to get the buttons fastened, but the fabric was pulling so tightly that it created huge gaps between them, exposing the undershirt he wore underneath. If he took even a moderately deep breath, Michael wouldn't be shocked to see one, or all, of the buttons come bursting off. Dropping his gaze to the pants, he laughed even harder. The hems stopped about four inches before his ankles.

"I think you're right," he gasped. "Good God, you look ridiculous."

"What do I do?"

"I don't know, but you can't go like that."

Boris nodded and turned his head, bellowing for Anya. A moment later they heard her coming up the old, creaky stairs.

"He's in here," Michael called.

"What—"

She broke off as she strode into the small bedroom and got a good look at Boris. To give her credit, any amusement that she had to feel at the sight of him didn't show on her face. Instead, she merely shook her head.

"No. That's no good. There's no point in even trying to make that work," she said decisively. "Nikita, you'll go in alone."

"And me?" Boris asked.

"You will have to go in through the fence the way we'd originally planned. Once Nikita is in, he can let you into the building through a back door."

"The warden is expecting two guards," Michael pointed out.

The Cuban

"Then improvise," she said shortly, turning to leave the room. "I'm sure you can think of something."

They watched her disappear out of the door and Boris glanced at Michael.

"I look like an overstuffed kielbasa, and she didn't even crack a smile," he said. "Is she always like that?"

Michael shrugged.

"I don't know. I don't know her that well," he said, pulling on the jacket.

He didn't miss the searching glance from Boris before he ripped the shirt open to take it off. Buttons flew around him and Michael raised his eyebrows.

"What? It's not as if there is any use for it now," Boris said with a shrug. "It's for the fire anyway."

Michael shook his head, chuckling. "True."

"I will be more comfortable in my own clothes, anyway." Boris turned for the door. He paused before leaving, turning to look at Michael. "Will you be able to convince them you're a guard?"

"I hope so, or we're all in deep shit."

Boris studied him for a minute, then grinned.

"As the lady says, I'm sure you will come up with something. It will be fine."

He left the room and Michael looked at himself in the mirror critically. He was sure it would be fine as well. He'd been trained for this. It wasn't the operation that was bothering him.

It was what would happen to The Cuban once he'd helped Viper get Hawk back.

Golubev closed his office door, exhaling as he removed his jacket. He'd made his rounds of the inmates, and had even looked into the infirmary to check on the prisoner causing the most disruption to his routine. He'd thought he was unconscious, but the medic attending him when he went in assured him that he was only sleeping. It was good, he was told, for the patient to rest. It would help his body fight the infection.

The warden grunted as he went over to sit behind his desk. He didn't like having inmates in the infirmary. There were too many opportunities for them to cause a disruption, and he prided himself on running a facility that never had any kind of trouble or disorder. The sooner that man recovered and moved back into his cell, the better. It was bad enough that someone was coming to try to break him out. He scoffed, reaching for his mouse to wake up his computer. It was perfectly ridiculous to attempt it, but when they came, his men would be ready.

The monitor came alive, and he started when the sound of a roar filled his office. His mouth dropped open as the monitor went black again and an animated T-Rex seemed to grow out of the bottom of the screen. Before he could even process the dinosaur taking over his computer, it disappeared on its own, leaving the screen black again.

"What the—"

He broke off when the black faded to gray and then blue. Chocolate chip cookies began raining down from the top of the screen as a cookie monster rose from the bottom, demanding cookies.

Golubev clicked his mouse, then hit the enter key on the keyboard, but nothing happened. The cookie monster was still demanding cookies as they fell all around him. After trying every keystroke he could think of with no result, the warden got up and went to the door. Throwing it open, he bellowed for his assistant, the sound of the cookie monster following him to the door.

A moment later, his assistant came running from the room next door, his face flushed.

"I know, sir, I know," he gasped, following him into his office. "There's something wrong with all the computers."

"I'd say so!" The warden exclaimed furiously, pointing at his screen. "Make it stop!"

"We're trying, sir." The younger man went around the desk and began hitting various keys. "I have a rubber chicken on mine. Everyone has something."

"What is it?"

"I don't know. Some kind of virus. One of the guys was able to clear his, but as soon as he opened his email, a porn bomb hit. He has enormous tits all over his screen, along with...well, other things."

The warden stared at him in disbelief.

"Tits?" he repeated.

The assistant nodded and risked a grin.

"I'd rather have his tits than my rubber chicken," he said.

"I'd rather not have any of it!"

The grin disappeared and he ducked his head again, trying in vain to get rid of the cookie monster. The warden picked up the phone and dialed a number, his fury mounting as he watched the cookies on his screen. When the call finally connected, he snapped into the receiver.

"What the hell is going on?"

"I assume you're referring to the computer system," a voice replied dryly. "What have you got? I've got Vladimir Putin singing on the back of a horse."

"I've got the damned cookie monster—wait, you have it too?"

"Yes. All the cellars have it. It's some kind of mutating virus. Once you get past one, another is right behind it. We're working on it."

"How the hell did this happen?"

"We don't know. We're working on that too."

Golubev swore and ran a hand through his hair.

"What do we do?"

"Shut everything down and leave it off until you hear from us," the voice advised. "As soon as we've cleared it out, we'll let you know."

He was silent for a moment, then he exhaled.

"Do you really have Putin singing?" he asked.

"Unfortunately."

"What's he singing?"

"I want to be a cowboy."

The warden choked back a laugh, then coughed to cover it up.

"Good God."

He hung up and looked at the younger man still desperately trying to get rid of the cookie monster.

"Don't bother. We've been instructed to shut everything down," he told him. "It's a network wide problem. Some kind of virus. All the cellars have it."

His assistant nodded and stepped back, watching as the warden powered the computer down at the tower.

"He has a singing Putin on a horse?" he asked, his voice trembling.

The warden nodded, trying to keep a straight face.

"Yes. Tits, rubber chickens, and Putin singing that he wants to be a cowboy. Who the hell has the balls to do this?"

The assistant swallowed a response and went towards the door instead, his shoulders shaking suspiciously.

"I'll let everyone know to shut the PCs down," he said, his voice still unsteady. "At least we know it's not just us, sir."

He disappeared out the door and the warden pulled his cigarette case out of his pocket, extracting a cigarette. No, it wasn't just them, and that was a good thing. If it had been, he would have suspected that the assassin coming for the prisoner was behind it to spread chaos. But it was impossible. The whole network was affected.

It had nothing to do with his high priority inmate.

Alina stood in front of the mirror in the master bedroom staring at the scars on her chest, the black thermal athletic shirt forgotten in her hand. Her eyes dropped to her abdomen and she absently touched the longer mark that was closer to her side. So many scars, and most from the same occasion. They were faded now, but as she touched the puckered line, her lips tightened. They were faded, but still potent reminders of what her fake death had almost cost her.

It had been months since she'd looked at them. The one on her leg was the worst of the lot, and she still refused to wear shorts or short skirts because of it. Damon said it wasn't bad at all, and it certainly didn't seem to affect the way he looked at her, but Alina was very conscious of the ragged remnant of one of the surgeries that had saved her life. While she had never given much thought to her appearance, especially after joining the Organization, there was still a woman somewhere inside Viper, and that woman was appalled at the disfigurement her body had endured. It looked like she'd been through hell, and while she supposed that she had, it didn't mean that she wanted the whole world to see it.

She had put her body through a lot over the years, and as she stared at the scars, Alina reflected wryly that she was still putting herself through hell. If the surgeon who'd told her she would never return to full activity again knew what she was doing, he would have a stroke. In fact, even Charlie had been surprised that she'd passed his grueling physical without any weakness or slowness. She was still demanding more from her body than perhaps was wise, but Alina knew that Viper would continue until she could no longer do the work effectively. If she'd learned anything in the past four years, it was that she was not built to sit by and watch the world spin out of control without at least trying to do something about it.

Unfortunately, that meant that more scars would undoubtedly join these. A memory, sudden and unbidden, exploded in her mind and she saw her childhood friend Angela as clearly as if she was standing in front of her. She was complaining about the single scar on her chest, the result of a bullet exiting after shattering her scapula. She had said it was hideous. Alina looked at her collection of scars and her lips twisted in amusement. What had she told Angela? To get a tattoo around it? Perhaps the answer to her own disfigurement was a body tattoo.

The Cuban

A knock fell on the door, jarring her away from the memory, and Alina started as Michael called out from the other side.

"Just a minute," she called, pulling the black long-sleeved shirt over her head quickly, covering the scars. As soon as they were out of sight, she pushed them out of her mind and reached for her bulletproof vest. "Come in."

Michael walked in carrying his laptop, raising his eyebrows as she dropped the vest over her head to settle over her torso.

"I never pictured you wearing a vest," he said in surprise.

"I never used to."

He waited for her to say more, making a face when she didn't continue. She watched him set his laptop down on the dresser as she did up the straps on the side of the vest.

"What's that for?" she asked.

"I know where they have Becker," he said over his shoulder, opening the computer. "This is a requisition form that was just submitted from #9 for vancomycin. The resident doctor needs it to treat an ill prisoner that was just transferred in."

Alina looked at him sharply and he nodded, stepping back so that she could take a look at the screen. She went over and leaned down to read the form. Fury went through her at the cold and clinical diagnosis: staph infection resulting from multiple lacerations on torso. Her jaw clenched, her heart pounding against her ribs as she forced the emotion down. It had no place here. There would be time enough to be angry later, when she had Hawk out of there. Taking a deep, calming breath, she straightened up.

"At least we know he's still alive," she said, her voice void of emotion.

"Alina," he began, his voice low and filled with compassion, but she threw up her hand and shook her head.

"Don't," she said harshly.

Michael stared at her for a beat, then nodded, wisely choosing to abandon whatever it was that he was going to say.

"He'll be in the infirmary," he said instead, going back to the laptop, "on an IV. The patient notes say that it's a severe infection. They won't risk moving him back to the cell, not if they want him alive in case you don't talk after all."

"Where's the infirmary?"

"On the main level, which is good. We won't have to try to move him up stairs in his condition."

Michael closed the laptop and turned to look at her, crossing his arms over his chest. His jaw was set and his face was grim.

"Do you really want to move him right now?" he asked, his green eyes probing hers. "The file says that the next twenty-four hours are critical. Maybe we should wait and give the antibiotic time to work."

Alina pressed her lips together, her eyes on his. He was trying to help, and he had a valid point. Every additional hour that Hawk was on the antibiotic increased his chances of fighting the infection.

But every hour that he remained in that hell hole was another hour that he could die there.

"No," she said, shaking her head. "He could be dead in twenty-four hours. I'll take my chances."

"And if he dies while we're transporting him?"

A surge of despair went through her and Alina sucked in a silent gulp of air.

"Then at least he didn't go in that hell hole." Her voice was hard. "If we can get him to the extraction point, I can have an IV waiting. At most, he'll be off it for two or three hours."

Michael was quiet for a long moment.

"Are you sure?" he asked softly.

"Yes. We continue as planned." She picked up her Ruger from the dresser and checked the magazine before sliding it into her back holster. "If he hasn't given up yet, he sure as hell won't when he knows he's getting out of there."

"I hope you're right." Michael picked up the laptop and turned to leave. "I'll let Boris know where he is. At least it will be easier to get him out from the main level than from the dungeons."

As he left, Alina clenched her jaw and exhaled.

I'll do my part, but you have to do yours, Hawk. Don't you dare prove me wrong.

Chapter Twenty-Six

Alina turned down an abandoned country lane in the darkness and slowed to a stop, looking at Boris. He was pulling his gloves over his hands and adjusting the fingers.

"I'm concerned about getting Becker out," he said, finishing and looking up. "Nikita says he is sick. It was going to be difficult enough getting out a man who may not be able to walk, but someone on an IV?" He shook his head. "It's not good."

"Nikita will remove the tube but keep the port in," she told him. "It will be wrapped securely with bandages. It'll be fine."

Boris was quiet for a moment, then nodded.

"That is better," he admitted. "If he is unconscious, I will throw him over my shoulder. It might even be better that way."

Alina bit back a laugh. Boris was large, but so was Hawk. She didn't think Boris would be quite so sanguine about it when he saw the patient. Unless, of course, Hawk had lost an immense amount of weight. Her lips tightened with the thought.

"Once the charges are set on the towers, how long before you're in position?" she asked, looking at her watch.

"No more than forty-five minutes," he replied. "Don't worry. I will be there."

He reached for the door handle, then paused.

"Why were you sent to do this?" he asked, turning his head and fixing her with an unnervingly sharp gaze. "You are not in the business of clean up and rescue. Why did they send you?"

"What do you know about my business?"

"Your business? Nothing. But I know people, and I have become very good at reading what their strengths are, particularly where it pertains to anything that would be a threat to myself. And you, Anya, are a killer. Why would your employer send a killer to rescue a man?"

"Why would yours send you to assist a foreign operative?" she countered, her voice even.

211

Boris looked surprised, but then he smiled slowly.

"Ah, so you don't believe that I am here out of the kindness of my heart and a desire to see these pigs suffer?"

"No."

The smile disappeared as quickly as it had come and he nodded.

"No. I didn't think that you would. We are both playing a very dangerous game, Anya. I hope you will trust that I mean no harm to you, or to Hans Becker."

She studied him in the dim light for a moment.

"I will trust that when we are on the extraction transport and away. Not a second sooner."

He chuckled and pushed the door open.

"That's fair, I suppose. One day, perhaps, I will be at liberty to explain to you why I am here." He got out of the Jeep and picked up his black duffel bag from the floor. "And perhaps one day, you will tell me what was so important about Hans Becker that I helped you break into a Russian prison to get to him."

"Perhaps."

"God willing, I will see you later."

He closed the door and Alina watched as he trudged into the trees. On the other side of the little wood stood the first cell phone tower. He would set the explosives, then move to the next tower, which was two miles away. She hadn't asked how he planned to get to the other tower, or how he would get back to the prison. She didn't have to. Boris was the man who could obtain anything. She assumed that also included a means of transportation.

After he'd disappeared into the night, Alina turned the Jeep around and headed back to the main road. Michael would arrive at the prison gates a few minutes after the power went out, and then there would be no turning back. Once Michael was inside, they were fully committed, regardless of what happened with the extra troops.

Pulling back onto the main road, Viper felt the old, familiar anticipation go through her. She was back in the field and, while not necessarily here out of choice, she couldn't deny that she was looking forward to the coming hours. The adrenaline rush, having to think on her feet in seconds, and using the skills that set her apart from 99% of the world's population had all been sorely missed.

As had Damon.

After three long weeks, she was finally going to get him back, or die trying.

The Cuban

The smells of crude oil and tuna fish hung in the small hut where a man sat with his boots propped up on a counter, a tuna fish sandwich in his hands, his eyes glued to the small television set. He was watching the soccer highlights from the day's matches, and every few moments he would emit either a grunt of approval or a curse of displeasure. Monitors lined the walls around him, displaying security camera feeds as well as pressure gauges and circuit boards. Every few minutes, he dragged his eyes away from the television and ran them over the monitors before returning to his highlights.

The last of the day crew had left the compound an hour before, leaving him as the sole human in charge. There was nothing new in that. He was the night security manager, and his duties encompassed everything from general security to monitoring the equipment that kept the power flowing to the prison camp a few miles away. He didn't mind the work. It was a job in a time and place where honest work was hard to come by. He was able to watch his sports, eat his dinner in peace, and stretch his legs when he got bored. The pay was crap, but it put food on the table and helped keep a roof over he and his wife. He had no right to complain.

The man sat up abruptly and let off a stream of curses directed at the television as the opposing team kicked a goal in the last few seconds of play. He dropped his sandwich onto the counter disgustedly, still muttering as he glanced at the monitors to the right. He turned back to the television only to frown suddenly and spin around to look at the monitors more closely.

"Oh, for God's sake," he muttered. "Not again."

One of the towers near the perimeter was flashing an alert, just as it had every night for the past week. He'd told them over and over again to replace the sensor, but here it was, flashing again.

"Like I've got nothing better to do than keep going out there to make sure the damn thing isn't overheating," he complained, getting up and reaching for his coat.

He took another bite of his sandwich before setting it down again and turning for the door of the hut. He would trudge all the way out there and it would be nothing. Just as it had been for the past week. He knew it, but he also knew that he had to go anyway. It would be just his luck that the one time he didn't investigate would be the one time that something would be very wrong.

Not that he could fix it if there was something the matter, he reflected, stepping outside into the cold and closing the hut door securely behind him. If anything went wrong, he called in the engineers that could fix it. But nothing ever went wrong. The day crew kept the plant running without any problems.

It was a few minutes later that he approached the offending tower on his motorized ATV. Right out near the perimeter, it was no small distance from his hut and he shivered as he climbed out of his open vehicle. The wind was whipping between the massive metal structures out here, and he hunched his shoulders as he made his way to the control panel on the base of the problem child. These towers were old. They still had manual access panels, whereas the newer ones were controlled from the warmth and comfort of the building. It couldn't be one of those. No. It had to be this one, out on the edge of nowhere.

The man was just reaching for the access door when a strange noise cut through the air. He spun around, looking for the source of the disturbance just as a massive explosion rocked the compound. The ground beneath him trembled violently and he gasped in shock as blinding orange flames shot hundreds of feet into the air, lighting up the night around him. His brain had only just processed the sight of an immense funnel of fire when the heat hit him in the face. He had the strangest sensation of flying for a second, then realized that he *was* flying! The force of the explosion had lifted him off his feet and hurtled him towards the perimeter fence. Orange and black blurred together as searing pain shot through his body and everything went black.

Michael turned off the main road and onto the winding avenue that led to the prison in the distance. The truck that the hapless guards had been driving the night before bounced along the pavement as the heater cranked out mediocre warmth to combat the freezing temperature outside. The bloodstains were covered with burlap draped over the seats and the windshield had been hastily replaced with new glass, courtesy of Boris and his seemingly endless ability to get anything they needed. As long as no one looked too closely at the seats, there would be no cause for alarm. And, given the eerily dark compound ahead of him, he didn't think there was any danger of anyone paying the least bit of attention to the inside of a truck cab.

As he drew closer to the gates, two trucks filled with soldiers

The Cuban

came barreling out at the highest speed that the older trucks could manage. Michael inched closer to the edge of the road to give them more room and slowed, watching as they sped past him in the other direction. His lips curved and he increased the pressure on the gas again. It was just as Viper had predicted. The warden wasn't taking any chances that the power plant may have been captured by the assassin coming for his prisoner. Human nature was human nature, and the warden hadn't disappointed.

A moment later, he rolled up to the gate, stopping at the checkpoint as a guard held up his hand in the universal signal to halt. The guard walked up to the driver's door and Michael unrolled his window, nodding to him as he shut off the engine.

"I'm reporting for duty," he told him, passing him his forged papers, his hand steady. "The warden is expecting me."

The guard took his papers, glancing at them, then reached behind him for a clipboard hanging just inside the small security hut.

"What's going on?" Michael asked as the guard checked his clipboard against the name on the papers.

"We've lost power," the man replied, glancing up. "Where's the other one? This says two guards."

"He got ill this morning. Flu, he thinks. If he is better, he will come tomorrow."

The guard nodded distractedly and handed his credentials back to him.

"It's the time of year for it. We have two down with it here," he said.

"When will the power be back on?" Michael asked, tucking his papers back into his inside pocket.

"Who knows. Something happened at the power plant." The man shook his head and shrugged. "That's where those two trucks went. The warden thinks it may have been attacked by Ukraine forces. They're going to find out. We're running on backup power for now." He motioned to the left of the main building. "You can park your truck around the side for now. Tomorrow, when it's light, you can move it to the back where the rest are. Go through the front doors and there's someone inside who will take you to the warden. They'll get you settled in."

"Thanks"

"Oh, and you might as well know, cell phones aren't getting signal either," he added as an afterthought as he turned away. "It's a shit show right now, so don't be surprised if your phone doesn't work."

"Sounds like a great time," Michael said with a laugh, starting

215

the engine again.

"Aren't you glad you got sent here?" the man asked with a grin. "Welcome to hell."

Michael nodded and shifted into gear, pulling forward and going to the area indicated by the guard. As he pulled around the side of the building, he saw that only a few exterior lights were on, illuminating the side of the bunker. The rest of the compound was dark. Guards were moving around quickly with flashlights to light their way, and there was a general feeling of controlled chaos around him. No one looked twice at the truck that was parking near a door midway down the length of the building. They were too busy trying to function without any source of electricity or communication.

Phase one had gone exactly as planned, right down to the cell towers being knocked out at the same time as the power. Everything was on schedule. Now all he had to do was convince the warden he was a guard from #2.

As Michael climbed out of the truck and turned towards the front of the building, two soldiers passed, complaining loudly.

"We don't have any protocol for this?" one was demanding of the other. "What kind of circus is this?"

"One without power," the other retorted.

"First the computers go berserk, now this. You think Ukraine was behind the virus too?"

"Wouldn't surprise me. Those bastards will do anything."

"This backup power is shit. I was in the supply hut when the power went. I couldn't find the door to get out!"

"You should be thankful. Igor was in the showers and slipped. He knocked himself right out and when he came too, it was pitch black and he was butt naked on the floor."

The other man grunted.

"Maybe the supply hut wasn't so bad after all."

The two continued past Michael with a brief nod of acknowledgement, their flashlights bobbing along in the darkness. He strode towards the front of the building, a grin pulling at his lips. It was even better than they'd hoped. None of these men seemed to be aware of any possible threat. They were too busy trying to cope with the sudden lack of light. If the warden was as distracted as everyone else, he'd have Boris inside in no time.

And then the real fun would begin.

The Cuban

Golubev looked up as his assistant came into the office. He was trying to work by the light of an old, battery-operated lantern, but the glow was barely enough to cover the desk and he rubbed his eyes tiredly.

"What is it?" he asked, sitting back in his chair. "Has something else gone wrong?"

The assistant shook his head.

"Not yet, sir. The new guard has arrived. Should I show him in?"

The warden scowled. He'd completely forgotten about the new guards that were coming to help with the security.

"I don't have time to deal with personnel right now," he muttered. "Look around! This place is in chaos, and I can't even see to work! Take him to his quarters and get him settled, then show him where things are. I'll deal with him later."

The younger man nodded and left, leaving the office door open. The emergency lighting in the corridor cast a soft glow into the office, helping to make him feel as if he wasn't sitting in a cave. Of all the infuriating things! They'd just got their computers back up after the virus had them shut down for most of the day, and then the power went out. It was like a nightmare!

The warden shook his head impatiently and reached for his cellphone, only to let out a string of curses at the no signal notification on the screen. The landlines were down, the network was down, and the cell phones were also down. The only thing working was the emergency generator in the building out back. It was making an ungodly racket out there, humming and clanking away, but it was providing the emergency lighting for the compound, and it was maintaining the servers. That sixty-odd year old piece of machinery was the only thing doing its job effectively at the moment.

Shaking his head, the warden pulled out his cigarette case with another curse. It was a fat lot of good the generator did for him. He couldn't get into the network to see what was happening at the power plant, or even to know if they were under attack from the Ukrainians. All he could do was sit in darkness and wonder what the hell was going on.

He understood the reasoning behind how the system controlling the backup generator had been designed. Its primary function in the event of an outage was to protect the servers and all the information held there. It wasn't to allow him access to it. The assumption when the system was put in place was that any outage would be short-lived, and wouldn't impede the functionality of the prison itself. And indeed, they'd had outages before during storms. The longest they'd been without power was eight hours, and that hadn't seemed that bad. They had known the cause of the outage was a storm, and that made all the difference. It was one thing to be caught in a snow and ice storm, and quite another to be facing the possibility of an enemy taking over the power plant and cutting the power.

"Sir! Sir! We were right!" A guard ran in breathlessly, waving a piece of paper in his hand. "I just heard it on my emergency radio!"

"Heard what?" The warden frowned. "Calm down! What did you hear?"

"The power, sir. They're saying it's a missile strike!"

"How does the state news know so quickly? Was it one of ours?"

"No, sir. I'm not listening to the news. I'm listening to the emergency bands." The guard looked sheepish and scratched his head. "I thought that given the circumstance, it was better than waiting for the news."

"And?" The warden prompted when he stopped.

"And they're saying it was a missile. The radar picked it up coming in just seconds before it hit. Emergency response is on their way to confirm, but they're saying it was the Ukrainians." The guard exhaled. "So you were right, sir. It *is* an attack by the Ukraine forces!"

Golubev was quiet for a moment, then he nodded.

"All right. Continue to listen and let me know as soon as they have definite confirmation of the missile strike," he commanded.

"Yes, sir." The guard turned to leave. "I have about three hours of battery left. I'll keep listening."

He disappeared into the corridor and the warden tapped his finger on the desk thoughtfully. Should he call the trucks back on the walkie-talkies? If it really was a missile that hit the power plant, there was nothing they could do to assist. But if it wasn't, and someone had taken over the plant in order to cut their power, then his men could retake the plant and get him back up and running.

After considering the problem for a minute, he shook his head. No. He would wait for confirmation either from his men or from the young guard monitoring the emergency band that it was really a missile strike. He needed to get his prison back online, and if there was any chance that the men he'd dispatched could do that, he had to take it.

As he pulled out a cigarette and lit it with a match, the warden

The Cuban

reflected that if it was, indeed, an attack from the Ukrainian army, then at least he didn't have to worry about an assassin trying to infiltrate his prison in the midst of all this chaos. And that, he admitted, sucking on his cigarette, was the thought making this whole situation that much more stressful. His prison was vulnerable right now, and the last thing he needed was to have them attacked with all of his men in disarray. At least if it was the Ukrainians, that was one less thing he had to worry about.

Chapter Twenty-Seven

Michael stood inside the door while he waited for the assistant warden to disappear around the corner. After showing Michael to the room he'd share with the other guard when he arrived, he'd given him a brief tour of the main areas of interest: the cafeteria, the recreational area, and the armory. After the quick tour, he'd left him in his sleeping quarters with the comment that he would want to unpack. He'd also given Michael a heavy duty flashlight with fresh batteries. Looking down at the heavy item in his hand, Michael smiled faintly. It had some serious heft to it, making it another weapon at his disposal, and he had absolutely no doubt that he would use it.

"Where are we?"

His ear bud came alive with the sound of Alina's voice as he slipped out of the small room.

"I'm in," he replied in a low voice.

"I'm through the fence," Boris said after a second. "I'm approaching the door on the south side corner."

"On my way."

Michael made his way along the dim corridor and turned the corner, following the path from memory. When he came to the end of the hallway, he paused, looking left before turning to his right. He looked at his watch, noting the direction with the tiny compass hand in the corner. He was heading in the right direction. Pulling out his phone, he swiped the screen and pulled up the rough blueprint he'd downloaded before leaving this afternoon. It was a copy of the emergency evacuation route in the event of a fire, and he'd pulled it from the prison's safety file. It was at least twenty years old, but the building hadn't changed. It was enough to get him around this level. Unfortunately, he had nothing on any of the subterranean levels. God willing, they wouldn't end up in the dungeon. If they did, it wouldn't end well.

Michael went past the recreation room, glancing in as he did. It looked like most of the personnel were gathered in there, smoking and

220

talking in low voices. He shook his head. Obviously the universal smoking laws hadn't penetrated into the walls of this place. Somehow he doubted that many of the international laws had made their way inside this hell hole.

A moment later, another guard emerged from the gloom in front of him, nodding in greeting. Then, suddenly, he stopped and turned back.

"Hey!"

A streak of fear went down Michael's spine and he froze, then turned slowly to face the other guard. His heart was suddenly pounding, but he forced his voice to remain steady.

"Yes?"

"Is the cell signal back?" The guard demanded, motioning to the phone in Michael's hand.

Michael looked down and let out a short laugh.

"No, I wish! It's a game."

The other man sighed comically. "Ah. I was excited for a minute."

"Sorry."

He nodded and turned to continue on his way and Michael exhaled silently in relief. Turning, he continued along the corridor, sliding the phone back into his pocket. Well, if nothing else, Viper had been right on the money when she said no one would look twice at a new guard. With all the new faces in the past two days, no one was batting an eyelid at another one.

He rounded another corner and was halfway along the corridor when a door opened behind him. Michael turned his head to look, his pulse leaping once again. He watched as another guard stepped out of a room, closing the door behind him. He nodded to Michael and turned to walk back the way Michael had just come. Michael hesitated, then turned around. The man was about the same size as Boris.

Moving swiftly and silently, he retraced his steps to come up behind the man. His fingers tightened on the flashlight in his hand as he raised it, bringing it down hard on the man's skull. Before the larger guard could do anything more than grunt, Michael had him in a neck lock with his hand covering his nose and mouth while he twisted his head sideways. A moment later, the guard slumped in his arms, unconscious.

Michael shone his light around him and then dragged the unconscious man towards a closed door a few feet away. Cracking it open, he directed the light inside to find that it was some kind of closet. Without further ado, he dragged the guard inside and held him up against a shelving unit while he pulled his jacket off of him. When he'd finished, he released him and the man fell to the floor. Bending down, Michael held his fingers to the side of his throat, checking his pulse. Satisfied that he was merely unconscious, he rapidly pulled the man's belt from his pants and secured his hands behind his back. Directing his attention to his boots, he swiftly tied his feet together with his laces.

"Sorry, my man," he murmured, patting him on his cheek. "Sleep well."

He straightened up and went out of the closet, pulling the door closed behind him. As he turned to continue down the corridor, he glanced down at the uniform jacket in his hand. It would be enough to get Boris past a cursory glance, but beyond that, they were screwed. However, if it could just buy them enough time to get Damon to the truck, then Michael would be happy.

A few minutes later, he reached the door on the south side corner and pushed it open. A blast of cold air came in along with Boris as he slipped through the opening.

"It's about time," he muttered. "Where were you?"

"Getting you this." Michael handed him the jacket as he pulled the door closed again. "It's not perfect, but with your dark pants, it should be enough in the dark for a quick glance."

Boris handed him his rifle to hold while he shrugged out of his own jacket and pulled the uniform on.

"Perfect fit," he said with a grin. He bent to stuff his own coat into the bag at his feet before picking it up and draping it across his body.

"What's in the bag?" Michael demanded in a low voice.

"Extra toys," Boris replied with a shrug. "I come prepared for anything."

"You come looking like someone who's up to no good."

Boris grinned again and clapped him on his shoulder.

"But we *are* up to no good, my friend," he said cheerfully. "Now, which way?"

"The infirmary is on this level," Michael said, turning to head down the corridor.

"Good. Where?"

"Well, that's the thing," he replied, glancing at the gorilla beside him. "It's in the north west quadrant, and beyond that, I have no idea. We have to get you all the way to the opposite side of the building without anyone noticing you."

"In this semi-darkness? No problem."

"Famous last words."

222

The Cuban

"You worry too much, Niki. You must learn to embrace the adventure."

"Is that what this is? An adventure?"

Boris grinned in the dim light from an emergency bulb above them.

"What else?"

"One of the stupidest things I've ever done," Michael retorted.

"It was your choice to come along, Nikita." Viper spoke in their ears, her tone amused. "Suck it up and stop your bitching."

Boris' shoulders shook with silent laughter as they moved rapidly through the corridor.

"I've always found the stupid things to be the most fun."

Hawk laid in darkness, confined to the uncomfortable bed and surrounded by the smell of antiseptic and plastic. The emergency lighting above the door didn't penetrate very far into the large infirmary, and he was positioned in the back corner, as far away from the door as they could place him. The room did have two windows, but that didn't help to provide light when the sun had gone down some hours before. Bars were installed on the outside, making it impossible to consider the windows as an exit strategy. Even if he was capable of it, there was no escaping the infirmary that way. He was still in a cell. It was just a much larger and slightly more comfortable one.

He shifted his gaze to the machines monitoring his vital signs and the tube running from his arm. The machines were still on, indicating that they were connected to the emergency power source. That was something, at least.

As soon as the power went out and the attending medic ran from the room, Hawk knew that Viper had arrived. The ensuing chaos only served to reinforce his conclusion, and he'd been wondering for the past hour or more how the hell she'd managed it. The doctor had come in a few minutes after the power initially went out to check the machines and secure him to the bedframe with a handcuff. While he'd been doing that, he and the attending medic had engaged in a lively discussion regarding the impossibility of them losing power so completely. The good doctor was of the opinion that it had to be an attack by the Ukrainians. Apparently their power was supplied by an exclusive power plant a few miles away, and no one would ever dare attack that plant. His lips trembled now.

There was one person who would dare, and they were about to meet her.

He lowered his gaze to the handcuff around his wrist and shook his head. Pathetic. He could have that off in less than ten seconds. That wasn't even a challenge. No, the challenge would be trying to move out of this bed. When they brought him here last night, he hadn't even been able to lift his head. This morning, he felt much stronger, but he didn't let them know that. He'd remained prone in the bed, his eyes closed, whenever someone was in the room. When they weren't, he tested moving his legs and sitting up. He thought he could probably get himself out of the bed, but moving was another story. He was in bad shape, and he knew it.

Damon had heard enough this morning to know that his condition was serious. He had a staph infection that he could only assume had resulted from the wounds on his torso being ripped open in the transport here. The doctor hadn't been worried about alarming his semi-comatose patient when he'd told the medic bluntly that he didn't know how he was still alive. He hadn't expected the antibiotic to work, but they had to try. The patient wasn't allowed to die.

Hawk's lips tightened grimly. No. It was crucial to keep him alive so that they had leverage when Viper showed up. He was no good to them dead until they got her to talk. Then they'd kill them both. In the meantime, they had to get him healthy enough to be of use to them.

Viper. He had thought he must be dreaming when the bastard who'd inflicted so much pain on him had said that someone was coming to save him. He thought perhaps it was another one of his mind games, but the following day, they'd moved him to a new location - a new hell hole. As soon as he realized they were moving him, he knew it was true. She'd found him. Against all the odds, she'd tracked him down. He knew he shouldn't be surprised, but he was. His wife was exceptional, but even people like them had their limits. His captors had convinced him that no one would ever know where he was.

He should have known better.

Damon shifted against the pillows. He had to conserve what little strength he had for the struggle that he knew was coming, but anticipation was surging through him, making him restless. It was insane for her to try to get him out of here, but he knew that she'd done it before. She'd pulled Jack out of a pit in the center of a Taliban camp, another insanely impossible operation, and had done it single-handedly. She wouldn't think twice about taking on the Russians in one of their Gulags. But oh God, if she failed...

Suppressed gunshots broke the silence in the room,

interrupting the thought, and Hawk lifted his head, his body tensing. Someone was running down the corridor, and another muffled shot was fired much closer. As what sounded like a body hitting the floor made its way to him in the bed, a tall man filled the doorway. The light from the emergency bulb above the door illuminated his face and Hawk sucked in his breath in surprise. The man lifted a flashlight and shone it around, landing on him in the corner a second later. Grimacing, Hawk squinted against the sudden bright light, relaxing when it moved from his face as the man crossed the room quickly.

"No offense, gunny, but your face is not what I was expecting to see coming through that door," he said dryly, his voice hoarse.

"Yeah, I know," Michael said, his eyes going to the monitors and IV beside the bed. "But if we don't get moving, it might be the last one you see."

"That would be supremely disappointing."

Michael stifled a laugh and turned to go over to the cabinets along the wall, holding the flashlight between his teeth as he began opening them. When he found the one he wanted, he put the light down and began gathering gauze bandages.

"I'm glad that you're still able to think clearly," he said over his shoulder.

"Was there doubt that I would?"

"We didn't know what they'd done to you. Anything was possible. I gotta tell you, Squid, I'm glad you're okay."

Hawk grimaced. "Okay might be a stretch, but I still have all my faculties, thank God. What's with all those bandages?"

"I have to disconnect the IV, but I'm leaving the port in. I'll wrap your arm to protect it until we can get you hooked back up."

"It's an antibiotic," Hawk said as Michael returned to the bed and began to disconnect the tube from the port in his arm.

"I know. You have a staph infection."

Hawk was impressed. How the hell had the gunny learned that? He watched as Michael finished with the IV, then looked at the handcuffs. When he looked up, he seemed amused.

"Seriously? This is their attempt to secure you?"

"In their defense, they don't think I'm much of a threat in my present condition."

Michael shook his head and pulled a pick out of the buckle of his belt.

"My, you *are* full of surprises," Hawk said, watching as Michael bent over the cuffs. A moment later, there was a click and he removed the handcuff.

Michael made a sound close to a grunt and began wrapping his arm with gauze bandages, covering the port with a thick layer of protection. Hawk watched him for a moment, his eyes on his face.

"What are you doing here, gunny?"

"Saving your ass." Michael glanced up. "I thought that was obvious."

"I have to give you credit. I know you were determined to find us, but I didn't think it would come to this. How the hell did you end up here?"

"Funny. I was about to ask how a dead man ended up in a Russian Gulag myself." Michael said with an edge to his voice. He finished with the bandage and straightened up, looking down at him. "Can you walk?"

"We're going to find out," Hawk muttered, throwing off the covers and sitting up. "I don't suppose you have any real clothes?"

Michael whistled and a moment later, a bag came flying through the door, sliding along the floor. He went to grab it, unzipping it and pulling out a pair of white ski pants. He tossed them to Hawk.

"Make it quick. We have to get moving."

Hawk nodded and pulled the ski pants on over the thin prison pants that he was wearing. When he was finished, Michael passed him the coat and he pulled it on, grimacing in pain as the movement pulled at the stitches on his torso.

"What is it?" Michael asked, seeing the flash of pain.

"The good doctor decided to stitch me up this morning," he said, zipping up the jacket. "Let's just say that I don't think much to his work."

Before Michael could answer, gun fire erupted in the hallway. Michael pulled out his Beretta and tossed Hawk the bag.

"There are boots in there. Put them on!" he ordered, turning towards the door.

Before he'd gone two steps, Boris stuck his head into the room, his face grim.

"Hurry up!" he exclaimed. "We have to move!"

Hawk glanced up at the behemoth in the door and raised his eyebrow.

"You brought a Ukrainian with you?" he demanded, pulling on a boot and tying it rapidly.

"Ukraine?" Michael looked from Boris to Hawk. "I think he's Russian."

"You think wrong." Hawk grabbed the second boot and Michael moved to get the bag, throwing it back to Boris. "He's

Ukrainian."

"He's right. I was born in Kyiv," Boris said, peering out the door. "Now, can we please get our asses moving? We have to go NOW!"

"Yes, we're coming."

Boris nodded and went back into the hallway as Hawk stood up. The whole room tilted on its axis. Michael's face swam in front of him and he sucked in his breath, reaching out to grab the side of the bed. Before his fingers could touch the frame, Michael was beside him. He put one arm around him and grabbed Hawk's hand, pulling his arm over his shoulders. Hawk shook his head, forcing himself to focus on one point until the room stopped spinning.

"You sure you want to do this, gunny?" he asked, glancing at the man supporting him. "I don't know how far I'll get."

"And face the wrath of Viper if I leave you behind?" Michael asked. "No thanks. I've got you. Focus on the door and move your feet, sailor. We're getting you out of here."

Charlie opened his eyes, pulled from his state of dozing when his phone rang, breaking the comfortable silence in the cabin. The quiet hum of the engines was soothing, and he sighed at the interruption. Sitting up, he reached into his suit jacket to pull it out, glancing at his watch. He'd been in the air for almost four hours. He was halfway to London.

"Yes?"

"Did you know about this?" a voice demanded unceremoniously.

Charlie blinked.

"Know about what? Really, Jack, for all my accomplishments, I'm not a mind reader."

"The missile strike in Donetsk. Did you know about it?"

Charlie was quiet for a moment, an involuntary grin pulling at his lips.

"You'll have to forgive me. I've been on a plane for four hours and you caught me in the middle of a nap," he said apologetically. "What missile strike?"

"A missile was fired into Donetsk half an hour ago," Jack told him. "It hit a power plant. We're still trying to get the details, but Ukraine is claiming that the Russians did it while the Russians, of course, are blaming Ukraine."

"And you're blaming me," Charlie said dryly, picking up the bottle of water in the cup holder of his arm chair.

"Not you. Viper."

Charlie's lips quivered again and were firmly repressed.

"I think you're seriously overestimating her resources."

"I don't overestimate anything when it comes to Maggie," Jack retorted. "I'm fully aware of what she's capable of, and of what you can facilitate when you're motivated to do so."

"And you think I was motivated to facilitate a missile strike on a power plant in Donetsk?" Charlie was grinning again. "You give me too much credit. Even I wouldn't be that bold."

"I question that. I really do." Jack's voice sounded just a little bit unsteady. "However, I'm relieved to hear that you apparently don't know anything about it. If it comes out that anyone fired that missile other than Moscow or Kyiv, it will cause one hell of an international kerfuffle, and possibly even World War Three."

"And yet you're just as amused by it as I am," Charlie said, sipping his water.

A chuckle sounded in his ear.

"I am," Jack admitted. "I do hope we learn what really happened. In the meantime, I've deployed a team for an extraction."

"Oh?"

"Yes. You didn't know?"

"I still haven't had any contact with her."

"Well, she'll contact me when she's enroute. We're pulling her out of Kopani, over the border from Donetsk. Tell me something, do any of your people ever return from their missions in one piece?"

Charlie raised his eyebrows. "What do you mean?"

"Your asset requested a medic, IV, and vancomycin to be on hand at the extraction," Jack said. "Charlie, if I'm saddled with another critically wounded operative, I'll not offer my services quite so readily in future. The last time was quite enough."

"An antibiotic is hardly indicative of someone being on death's door," Charlie said, frowning nonetheless. "What time is the extraction?"

"2240."

Charlie looked at his watch.

"You'll keep me informed? I'll be in London in three hours."

"Of course." Jack cleared his throat. "You know, I had to get permission directly from Zelensky's people. I sincerely hope that it will be worth it."

The Cuban

"It will," Charlie said calmly. "Have patience and trust us, Jack. We'll get The Cuban. I give you my word."

"And Viper's op will get us closer?"

"I certainly hope so, or I'll have to wonder what the hell she spent all this time doing."

Chapter Twenty-Eight

H awk winced and grit his teeth as Michael shoved him up against the wall in the shadows of an unlit part of the corridor before turning to fire behind them. The gorilla had already shot two guards and was in the process of beating the daylights out of a third. Four more were charging down the corridor towards them and he grunted, forcing himself to stand upright.

"If you give me a gun, I can give you a hand," he rasped out.

Michael didn't even spare him a glance.

"This will only take a second," he said. "Concentrate on keeping yourself upright."

Hawk made a face, but was forced to admit that it was taking everything he had to keep himself supported by the wall without sliding down. In fact, if it weren't for the adrenaline pumping through him, he doubted if he would have made it this far.

Michael moved down the corridor, shooting two of the guards in the forehead as his companion finished with his opponent. Hawk watched as he pulled out a Glock and turned to help Michael.

"Get him to the door!" Michael ordered over his shoulder. "Go!"

The gorilla nodded and turned towards Hawk. He grabbed one arm and hoisted it over his massive shoulders, sending pain shooting through Hawk's torso.

"Can you walk? Or should I carry you?" he asked in a deep voice that seemed to boom out of his chest.

"I can walk," Hawk said, turning with him towards the door at the end of the corridor.

"I am Boris."

"Hans."

"I know." Boris glanced down at him. "You're not what I was expecting."

A wave of amusement went through him and Hawk's lips quivered.

"You're not exactly what I was expecting either."

230

The Cuban

Boris grinned, then looked behind them when the shooting stopped. A moment later, Michael joined them and moved to Hawk's other side.

"How're you holding up?"

"I feel like a rag doll," Hawk replied. "This is pathetic."

"After what you've undoubtedly been through, I think you're doing exceptionally well," Boris told him. "I was prepared to carry you out like a sack of feed."

"Over my dead body," Hawk muttered, appalled.

"That's what we were half expecting to find," Michael said. "I'm glad we were wrong."

"Day's not over yet." Hawk stopped himself before adding gunny and shot Michael a hooded look. "How are we getting out of here? I'm assuming that door leads outside, but then there are over forty extra soldiers. They brought them in especially for you."

"So we heard. As much as we would have loved the welcoming committee, we made arrangements for half of them to miss the party." Michael looked at Boris over his head. "They'll have regrouped by now and know where we're going. Time for some fireworks."

Boris reached into his pocket with his free hand and pulled out a detonator. Hawk smiled faintly.

"Distraction?" he asked Michael.

"Yes."

"Your idea?"

"Not exactly."

Hawk chuckled, his spirits lifting abruptly.

"She's always so dramatic," he murmured with a grin.

"She's not the only one," Michael replied, shooting him an amused look. "I've heard stories over the years."

"All lies."

They reached the door just as there was a muffled explosion and the entire building trembled. Michael looked at Boris.

"Where the hell was it?!"

"That one was near the front door," he said cheerfully. "The next one is behind the building, where the trucks are parked."

Hawk choked back a laugh.

"How many distractions do we have?" he demanded.

"As many as it takes," Michael said.

"And more, if we need them," Boris said with a nod, tucking the detonator back into his pocket and swinging the rifle hanging on his back into his free hand easily. "Are we going out, or do we wait for more to come this way?"

Michael pushed open the door and a blast of frigid air washed over the trio as they stepped outside. Instead of the instant hail of gunfire that Damon was half expecting, there was nothing but the distant sound of yelling. They were trying to find the threat in front of the building. He exhaled in relief when he saw the truck a few feet away. Despite the energy and adrenaline running through him, he knew he wouldn't last much longer on his feet, even with two large men supporting him.

"You're going in the back of the truck," Michael told him. "It'll be uncomfortable."

"I think I'll manage," he said dryly, and Michael chuckled.

"I'm sure you will."

Boris released him and Michael spun him around so they could lift him over the edge of the open tailgate. Hawk was straining to pull himself backwards into the bed when he saw the door they'd just exited open.

"Behind you!" he gasped.

Boris spun around and shot the two soldiers coming out of the door while Michael finished helping Damon into the truck. Grabbing the rifles from the dead men, Boris turned to toss one to Michael. Coming back to the truck, he looked at Hawk.

"Can you shoot one of these?" he asked, holding it up.

Hawk saw Michael turn away swiftly and felt his lips tremble. He began to laugh, but choked and ended up coughing instead. As he bent over, gasping for breath as coughs racked through him, Michael turned back and took the rifle from Boris, tossing it into the truck with Hawk.

"He'll figure it out," he said, his voice unsteady. "Let's get moving before the rest of them get here."

Boris nodded and put the tailgate up, nodding to Hawk before going towards the passenger's door of the cab. The coughing subsided and Hawk reached for the rifle. Fresh adrenaline was coursing through him, making his movements much quicker and sharper than they had been a few minutes before. He pulled the magazine out, checking it quickly before clipping it back in and taking off the safety. The actions were mechanical, and he exhaled as the comforting, familiar weight of a rifle settled into his hands.

The engine roared to life, making the bed vibrate, and he shifted backwards to brace himself against the cab. As he did, the door opened and three more guards ran out, weapons ready in their hands. Hawk swung up the rifle and fired rapidly, hitting them all before they had a chance to pull their triggers. Boris looked out the back window of the cab and grunted in approval.

"Good. You cover our ass," he said as Michael shifted the truck into gear and pressed the accelerator.

"How exactly do you plan to get out?" Hawk called over his shoulder. "They'll be covering the gate, and we're not plowing through all of them with three rifles and a couple of pistols."

"We're going through the fence," Michael called back.

Before Hawk could respond, machine gun fire erupted from the darkness near a smaller building on his right. As Michael gunned the engine, Hawk swung the rifle up and began shooting. While he engaged the guards on the right, Boris aimed at more on the left. Bullets were raining all around them and Hawk shook his head, wincing as several of them hit the sides of the truck.

"Get us out of here, Niki," Boris cried. "We're right in the line of fire!"

"Blow the next charge!" Michael commanded, steering to the right and moving them closer to the main building for some added protection.

As the truck moved to the right, a soldier sped up behind them on a motorcycle. Hawk pulled the trigger only to hear the tell-tale click of an empty magazine.

"Damn!"

The soldier pulled alongside the truck, coming up on the driver side and pointing a gun at the back of Michael's head. Hawk grit his teeth and, summoning every last ounce of energy that he had, threw himself half over the side of the truck bed, grabbing the guard. Heaving and straining with exertion, he yanked the man off his motorcycle and pulled him half into the truck bed. He brought the butt of the empty rifle down sharply on his head, wrenching the man's rifle away from suddenly slack fingers. Running his hands over his torso, Hawk found the extra magazines and grabbed them before unceremoniously throwing the guard out of the truck. Raising the new rifle, he braced it against his shoulder and began shooting as more motorcycles came from the front of the building.

Michael pulled suddenly to the left, throwing Hawk off balance and he missed his shot at the lead motorcycle. Letting out a low curse, he fired again, satisfaction coursing through him as the man flew backwards off the bike, blood pouring from the hole in his forehead. The truck was veering across the open space towards the back of another smaller building behind the prison, and out of the corner of his eye, Hawk saw another group of motorcycles coming from the other direction. He shook his head grimly. They were trapped between two groups of heavily armed and mobile soldiers. They wouldn't last a minute under fire from both of them.

"Any more tricks you want to pull out?" he called through the open back window before he began unloading his magazine on the group to their right.

He looked up at the roof of the main prison and shook his head again. Snipers were running along the edge to get into position. Once they stopped, it was all over. He'd made enough of those shots himself to know that even a mediocre shooter couldn't miss at that distance.

"The sooner the better!" he added, swinging his rifle towards the snipers on the rooftop.

"Just one," Michael called back.

Hawk lowered his eye to the sight on the rifle, trying to get a steady shot off, but he never had to pull the trigger. Before he could center the sight, the man he was going to aim for suddenly pitched forward, falling off the edge of the roof. He lifted his head, watching as another sniper dropped on the rooftop, and then another. Relief coursed through him and he sagged against the cab for a second before turning his gun back to the men on the motorcycles. His heart settled down into a steady, strong rhythm and his breath came more easily as he began picking off their pursuers. They were going to make it.

Viper was here.

Viper exhaled softly as she squeezed the trigger, dropping a soldier carrying what looked like an Uzi before he could fire it towards the truck careening through the compound. Michael was heading for the side fence where Boris set an explosive on his way in earlier. It was their exit point, but they were rapidly being surrounded, despite the two explosions that had pulled guards away from them. Her jaw tightened as she watched a guard get close to the truck on a motorcycle. She was about to fire when he was suddenly yanked from his bike and half into the truck bed. Sliding her finger off the trigger, Alina watched as he hung draped over the side of the truck, then laughed when he was unceremoniously thrown out a moment later. Relief rolled through her, causing her heart to skip a beat. Not only was Hawk apparently still conscious, but he was doing just fine for the moment.

Pulling her attention from the truck, she shifted her scope a little to the right, her lips tightening at the sight of five snipers running across the roof of the prison to get into position. After making a slight adjustment, she squeezed the trigger rapidly in succession. One by one, each man fell, her bullets finding their mark in their foreheads. She only had time to feel a brief shot of satisfaction before movement on the roof of the generator hut alerted her to the presence of more snipers. She shifted her weight on her stomach, turning her focus on the new threats. A moment later, the roof was cleared.

She glanced at her watch, then directed her scope over the road approaching the prison. Her lips tightened as she watched two trucks barreling along the road at top speed. The other half of the contingent was returning.

"Step on it," she said into the mic at her collar. "Company's coming."

"I'm going as fast as this old heap will go," Michael retorted, his voice tight.

Viper looked back at them and measured the distance between the truck and the fence. Shaking her head, she shifted her gaze back to the returning guards. They were almost at the gates now, and she was in the wrong position and angle to shoot. If she were to have any success, she would have to reposition herself altogether. Given the surprising number of snipers that the prison seemed to have available, that wasn't the wisest of choices. Michael needed her cover fire to help get them out of there.

She hesitated for a second, then let out a low curse. They wouldn't make the fence before the reinforcements could make an impact, and they had to be running out of ammunition. Lifting her head, Viper turned to a box on the floor beside her and opened it quickly.

"I'll give you some cover, but it'll be loud," she said cheerfully, lifting out Boris' rocket launcher. "Get ready for kablooey."

"Kablooey?" Boris repeated breathlessly. "What is kablooey?"

Viper sat up and knelt on one knee, bracing herself as she hefted the launcher onto her shoulder. She adjusted the scope until she had a good fix on the generator hut, then smiled.

"It's what happens when you give me a rocket launcher."

She fired the weapon, watching through the scope as, a few seconds later, the building with the generator and servers exploded, sending a fireball and debris high into the night sky.

"Oh shit!" Boris exclaimed.

"You boys haul ass. I just bought you a thirty second wall of fire to cover you," she said, setting the rocket launcher down and getting back onto her stomach before her rifle. "I'm blowing the fence now."

She reached into her pocket and pulled out the detonator Boris had given her, pressing the button. A smaller explosion ripped through the fence, creating a hole just large enough for the truck to go through. Sliding her finger over the trigger, Viper calmly waited to see if any of the soldiers were willing to venture through the wall of flames to pursue the prisoner. Not surprisingly, none seemed inclined to do so.

She watched as the truck went through the opening in the fence a minute later, plowing into the crater left by the explosive before rumbling out on the other side of the fence. By the time Michael was on his way into the trees behind the compound, the flames had decreased in size and ferocity, allowing some of the guards to follow on motorcycles. Exhaling, Viper picked them off one by one as they emerged until, at last, no more followed.

Lifting her rifle off the mount, she shifted and turned to the gates, bracing the butt against her shoulder. The reinforcements were on their way towards the fire in the back of the compound when her bullets ripped into the front tires of both trucks. They careened out of control, one hitting the side of the prison and the other veering into a cement barrier beside the supply hut, but Viper wasn't even watching.

Thirty seconds later, she was on her way out of the bell tower in the church half a mile away, leaving no trace that she'd ever been there.

Chapter Twenty-Nine

Alina watched as Boris laid Hawk down as gently as he could in the confined space.

"He passed out sometime after we left the compound," Michael told her, speaking loudly over the sound from the propellers. "I don't know how long he's been out."

The helicopter lifted into the air and Boris nodded to her as he maneuvered by her.

"There isn't any blood and he's breathing," he said. "It's probably the adrenaline crash along with his weakness."

As he moved past her, Alina saw the blood soaking his coat and looked up at his face sharply.

"You were hit," she said, unnecessarily.

"Yes. I will take care of it."

She nodded and perched on the edge of the bench where he'd laid Damon. Her heart had surged into her throat a few minutes before when Boris had carried him from the truck to the waiting helicopter. Her first thought was that he was shot, but one glance had been enough to dispel that idea. His white ski suit was dirty, but not bloody. On the heels of relief, however, had come the thought that they had no idea what kind of wounds had been inflicted over the past few weeks. For all they knew, he could be bleeding internally.

With that thought foremost in her mind, she reached out and unzipped his jacket, unceremoniously pulling up his prison scrubs to examine his abdomen and chest. Her jaw clenched and anger tightened her gut as she stared down at him. The skin from his waistband to his neck was various shades of black, blue, green and purple, and swelling on his left ribs suggested at least one, and probably more, broken ribs. Three of the deeper lacerations on his abdomen and chest had been stitched, but the smaller ones were left to heal on their own. She was surprised that they'd bothered to close up the three larger ones at all, but she was grateful that they had. They were probably the source of the infection.

All of those she'd been expecting. It was the burn marks on

237

either side of his chest cavity that caused fury to take hold of her. They had shocked him back to life and, judging by the patterns of the burns, they had done it multiple times.

"My God," Michael breathed behind her, his hand coming to rest on her shoulder in a silent gesture of support.

The touch quelled the fury burning inside her and Viper inhaled silently before reaching out to press her fingers against the pulse in Damon's neck. It was slow, but steady, and she exhaled, moving her hand to the side of his face. His skin was hot to the touch.

"How long before we reach Voskresenka?" she asked loudly, looking over to Boris.

"About fifty minutes," he called back.

"Is there a sedative onboard?"

"I'll see."

He went towards the cockpit and Michael moved to crouch down near Hawk's head.

"Do you think that's a good idea?" he asked. "You don't want to risk his pulse dropping too low."

"I also don't want to risk him waking up and doing more damage to himself," she replied. "We don't know what's happening. He may have internal bleeding from some other injury we don't know about, or the infection could be attacking his organs. We don't know, and if he comes to and makes something worse…"

"He definitely has at least two broken ribs." Michael's lips tightened. "The pain when we moved him must have been extreme. It never occurred to me that…"

"Don't think about it," she advised, her face grim. "You couldn't know, and he wouldn't tell you. He's a stubborn bastard. He would have walked out himself if there was any physical way for him to do it."

Michael grinned. "Oh, I know he would. He wasn't happy about us helping him."

Boris made his way back to them, holding on to the side of the cabin as turbulence caused the helicopter to drop suddenly.

"They have a mild sedative that they use if they are wounded," he announced. "It won't knock him out, but it might keep him under if that's what you want."

Alina nodded. "That's fine."

He motioned to the first aid box attached to the wall above the bench where Hawk was laying.

"It's in there." He sat down on the bench opposite them and began to pull off his jacket, grimacing in pain. "Perhaps you could pass

238

me the box when you're finished."

Michael waited for Alina to find the sedative, then took the kit from her and turned to Boris. He helped him the rest of the way out of the jacket, then tore open the black shirt at his shoulder. When Boris tried to protest, he looked up in exasperation.

"Don't be stupid, Boris. I can see a hell of a lot better than you can. Or, at least, I could if I had some light."

"Here." Alina passed him a Maglite from her jacket pocket. "Use this. If you give me a minute, I'll help."

"I've got it. You take care of him." Michael took the flashlight and switched it on, examining Boris' shoulder. "The bullet's still in there. I'll have to dig it out."

"Like hell," Boris said with a scowl. "No one's digging around in me but me. I'll do it."

Michael looked up at him and, after a slight hesitation, nodded. "All right."

"Ask the pilot where he keeps his vodka. I know he has some stashed somewhere."

Michael nodded and turned to make his way to the cockpit. Boris watched Alina for a second, then cleared his throat.

"Who is he?" he asked, nodding to Hawk. "He's no businessman."

"He's none of your concern," she said shortly as she ripped open the protective packaging around the syringe.

"Perhaps not, but he knew I was Ukrainian. No one ever knows that. Everyone thinks that I am Russian."

"They think that because you let them," she said, glancing at him in amusement.

"There was no point in denying it. He knew." Boris fished in the first aid kit for a pair of tweezers. "How?"

"You would have to ask him."

He grunted, looking at her sharply under his bushy brows. "I would, but you're keeping him under. Convenient, that."

"It's better this way," she said after she'd finished injecting Damon with the sedative. "For everyone."

"No vodka," Michael said, returning. "They finished it and haven't replaced it yet. He said there's a bottle of alcohol in the kit for sterilization."

"I didn't want the vodka for sterilization. I wanted it to drink."

"Then you're out of luck."

Michael sat on the floor, leaning against the side of the cabin near Damon's head, and watched as Alina pulled his shirt down and zipped up his jacket again.

"It's a miracle he made it out without any extra injuries," he said after a moment, his eyes on her face. "He held his own back there in the truck."

"I would hope so."

"Even so, it was a messy job. We should have waited."

"There was no time to wait. You saw what they did to him, and those are only the wounds we can see right now."

Michael looked like he wanted to say something, but a grunt of pain from Boris reminded him of the other man's presence, and he changed his mind. He looked over to see Boris digging around in his shoulder with the tweezers while he held a small mirror with his other hand.

"Sure you don't want help?" he asked.

"Yes." Boris was frowning into the mirror and, after another minute, he cursed. "No. Come and hold the mirror."

"Some light would help," Alina offered dryly. "You're trying to dig a bullet out blind."

Boris shot her a disgruntled look and she laughed, turning to take the Maglite from the floor where it had been dropped.

"You're a stubborn ass, you know that?" she asked, switching it on and holding the beam on the wound in his shoulder.

"So everyone says. But you know what? I am still alive."

Michael held the mirror and Alina held the light as he went back to digging around with the tweezers, letting out an occasional grunt of pain. After a few minutes, he finally pulled a mangled lump of metal out and dropped it into his hand.

"Ah! Got it."

"Congratulations," Alina murmured. "That was the most painful thing I've ever watched."

"It is not so bad. After some time, you don't even feel it anymore."

"I was talking about the mess you made of the entry wound," she said, switching the light off.

"And you would do better?" Boris demanded.

"I *have* done better, a few times."

"Hey," Michael interrupted, shushing them and motioning towards the cockpit. "Listen."

Alina frowned and glanced at the pilots. Over the noise of the propellers, they heard the pilot yelling into his headset.

"Negative. We don't see anything," he was saying. "It's all quiet here. I'll move west and continue looking."

The Cuban

Michael scowled and looked at Boris sharply.

"What's going on?" he demanded in a low voice. "What are they talking about?"

Boris grinned, pressing gauze against his wound.

"They are doing their job," he said. "We are onboard one of the helicopters that are looking for an escaped prisoner."

Michael stared at him, speechless, and Alina felt a laugh bubble up inside her.

"You're joking!" Michael finally got out.

"I do not joke about things like this," Boris muttered, ripping open a bandage with his teeth. "I knew they would use air support. Lucky for us, I'm good friends with one of their pilots."

"So they're...looking for us?"

Boris looked up with a flash of white teeth.

"Yes. Unfortunately, they will find no trace."

Alina felt her lips curling up and she began to laugh.

"Oh Boris, I wish there were more of you in the world," she chortled. "You're a man after my own heart."

"Who *are* you?" Michael demanded. "First you arrange a Ukrainian missile strike on a Russian-held power plant, and now we're in a search chopper?!"

"Russian military chopper," Boris corrected him with a wink. "I am someone who has made several connections in my time. It is very useful in my line of work."

"Well I, for one, am grateful for your connections," Alina told him with a nod, still chuckling. "I am eternally indebted to Yakiv for our introduction."

"But you are not indebted to me? Without me, you would not be here."

"I distinctly recall you saying that you did not deal in debt and favors."

He nodded. "You're right. I do not."

"Besides, I would have managed without you. It would have taken longer, but I would have managed."

Boris studied her for a minute, then smiled.

"I believe you would have."

Alina leaned against the side of the SUV, staring pensively

across the expanse of darkness. They had arrived at the coordinates that Jack had given her ahead of schedule. Michael was sitting in the back with a still-unconscious Damon while Boris had disappeared into the darkness in the other direction to relieve himself. Every muscle in her body was tense, and a headache was starting behind her eyes. She was on edge, and she knew she wouldn't relax until they were out of Ukraine altogether. As far as she was concerned, they were still in enemy territory. It would be too easy for them to be captured here.

"Anything yet?"

She turned her head to watch Michael climb out of the back of the SUV.

"Not yet."

"What time are they supposed to get here?"

"Getting worried, gunny?"

"Just asking a question."

Alina looked at her watch.

"Any minute," she relented. "We were early."

"Did Charlie arrange it?"

"No."

Michael looked at her, a frown on his face.

"Who, then?"

She exhaled and turned to look at him.

"I don't remember you asking so many questions. Were you always like this?"

"Yes, but you never had me with you on an op," he said, undisturbed. "MI6?"

She cast him an amused glance.

"You're not going to leave it alone until I tell you, are you?"

He grinned at her. "Nope."

"Yes. Happy?"

"Not as happy as I would be if it was our boys, but I'll take it."

Alina shook her head, a reluctant smile pulling at her lips.

"I'm so glad you approve."

"Any sign of your friends yet?" Boris called, emerging from the darkness behind them.

Alina turned to look over the hood of the SUV.

"They'll be here."

He came around to join them, looking out over the darkness. As he did so, the frigid wind carried the welcome sound of a low hum with it. A few seconds later, Alina saw tiny lights in the distance.

"There she is," Michael said, straightening up and turning towards the back of the SUV. "Coming in low and fast."

The Cuban

Alina nodded, watching as the faint lights on the horizon grew closer. While she wouldn't fully relax until she was onboard, she was relieved to see the helicopter flying in at last.

"Anya, it has been one hell of a ride," Boris said, turning to her, "but this is where we part company."

She frowned and looked at him.

"You'll come with us," she said shortly. "The transport is for four."

"I appreciate it, but I will remain here, in Ukraine."

"If you stay, they'll find you," she said, shaking her head. "Not to mention that you're sporting a gunshot wound in your shoulder. It isn't safe to remain. You can return later."

"They will look for me, yes, but they won't find me." He held out his hand to her. "I will be fine. If you are ever in need of assistance again, I'll be happy to help. Yakiv knows how to contact me."

Alina sighed and grasped his hand, her eyes meeting his in the darkness.

"If you insist," she said. "Take care of yourself, Boris."

"Always."

The helicopter was coming to land in the field next to them, the sound deafening in the silence. It hovered for a moment above the ground, then settled down onto the grass, the propellers spinning above. The side door opened and two men in full gear jumped out, running towards them. Alina bent to pick up her bag and strode forward.

"I have an unconscious man," she called to them. "He's in the back of the SUV."

The one closest to her nodded and pressed a button on the radio on his chest, requesting a stretcher.

"This is the medic," he said, motioning to his companion. "He'll see to him."

Alina nodded and turned to watch as the medic ran to the back of the SUV. A second later, another soldier emerged from the helicopter carrying a folding stretcher.

"I'm Captain Martin," the soldier next to her said with a nod.

"Anya." Alina nodded to him.

"Let's get you onboard," he said. "We have a very small window. We need everyone to move."

"There are just three of us," she said. "One is staying behind."

Michael came around the back of the SUV carrying two bags, and she motioned to him.

"Let's move!"

He looked at Boris questioningly, then went over to speak to him. Alina couldn't hear what was being said over the sound from the chopper behind her, but she didn't need to hear to know that Michael was trying to convince him to come with them. No one left behind, that was Michael's creed. He was always a Marine to the end.

After a quick conversation, Michael shook Boris' hand, then came towards them as the two men came away from the SUV bearing Hawk on a stretcher. As soon as she saw Damon, Alina turned towards the helicopter. She ran beside Captain Martin as Michael jogged next to the stretcher and, a moment later, she was climbing into the belly of the gunship. Pausing in the door, she turned to look back at Boris. He was getting behind the wheel of the SUV, but when she looked back, he held up a hand in a wave. After a second's hesitation, Alina returned the wave before ducking into the helicopter.

A few minutes later, they were lifting into the air as the medic began to undo Damon's jacket.

"What am I looking at here?" he called over to her.

"Staph infection, multiple lacerations to the torso, broken ribs, and burn patterns most likely from a defibrillator," she replied.

"Heart condition?"

"He didn't have one before."

"How long has he been unconscious?"

"A little over two hours. I gave him a sedative to keep him under." Alina pulled the packaging from the syringe from her pocket and handed it to him. "I don't know if there are other injuries. They put him on vancomycin. The port is still in. It's under the bandage on his arm."

The medic nodded. He took the packaging, glanced at it, then reached for an IV cart. She watched as he got to work, removing Damon's jacket and shirt while he examined the wounds on his torso. Michael touched her arm and she looked at him questioningly.

"Sit down," he told her from his seat on a bench. "He's in good hands now."

She smiled ruefully and sat beside him, her eyes going back to the medic.

"I just…"

She stopped suddenly as her throat closed up, and Michael reached over to cover her hand with his.

"I know."

"We'll be in Kyiv in four hours," Captain Martin told them, returning from the cockpit. "When we land, you'll be transferred to a Red Cross flight to Poland. Someone will meet you in Warsaw. I'm told you'll know them."

Alina nodded and smiled for the first time since reaching Kopani.

"Thank you."

Captain Martin nodded back, his face softening.

"It's good to have you onboard," he said. "Try to relax. We'll have you in friendly territory before you know it."

Chapter Thirty

C harlie looked up from his tablet when a shadow fell across his chair in the first class lounge. He smiled and stood up, holding out his hand.

"You got here faster than I expected," he said, shaking Jack's hand. "Thank you for meeting me here. We're refueling, then I'm off again."

"My people have yours, safe and sound, and they're on their way to Kyiv as we speak," Jack told him, sitting down in the leather chair next to him. "Once they land, they'll get onto a Red Cross flight to Warsaw."

Charlie nodded and slid his tablet into his leather bag.

"Thank you, my friend. We will take it from there."

Jack nodded and crossed his legs.

"There's one other thing. I've received intel on Sophia Morozov."

Charlie raised his eyebrows. "Really?"

"Yes. We've found her. She's hiding in Nice, in France." Jack pulled out his phone, swiped the screen, and held it out for Charlie to see. "My people found her this morning."

Charlie leaned forward to examine the photograph of a woman wearing a linen suit walking into a hotel.

"Is she alone?"

"Yes." Jack tucked his phone away again. "I've already made contact with her. We had a conversation before I came here. She's agreed to a joint protective detail between us and Interpol."

"Someone *is* trying to kill her?"

"She thinks so. Someone tried to take her from her apartment in Brussels. She got away from them before they could get her into a van. She's been running ever since. She's frightened, and shaken up."

"And she has no idea who?"

"She never saw their faces, but it wouldn't have made a difference if she had. You and I both know that the people doing this are using paid assassins."

The Cuban

Charlie nodded slowly, his lips pressed together thoughtfully.

"And she's willing to stop her work and hide indefinitely?" he asked after a long moment.

"Well, it won't be indefinitely, will it?" Jack shrugged. "I've assured her that we can guarantee her safety until it's safe for her to return to her life. She agreed."

"Just like that?"

"I told you, the woman is frightened. Someone tried to kidnap her, for God's sake. She knows what's been happening all year to her fellow executives. She's convinced that they would have killed her."

Charlie was silent for a long time before he glanced at Jack.

"Would you mind if I added one of my assets to the security surveillance?" he asked, his voice mild.

"I don't see why it would cause a problem," Jack said slowly. "But why do you want to? It's hardly your area of expertise."

Charlie smiled faintly.

"No, but I find I'm very anxious to see who comes looking for her."

Boris watched as the helicopter lifted into the air and turned northwest, tapping one finger on the steering wheel. The helicopter was a Mil Mi-24P, a Russian-made gunship with the ability to transport a very limited number of troops. Ukraine had been using it for years, along with several other nations. It was the premier helicopter that could be used both as a gunship and to transport soldiers. Whoever it was that Anya contacted for extraction, they had the ear and support of Kyiv. That was the only way that gunship could operate in Ukrainian airspace without being shot down as the enemy.

As the lights disappeared into the distance, he put the SUV into gear and pulled onto the road. Pulling out his cell phone, he pressed a button and then set the phone into a mount on the dash. He listened to the phone ring on the other end, his lips pressed together thoughtfully. Perhaps he should have accompanied them to wherever they were going. He moved his shoulder uncomfortably and shook his head. No. He'd already been shot once in this affair. He didn't want to risk more trouble, and something told him that trouble followed wherever Anya went.

The call connected and he gave his access code, then waited

while the call transferred. After another moment, a man picked up.

"What is your status?" he asked briskly.

"Alone."

There was a very faint click on the line, then the man spoke again.

"Good. How are you?"

"Wounded, but mobile," Boris said, moving his shoulder with a grimace. "I dug a bullet out of my shoulder."

"Are you coming in?"

"Yes."

"We'll have a doctor waiting. What do you know?"

"Nothing very much." Boris rubbed his forehead tiredly, his eyes on the dark road in front of him. "Hans Becker is definitely *not* a businessman from Austria. He's an operative of some kind, but I was unable to determine whose. Possibly MI6, but his Russian is very good. He could just as easily be working for Moscow. He's had special forces training. Even half dead, he was lethal, and unbelievably efficient. What I saw him do with a high fever and severe injuries from repeated interrogations was enough to make me hope that I never have to go against him at full strength."

"Does he know how to get to The Cuban?" The man asked after a short silence.

"I don't think so," Boris said slowly, "but I would bet anything that the woman does."

"Tell me about her."

"She's an assassin, and also very well trained. She doesn't have any weaknesses that I could find, but I was only with her for a few days. I wasn't able to determine which country she's from, or even whose side she's on. She was guarded and didn't talk much."

"Did she know Becker?"

"I think so. She seemed overly concerned about his injuries, more than a stranger would have been. He certainly seemed to know her, or at least know of her. He knew she was there, and he never even saw her."

"And the other one?"

"Nikita. He was an operative, and she *did* know him. She said they weren't friends, and they didn't appear to be overly friendly. I think they probably have had some dealings with each other in the past, perhaps as a contact or supplier." Boris thought for a minute, then shook his head. "I don't think that they're a threat together, but I do think that if she and Becker ever teamed up, that would be a problem."

"Do you think you have enough for us to stop them in Kyiv?"

The Cuban

Boris frowned and was silent for a long time, then he let out a frustrated sigh.

"No. Let them go," he finally said. "I don't know what Becker was doing here, but they're not staying. She's getting him out of the country and somewhere safe to heal."

"This might be our only chance to find out what they know."

"I think they'll show up again," Boris said confidently. "These are high stakes players. The kind that only come out when things get really bad. They'll be back. We'll learn more then, when they're not on their guard."

"If they're what you say, we won't know if they come back," the man pointed out dryly. "If they're that well-trained, they won't allow themselves to be seen again."

A small smile pulled at Boris' lips.

"No need to worry on that account. When she returns, she'll find me."

"How do you know?"

"Because she will need weapons, and now she knows just how useful I can be."

"You sure took your sweet time."

Alina turned away from the window swiftly at the sound of Damon's voice. His blue eyes were open and, as she turned, he smiled tiredly. Her heart thumped as she met his gaze, her own lips curving in response.

"If you'd left a better trail, I would have been there sooner," she retorted, crossing to the bedside. "If it weren't for an Interpol contact of mine, I might still be looking."

"Remind me to send him a bottle of something." Damon coughed and shifted against his pillows. "If you'd been a day longer, I don't know if I'd be here."

"A bottle won't be any use to him now," she said, leaning forward to bank up his pillows so that he could sit up. "He's dead. He was killed before he could get the information to me."

She felt Damon studying her face as he pulled himself into a sitting position.

"Then how did you find me?"

"I followed his trail." Alina watched as Damon sank against

the pillows with a sigh of relief. "How are you feeling?"

"Like I've been beaten." He shook his head and reached out his hand, his fingers closing around hers with surprising strength. "The last thing I remember was going into the woods after we got out of there. How long was I out?"

"A little over twenty-four hours." She sat on the edge of the bed and glanced at the monitors, watching his steady pulse and blood pressure. "You woke up when we were boarding a plane in Kyiv, but the attending medic put you under again."

"I was sedated? Why?"

She smiled ruefully.

"You passed out yourself on the way to the rendezvous, but I gave you something to keep you under. The gunny was a little too determined to debrief you. I wanted you to have some warning first." She looked down at their hands and played with his long fingers. "Then the medics wanted to keep you under because your body was trying to fight a staph infection. They felt the more rest you got, the better your chances."

"What the hell was O'Reilly doing there?" he asked, his face grim. "Was that Charlie?"

"I think so. He showed up in Belarus the same time I did."

"And he saw you?"

"I went to him." Alina shrugged. "I was afraid he would do something that would prevent me from getting to you."

"And now he knows you're still alive."

"To be fair, he knew before this. He just didn't have any proof. We've been dodging him for four years."

"And we would have continued to dodge him indefinitely." Damon ran a hand over his face. "What the hell was Charlie thinking?"

"I don't know, but he's only gone out for coffee, so we need to decide now how much we tell him."

"How much does he already know?"

Alina let out a short laugh and pulled her hand away, standing restlessly.

"I don't know," she admitted. "He initially thought that you ended up in that hell hole because The Cuban put you there. I let him believe that. But then Boris told him that an assassin had been sent to kill The Cuban, and asked if you - Becker - were the assassin."

"Damn."

"Exactly. That was the day we stormed the prison. I haven't had time to talk to Michael since, so I don't know what he's figured out. Until then, I honestly don't think he'd considered the possibility

250

The Cuban

that you might be more heavily involved with The Cuban." She frowned. "Although, given how much he knows about us, I'm surprised that he didn't figure it out from the very beginning."

Before Damon could say anything, the door to the hospital room opened unceremoniously and the subject of their conversation walked in carrying two large paper cups with heat sleeves.

"You're awake!" he exclaimed, crossing the room to hand Alina one of the cups. "It's about time."

"Where's mine?" Damon asked, looking from one coffee cup to the other.

"You don't need it," Alina said, sipping hers thankfully. "You've been asleep for over twenty-four hours. We've been awake for longer than that."

"How're you feeling?" Michael asked, pulling a chair over and sitting down comfortably. "You look a hell of a lot better than when I found you."

"I'll live." Damon watched him sip his coffee, then looked from him to Alina. "Where are we?"

"Warsaw. As soon as you're cleared to travel, I'm moving you," she said.

"I can move now."

"Not until all the scans come back. I want to be sure you're not bleeding from the inside out."

"I'm fine," Damon muttered with a frown. "It takes more than a Russian bastard to kill me."

"Just so that we're clear, if you ever do anything like this again, I'll kill you myself," she promised him. "And it won't be pretty."

Damon winked at her.

"You missed me."

Alina felt her heart skip and she couldn't stop herself from smiling. After the weeks of worrying that he was already dead, or that she would be too late if he wasn't, she almost couldn't believe that he was laying there, giving her that old sexy wink that always drew a laugh from her.

"Maybe so, but we can't keep doing this, Hawk," she said, the smile fading. "We're running out of lives."

"In my defense, getting thrown into a dungeon wasn't part of my plan."

"How, exactly, *did* you end up in a Russian Gulag?" Michael asked.

Damon turned his gaze to him and he considered him thoughtfully for a moment.

"How did you?" he asked softly.

"I was helping Lina get you out. She seemed to think that she could take on the whole place by herself."

Damon shot her a look filled with amusement.

"Again? Once wasn't enough for you?"

"Well, if you find something that works," she said with a shrug.

"I'm glad the gunny showed up to talk some sense into you," he muttered. "It wouldn't have worked. They were waiting for you."

"Oh, I know."

He shot her an inscrutable look, but then turned his blue gaze back to Michael.

"As much as it pains me to say it, I owe you, gunny. If you weren't there, we'd both be in that hell hole right now."

"Pozhaluysta."

"Not bad." Damon shifted on his pillows with a grimace of pain. "You've learned a southern dialect. That's good. The Organization trained you well. Do you spend a lot of time in the old Soviet bloc?"

"No. I'm primarily in Europe and the Middle East."

Damon raised an eyebrow.

"Then what the hell were you doing in Ukraine?"

"Looking for The Cuban."

Damon studied him in silence for a long moment, then smiled faintly.

"Well, you found him."

Chapter Thirty-One

A heavy silence fell over the room with Damon's words, and Alina let out an imperceptible sigh. There it was. Hawk had obviously decided to attack the bull head-on. She shook her head and turned to walk over to the window again, staring at the rain outside. She shouldn't be surprised, she supposed. She knew her husband well. He wouldn't have the patience to play games with the gunny, not after Michael had pulled him out of hell.

"Excuse me?"

Michael's voice sounded tight behind her and she raised her coffee to her lips, suddenly wishing it was something stronger. This wasn't going to be pretty, no matter which way they spun it. Michael was about to be pulled over the point of no turning back, whether any of them liked it or not.

"You heard me just fine," Damon said, amused.

"You're...it's not possible!"

"Oh, but it is."

There was silence behind her and Alina waited for the explosion. It wasn't long in coming.

"Son of a bitch!" Michael was on his feet now. "You knew?" he demanded, looking over at her.

She turned her head to look at him, her face carefully void of any expression that might escalate the situation further.

"Of course you knew!" he exclaimed, his eyes narrowing in anger. "Do you ever *not* lie to me?"

"I didn't lie to you, Michael," she said, her voice steady. "I just didn't tell you."

"Why?"

"It wasn't her place to say anything," Damon said, his voice stronger than either of them expected. "Sit down, gunny."

The steel in his voice brooked no argument and Michael hesitated, glancing from Alina to Damon, before reluctantly seating himself again.

"I'm assuming Charlie knows?" he asked after a moment, the

muscle in his jaw still ticking.

"Of course."

"Then why the hell did he send me on a wild good chase?"

"You'll have to ask him that," Alina said.

"You don't know?"

She shook her head. "No. I certainly wasn't expecting to see you in Dachnyi 6."

Michael ran a hand through his hair and shook his head.

"Why send me after you? It was all a waste of time!"

"Not such a waste of time," Damon murmured. "At least, not from my perspective."

Michael looked at him, his brows drawn together in a scowl, then he exhaled loudly and sat back.

"Tell me," he said. "Tell me what the hell is going on. And don't try to pull that classified bullshit with me. We're on the same playing level now."

Damon chuckled, then winced at the pain it caused.

"How much do you already know about The Cuban?" he asked.

"You mean about you?"

"I mean about The Cuban," Damon replied, that faint smile back on his lips.

"I've been following him for the past six months. After the first four executives died, it was clear that they weren't suicides. I started asking questions, discreet ones, and looking for information. None of my usual sources could dig up anything, so I decided to tackle it from the opposite side. If there were assassins killing people, they had to be well paid, and they had to have clean weapons."

"And that's when you stumbled across The Cuban."

"Yes." Michael hesitated, then flushed. "I also had an idea that…well, it doesn't matter."

Alina turned around, her attention caught.

"What?"

"I told you, it doesn't matter."

"Show and tell goes both ways, O'Reilly," Damon murmured. "Spit it out."

Michael looked from one to the other, then exhaled loudly.

"When I couldn't find any trace of Lina, I switched to looking for you," he told him reluctantly. "I knew if you both were still alive, you'd be together."

Damon grinned.

"Obviously. We're stuck with each other until death do us

part."

"Well, I got intel that The Cuban kept an assassin on his payroll, one that was reportedly the best there is."

"And you thought it was me?" Damon's grin grew. "I'm flattered."

"I'm not," Alina muttered. "What about me?"

"I didn't think it was your type of gig."

She raised an eyebrow, then looked at Damon.

"See? I told you. Men always underestimate women. They never dream that a woman can be that good."

"I don't think that's what he's saying," he said soothingly, his eyes dancing. "I think he's saying that you don't seem like the type to hire yourself out."

"Actually, it's more that I don't believe you're a true killer," Michael said with a shrug.

Alina choked on her coffee.

"What?" she sputtered. "I'm not a…are you feeling all right?"

Michael made a face as Damon's shoulders shook in silent laughter.

"You're not a mercenary," he snapped. "You have a moral standard, or at least you used to."

"Oh, she still does," Damon assured him, his voice unsteady. "It's gotten pretty flexible, kind of like Gumby, but it's there."

"How are the ribs feeling?" Alina asked, her voice mild. "Do they need adjusting?"

Damon burst out laughing, then started coughing painfully. When he finished, he looked at Michael, his eyes streaming.

"So you thought if you found The Cuban, you'd find me."

"Something like that."

"Well, you weren't wrong."

"When Charlie found out I was already looking for The Cuban, he began feeding me what information he got. Then, last week, he told me to find you."

Damon and Alina glanced at each other. Catching the look, Michael frowned.

"If Charlie knows you're The Cuban, why did he send me?"

"My best guess? Because he knew you'd find Viper, and that she would lead you to me." Damon rubbed his eyes and shook his head. "I don't know why. Charlie is…well, he's Charlie. He never does anything without a reason. I can tell you this much, he must have had a damn good one for wanting you in on this."

"The hard-drive," Alina said suddenly, looking at Michael.

"You're probably the only one with the skills to go through that hard-drive and pull relevant intel off of it."

"Any of the computer guys in Langley can do it faster," Michael objected, shaking his head.

"But they wouldn't know what they were looking for. You do."

"I do?" He stared at her. "I don't even know what the hell is going on here!"

"You know more than you think."

"I might once you two tell me your side," he muttered.

"When the first executive was found dead of an apparent suicide a year ago, I knew it wasn't suicide," Damon told him. "I'd been approached two weeks before with an offer. I declined."

"Someone wanted you to kill him?" Michael's head snapped up. "They were going to hire you?"

"Yes. Unfortunately, contrary to your somewhat low impression of me, I refuse to work freelance." Damon shrugged. "Some of my wife's moral accountability has clearly rubbed off onto me. I only offer my services to certain governments, and all with Charlie's approval."

Michael stared at him speechlessly for a minute, then shook his head in disbelief.

"Dammit, you could have been in!" he exclaimed. "You could have found out who's behind all of this months ago!"

Damon's lips twisted.

"Oh, trust me, I'm aware of that. At the time, though, I didn't know something was starting. Someone offered me a contract, I declined it. After the second one was found dead, Charlie contacted me. That's when I realized my mistake."

"You've been working this from the beginning?"

"Yes." Damon sighed and looked around. "Is there any water to be had?"

Alina set her coffee down on a table and went to get the bottle of water that a nurse had left on a side table. Pouring it into a cup, she carried it back to him.

"Thanks." He drank some, then set the cup on the table beside the bed. "Charlie believed, and so did I, that this was the start of something much larger than just a power play within the energy sector. I created The Cuban as a way to gather information."

"How is an arms dealer relevant to energy executives getting killed?"

"If this was truly something bigger, then people would need weapons. I set myself out to supply them. But I couldn't just be an average supplier. I had to make myself the only supplier that whoever was behind this would come to. They had to trust me, so I had to create a legend."

"When you say something bigger than a power play in the energy sector, you mean..."

"Something that would cause unrest over several continents."

Michael was staring at him with a frown and Alina sat on the edge of the bed, watching him thoughtfully. He was figuring it out on his own, she realized. All the pieces of the puzzle were fitting together, and Michael was about to realize just what he'd stumbled into.

"A world war?" Michael stared at them. "You think these people want to cause an energy crisis that will result in another war?"

"Global conflict is worth billions to the right people," Alina told him. "Cause a crisis that will turn citizens into activists, and populations against their governments..."

"And groups all over the world would need to be weaponized," he breathed. "Holy shit."

"Exactly."

"So you became a global arms dealer." He looked at Damon. "And the cigars?"

Damon grinned.

"A tracking device is in the lining of the boxes. We know where the buyers live and work, and we keep track of the weapons. Several have suddenly gone missing or been destroyed in enemy attacks when they were about be utilized in ways not consistent with western policy."

Michael exhaled and got up restlessly, running a hand through his hair.

"Who found out?" he asked, looking over at the bed as he paced across the room.

"No one."

He frowned.

"Then how did you get caught?"

Damon's lips tightened.

"They didn't know who they had," he said grimly. "As for how I got caught, I was betrayed by a rather intelligent energy executive, of course."

Alina caught her breath and looked at him sharply. "What?"

"I was asking questions about the wrong person and, as it turns out, ended up talking to someone who knew a lot more than I did."

"Will you stop talking in riddles?" Michael demanded from across the room. "God, I hate when you people do that! And, just so you know, I've learned that it's only the dramatic and arrogant assets who talk like that. The rest of us just say what people need to know."

Alina blinked and felt a laugh bubble inside her.

"I think the gunny is getting impatient," she said in a stage whisper to Damon. "He doesn't appreciate your dramatics."

"My dramatics?" Damon stared at her, his lips trembling "You're the dramatic one! You and your over-the-top explosions!"

"I have no idea what you're talking about."

"How. Did. You. Get. Caught?" Michael bit out each word through clenched teeth, drawing a laugh from Damon.

"I came across another missing energy exec, but one that no one knew about," he said. "His name was Yuri Morozov, and he lived in Minsk."

Michael frowned.

"Morozov?" he repeated. "As in—"

"Sophia Morozov? Yes. He's her father, if he's still alive. I spoke to her briefly in Brussels, and she said that he'd disappeared a few months ago. She seemed to be under the impression that he was dead." Damon looked at Alina ruefully. "That was my mistake."

"Looking for Morozov?"

He nodded.

"When I returned to Minsk, they were waiting for me."

"And the tracker in your leg?" she asked with a frown.

"Removed before we ever left Minsk. At least, I assume it was. I was unconscious, and when I came to, it was gone. We were in a truck at that point."

Michael walked over to stand at the foot of the bed, frowning in consternation.

"So you were taken because you stumbled across another missing executive?" he demanded. "Not because of anything to do with The Cuban?"

Damon nodded, his lips twisting into a sardonic smile.

"They really had no idea. Their line of questioning made that very clear. I think they thought that I was an assassin, but who I was supposed to be after is anyone's guess."

"Or they assumed you were an enemy operative," Alina murmured.

"Or that."

"But…how did they find out you knew about Morozov?" Michael asked. "I know you didn't tell anyone."

"I told one person: his daughter."

Michael sucked in his breath sharply. "Sophia? But why?"

258

The Cuban

"Gunny, you might want to sit down," Damon advised. "You're looking a little stunned."

"I *am* stunned." Michael dropped into his chair heavily. "And confused."

"I can see that. Who do you think Sophia Morozov is?"

Michael shook his head, rubbing his forehead.

"I don't know very much about her, to be honest. Her name came up in some files from the hard drive in Dachnyi 6, and then Charlie mentioned her a few hours ago when I spoke to him. She works for BenuTec, one of the top oil and gas companies in Eastern Europe, and works out of their headquarters in Brussels. She disappeared from her apartment a few days ago. The general consensus seems to be that she's the latest target."

Damon snorted.

"She's no target. If she's disappeared, it's because she wanted to disappear. Yuri Morozov was thrown into a Russian prison because he discovered that his daughter was involved with the deaths of over twelve energy executives, and even more since."

Michael stared at him. "She's the one behind all of this?"

Damon shook his head.

"Not *the* one," he said, "one of the ones. They're called Les Cinq, The Five."

Alina looked at him sharply.

"You have proof?"

"I did before I was taken. I was able to access one of their servers in Prague. The city grid just happened to experience a power outage that enabled me to bypass all their security." Damon grinned. "And I did it without blowing anything up. Which reminds me, how did you kill the power at the prison?"

"She blew up the power plant," Michael said with a grin.

"Oh no, you're not dramatic at all," Damon murmured, his dancing eyes meeting hers. "How the hell did you blow up a whole plant?"

"I don't know what either of you are talking about," Alina said calmly, sipping her coffee. "That plant was hit with a missile strike from Ukraine."

Damon stared at her for a beat, then threw his head back and burst into laughter. He clutched his left side as he laughed, the pain clearly not having any effect on his amusement.

"My God, Viper," he gasped, "only you! Now how the hell am I supposed to top that?!"

Alina chuckled, her spirit lifting at the reminder of their

ongoing competition that had begun years before in boot camp.

"Oh, I'm sure you'll think of something." She watched as he got his laughter under control. "Do you still have what you pulled off that server?"

The laughter disappeared.

"No. They took it from me, but I know how to get to them. I know how to get through their layers of security and decoys."

"It won't do any good without proof," she said. "You know that."

"I'll get the proof Charlie needs," he said grimly.

"So you're saying it's not just one person doing all of this?" Michael asked. "It's a group?"

"More of an organization," Damon told him. "They've been around for years, manipulating stock markets, governments, health providers; you name it. They've even recently gotten into the arms market," he added with a cold smile. "And that is where *they* made *their* mistake."

"Well, that and not killing you outright when they had you," Alina said. "If they'd put a bullet in your head, it would have been months before I picked up your trail, if I ever did."

Michael looked at her with a frown.

"What do you mean? How are you involved in all of this?"

She smiled at him in genuine amusement.

"Really? You haven't figured it out yet?"

Michael scowled at her.

"I'm still processing the fact that your husband is The Cuban!"

"You'd have thought that the training would have taught him to think faster on his feet," Damon murmured, glancing at Alina. "Yet he doesn't seem to have improved in that regard. Are we inordinately good, or is he just slow?"

She bit back a laugh at the look on Michael's face.

"In his defense, his training stopped before ours did," she said. "He's a spook, not an asset. I don't think that he had to go through the last three weeks."

Damon raised his eyebrows and looked at Michael.

"You lucky bastard."

"Thank you. Now will you please clue me into what my slow ass missed?"

Alina burst out laughing and got off the bed, going for her coffee again.

"Hawk is the bait," she said over her shoulder. "The Cuban will draw them out and reveal their identity, or in this case, their identities. I'm the tip of the sword."

The confusion on Michael's face cleared.

"You're the one who will eliminate them. But what if he'd been killed in that prison?"

"Then I would become both the bait and the sword."

Michael shook his head, looking from one to the other in bemusement.

"You two really do love to get embroiled in shit shows, don't you?" he asked.

"Well, we did *try* retirement," Damon pointed out. "It just wasn't for us."

"And now I'm embroiled in it as well."

Alina's lips tightened.

"I tried to warn you, gunny," she said softly. "You don't belong here."

His jaw clenched and he looked up, his eyes narrowing.

"Well, I'm here now, whether you like it or not."

"Mm. I suppose I can thank Charlie for that. I can't wait to discuss it with him," she added, her voice hardening.

"That's not all you'll have to discuss with him," Michael said, finishing his coffee. He looked at Damon. "You have to tell him about Sophia Morozov. He needs to know what she is. He thinks that she's a target, and one of the good guys."

"Why do you think that?" Damon asked, raising an eyebrow.

Michael frowned.

"Because he's got her under protective surveillance," he said. "He obviously thinks…"

His voice trailed off at the looks on both their faces, and he sucked in his breath as Viper smiled that cold and deadly smile that didn't quite reach her eyes.

"It's not protective surveillance, gunny," she said softly.

Michael exhaled. "He already knows."

"Yes."

He looked at Alina and she saw the resignation in his eyes.

"And you?"

Her face softened for a moment as her eyes met his, then the mask that Viper wore so well slid into place.

"I have a plane to catch."

Epilogue

Nice, France
Three days later

Viper watched as the small boat sped towards the dock, then shifted her gaze to the yacht anchored just outside the bay. She considered it thoughtfully for a moment, remembering another yacht similar in size and expense. She'd blown that one to pieces in the Atlantic Ocean. This one she wasn't permitted to touch. Not yet.

She moved her attention back to the speedboat and lowered her eye to her rifle scope, zooming in on the woman sitting next to a handsome Frenchman. She was holding a wide-brimmed hat onto her head with one hand while the other was tucked into the crook of his arm. There were two others in the boat with them, security by the looks of them, but Viper wasn't concerned with them. They weren't her target.

The Frenchman's name was Pierre Marne, and he was a diamond broker for one of the larger jewelers in France. She could see why the woman on his arm was so enthralled with him. He was very good-looking, and as rich as any woman could want. He was also twice divorced, currently single, and owned a nice little chateau on an island in the Mediterranean. He was the perfect catch.

Viper's lips twisted humorlessly. He should really be more selective about whose company he kept.

The boat pulled up to the dock and there was a moment for the driver to secure the ropes before the party began to disembark. The two security guards went first, serious and intimidating as they scanned the dock slowly before turning and nodding to the couple in the boat. Pierre climbed out, then turned and held his hand out for the woman.

Sophia Morozov.

As she made a slight adjustment and zoomed in on her face, Viper felt a hot wave of anger go through her. That woman was the reason Hawk had endured brutal beatings and torture at the hands of a

The Cuban

Russian interrogator. If not for Marcel, Viper would never have got to him before they broke his body, if not his will.

It was also that woman who had caused Michael to get dragged into a situation that had always had the potential to become a suicide mission. Alina saved his life four years ago only to have him sucked into another one of her impossible operations, and all thanks to a woman whom she'd never even heard of until last week.

The target stepped out of the boat, smiling up at Pierre as she held his hand for support. Viper squeezed the trigger, exhaling as the recoil pushed her rifle against her shoulder. A second later, the smile froze on Sophia Morozov's face and a hole appeared on her forehead. Her pupils dilated suddenly in response to the trauma ripping through her brain, and everything seemed to freeze for a second.

Then all hell let loose as she fell backwards into the boat, dead.

The security guards turned and pulled their weapons, looking around frantically. Realizing that the shot wasn't made from the dock, they lifted their eyes, searching for a glint of sunlight to give away the position of a shooter.

But there was nothing.

The bathroom window of the beach front hotel was empty, and Viper was gone.

Other Titles by CW Browning:

Next Exit, Three Miles (Exit #1)

Next Exit, Pay Toll (Exit #2)

Next Exit, Dead Ahead (Exit #3)

Next Exit, Quarter Mile (Exit #4)

Next Exit, Use Caution (Exit #5)

Next Exit, One Way (Exit #6)

Next Exit, No Outlet (Exit #7)

Games of Deceit (Kai Corbyn #1)

Close Target (Kai Corbyn #2)

The Courier (Shadows of War #1)

The Oslo Affair (Shadows of War #2)

Night Falls on Norway (Shadows of War #3)

The Iron Storm (Shadows of War #4)

Into the Iron Shadows (Shadows of War #5)

When Wolves Gather (Shadows of War #6)

Available on Amazon

About the Author

CW Browning was writing before she could spell. Making up stories with her childhood best friend in the backyard in Olathe, Kansas, imagination ran wild from the very beginning. At the age of eight, she printed out her first full-length novel on a dot-matrix printer. All eighteen chapters of it. Through the years, the writing took a backseat to the mechanics of life as she pursued other avenues of interest. Those mechanics, however, have a great way of underlining what truly lifts a spirt and makes the soul sing. After attending Rutgers University and studying History, her love for writing was rekindled. It became apparent where her heart lay. Picking up an old manuscript, she dusted it off and went back to what made her whole. CW still makes up stories in her backyard, but now she crafts them for her readers to enjoy. She makes her home in Southern New Jersey, where she loves to grill steak and sip red wine on the patio.

Visit her at: www.cwbrowning.com
Also find her on Facebook, Instagram and Twitter!